"*These Blue Mountains* is a ... two continents, two wars, and two lives defined by longing and resilience. Sarah Loudin Thomas has crafted a story as rich and layered as the Blue Ridge Mountains themselves, where every twist reveals deeper truths about love, loss, and identity. When Hedda Schlagel, a German woman caught between the shadows of the Great War and the ominous rise of Hitler, embarks on a journey to America to uncover what truly happened to her fiancé, Fritz, she discovers that home is not just a place but a truth we carry in our hearts. *These Blue Mountains* explores the transformative power of art, the meaning of home, and the redemptive beauty of risking the heart. S. L. Thomas has gifted us with a story to savor, a journey to take, and a reminder of how history shapes—and redeems—us all."

Patti Callahan Henry, *New York Times* bestselling author
of *The Secret Book of Flora Lea*

"North Carolina's mountains hide the secrets of a war long past and a young love cut short in this atmospheric tale of unexpected hope and the gentle reminder that only by releasing the past can we embrace a new and unexpected future. Sarah Loudin Thomas brings the Blue Ridge and its history to life in intimate and fascinating detail."

Lisa Wingate, *New York Times* bestselling
author of *Shelterwood*

"The perfect blend of pre-WWII history, second chances, and the quest for love, acceptance, and honesty. A great read not only for lovers of historical romance, but for anyone who sees mountains as a metaphor for pursuing—and achieving—your dreams."

Susan Meissner, *USA Today* bestselling
author of *Only the Beautiful*

these
BLUE
MOUNTAINS

these BLUE MOUNTAINS

SARAH LOUDIN THOMAS

BETHANYHOUSE
a division of Baker Publishing Group
Minneapolis, Minnesota

Published by Bethany House Publishers
Minneapolis, Minnesota
BethanyHouse.com

Bethany House Publishers is a division of
Baker Publishing Group, Grand Rapids, Michigan

Printed in the United States of America

Library of Congress Cataloging-in-Publication Data
Names: Thomas, Sarah Loudin, author.
Title: These blue mountains / Sarah Loudin Thomas.
Description: Minneapolis, Minnesota : Bethany House Publishers, a division of
    Baker Publishing Group, 2025.
Identifiers: LCCN 2024052033 | ISBN 9780764242021 (paperback) | ISBN
    9780764245121 (casebound) | ISBN 9781493450909 (ebook)
Subjects: LCGFT: Christian fiction. | Historical fiction. | Novels. Classification: LCC
    PS3620.H64226 T43 2025 | DDC 813/.6—dc23/eng/20241108
LC record available at https://lccn.loc.gov/2024052033

Scripture quotations are from the King James Version of the Bible.

This is a work of historical reconstruction; the appearances of certain historical figures are therefore inevitable. All other characters, however, are products of the author's imagination, and any resemblance to actual persons, living or dead, is coincidental.

Cover image © Ildiko Neer / Trevillion Images

Published in association with Books & Such Literary Management,
www.booksandsuch.com.

Baker Publishing Group publications use paper produced from sustainable forestry practices and postconsumer waste whenever possible.

25 26 27 28 29 30 31   7 6 5 4 3 2 1

For the Dr. Rices in my life,
Paul and Nelljean

*One gone too soon,
and the other still cheering me on.*

Art is a province in which one finds all the problems of life reflected.

—Josef Albers, *Black Mountain Bulletin*

1

Hedda slipped from the frigid air into the warmth of the kitchen and snugged the door shut behind her. She closed the dead bolt. Opened it. And closed it again, nearly dropping the newspaper beneath her arm. She reached for the lock a third time but then lowered her hand.

No. It wasn't necessary.

Turning, Hedda took a few steps into the kitchen, placing the newspaper on the table. Quietly, she began to heat water for a *Köppke Tee*, savoring each step in her routine. She took down her favorite cup and saucer—the one with violets—and scooped tea leaves into an infuser. She added an extravagant lump of rock sugar to her cup, followed by the little silver basket. She poured steaming water over it, watching the dried leaves unfurl. She'd once read this was called "the agony of the leaf." She chuckled softly. Agony indeed to get a decent cup of tea with a little sugar in these lean days.

When the tea was a deep amber, she removed the infuser and added a splash of milk, watching it billow through the dark liquid. Sighing deeply, she lifted the cup and took a careful sip.

Sweetness, warmth, and dare she say peace seeped into her spirit. She exhaled slowly and settled the cup in its saucer with a click. It was always like this when she ventured out. Such relief to be safe in the shell of Lotte's house once again. Like a turtle, she thought as she dropped into a chair at the table and drew the newspaper toward her.

She'd read the front page on the train home to this comfortable house that she still struggled to think of as *home*, even though it had been familiar to her before she came to stay. The woman she'd once expected to become her mother-in-law was not well. When Lotte's sister asked Hedda if she would consider moving in, she hadn't known how to say no. And why would she? She loved Lotte, and it was certainly more economical to live here. Hedda still wasn't clear on what ailed her—perhaps because Lotte wasn't clear herself. But each week she could see the burden of her sixty-two years pressing down harder. It was a shame to be so old while still relatively young.

She knew she should check on Lotte even now, but the peace of the kitchen after the bracing air and the bustle of the train was too enticing. Glancing at the clock, she felt certain Lotte would still be napping. Exhaling the tension of the outside world, she folded the front page of the newspaper back, meaning to read page two—she always started on page one and read through to the end—but a photograph on page three caught her eye. A dignified man with a hat in his hand was placing a wreath on a large monument. But that wasn't what made her gasp and slosh tea into the saucer.

10

The name. Right there in the foreground. There was a small white cross with a name she knew like the beat of her own heart: *Fritz Meyer*. But no. Surely it wasn't her Fritz. It was a common enough name, she told herself even as her breath came short and tight.

She pushed the tea away and drew the paper closer, getting smudges of ink on her fingers. She read greedily, eyes tumbling over the words. The man in the picture was the German ambassador to the United States, Friederich von Prittwitz, and he was placing a wreath on a memorial to eighteen German seamen who had died in a typhoid outbreak at a camp in Hot Springs, North Carolina, in 1918. The names of the soldiers were listed, and there it was, the name she'd been mourning for more than fourteen years. Fritz Meyer, her fiancé. Lotte's missing son.

"Hedda, you are as unsettled as a hen that has lost her chicks." Lotte shuffled into the *Wintergarten* and sank into a chair with a soft moan. She lifted her legs, one at a time, onto a footstool. Hedda could see how swollen her ankles were.

"Do you think so? I suppose the waiting is making me anxious."

"Waiting. It seems that is what life is about in the end. If there's an answer to your letter, it will likely be to tell us this is some other Fritz Meyer. Don't be anxious, *Liebling*."

Hedda knew Lotte was right. But it had been two weeks since she sent the letter to *The American Legion, Asheville, North America*. Since then, she'd felt as though her life were a simple melody being played on a badly out-of-tune instrument. Her previously ordered life now revolved around checking the post each day in hopes of receiving a response.

11

Had her letter even arrived? It seemed as if a lifetime had passed since she had seen the newspaper photo that she'd clipped and tucked into a corner of her vanity mirror. It was now December—surely this was long enough for an answer.

She glanced at the clock. The post almost always arrived by two in the afternoon. But she would be giving young Liesl from down the street a piano lesson at two. She was one of six students whose fees made it possible for Hedda to live comfortably without having to depend on Lotte for every little thing.

She twisted a bit of hair at the nape of her neck around and around her finger until it tangled. She tugged her hand free, stifling a yelp. It was a terrible habit, one she thought she'd finally conquered.

The doorbell sounded, and she hurried down the hall to open the door. Liesl stood there, music book under one arm and crutch under the other. Hedda peered down the street, hoping the mail might arrive early for once, but alas, no sign of the postman.

She motioned for Liesl to come in and settle beside her on the piano bench. The child leaned her crutch against the sofa and hopped onto the bench. Liesl, having been born missing a foot, had started learning to play the piano early in life, this at the insistence of her mother. Now, at ten years old, the girl was clearly demonstrating her remarkable gift.

Hedda opened the book to the music she'd assigned the previous week and folded her hands in her lap, Liesl's signal to begin playing. They hardly needed to speak anymore, which seemed to suit them both. Hedda settled in to listen and critique.

As Liesl played, Hedda tapped her finger to the correct tempo. Her student was lagging. She unfolded her hands and

12

tapped the same finger on the case, where Liesl could see it. She grimaced and played a bit more quickly.

"Allegro," Hedda murmured.

Then she heard the clink of the mail slot. Her finger stuttered, losing the rhythm. Liesl frowned and glanced toward her.

Hedda took a deep breath and smiled at her student. "Forgive me. Let's begin again, shall we?" Liesl nodded and started the piece over. Hedda gritted her teeth, deciding this would be an excellent exercise in delayed gratification. Lotte was surely sleeping now and wouldn't stir to collect the mail. Most likely there was nothing of importance in the post anyway.

The next thirty minutes passed with grinding slowness. Liesl seemed unusually clumsy. Or perhaps Hedda's nerves were catching. Either way, they were both relieved when the lesson came to an end. Hedda closed the book, and Liesl scooped up her crutch with surprising agility, scampering for the door. She grabbed the two envelopes lying there and spun to hand them to Hedda.

"Your mail, *Fräulein*," she said with a cheeky grin.

Hedda traded the book of music for the post and closed the door behind Liesl. She leaned against it, suddenly afraid to examine the envelope in her hand that she thought bore the word *Flugpost*. Airmail. From America.

She dared to look, her hands shaking. And there it was, a letter from North Carolina. She tore it open, immediately regretting the ragged edge. She always slit her envelopes neatly. But never mind. Inside was a single sheet of paper. She glanced at the signature. It was from Thomas B. Black, former commander of the Kiffin Rockwell Legion Post in Asheville, North Carolina.

Hedda slid to the floor, drawing her knees up and bracing

her hands against them so she could steady the page. There were a few preliminaries, and then this:

> *Your letter of November 25 to the American Legion has been referred to me. I can confirm to you that Fritz Meyer died of typhoid, August 17, 1918, age 25, at an internment camp in Hot Springs, North Carolina. He had been in service as a seaman on the ocean liner* Vaterland *and was buried in Riverside Cemetery, plot 76, grave 4.*

There was more about the dedication of the monument and how more than four thousand people had come for the ceremony, but Hedda could barely absorb the information. She was too much occupied tallying the facts that pointed to this man being her fiancé.

Fritz had indeed signed on as a seaman for the *Vaterland*, the world's largest ship, in 1914, soon after asking her to be his wife. He was nineteen to her sixteen, and his plan was to earn as much as he could until her parents would allow her to marry at eighteen. Then they would wed and live in his grandparents' home near Potsdam just outside of Berlin. She'd received several letters from him extolling the wonders of the immense vessel he helped sail. Hedda smiled, remembering his description of the flocked carpet and tufted velvet chairs in the lounge. She'd dared to dream that she might one day sail on such a fine ship.

But their plans came to a crashing halt when Great Britain declared war on Germany in August 1914. Fritz and everyone else on board the *Vaterland* were ordered to remain in New York Harbor. Eventually, the ship was commandeered by the

United States Navy and renamed *Leviathan*, while the men were scattered to internment facilities. This much she knew.

She and Lotte had a smattering of letters from Fritz over the next three years. They were always cheerful and full of the wonders he was seeing in America. The last letter mentioned the possibility of being sent to an American state called North Carolina. And then . . . nothing. She'd heard other seamen were allowed to come home, yet there was no word from Fritz. Not to her. Not to his mother. She'd feared the worst, and now this letter seemed to confirm it.

But still she doubted. The Fritz Meyer buried in the United States was twenty-five—two years older than her Fritz would have been in 1918. Could that be a mistake? Also, there had been a letter from Fritz, joking about how many of the seamen had the same names. Johann or Hans or Fritz. *"There are five of us Fritzes,"* he'd written. *"I am Fritz-zwei, which I think has a certain ring to it."* At the time she'd thought that perhaps when they were married, she would adopt this as her pet name for him.

Hedda looked up as though awakening from sleep. Why was she sitting on the floor like this? She climbed to her feet and carried the letter with her to Lotte's favorite chair. She needed to think. If this was her Fritz—Lotte's Fritz—what did that mean? She'd long assumed he was dead but now recognized that she'd also been holding on to the thinnest sliver of hope.

She snorted. Hope of what? That he was alive and well and carrying on without her? That he had been horribly injured and was too ashamed to return home? That he had been hit on the head and had forgotten his family and his homeland?

Lotte needed to know. Perhaps there was a detail here she was missing that would confirm the truth once and for all.

And if so, they could mourn Fritz together. After that . . . well, perhaps she would move on with her life.

Hedda let the page drop to her lap and gazed out a window at the gray houses and grayer street of this part of Berlin. She rarely ventured more than a few blocks away. To the market, to the church or to the library. Sometimes, when she wanted to feel the energy of the city around her, to a nearby coffee shop where they knew her order before she placed it. Perhaps, if she could put this sorrow she'd been carrying for so long behind her, she might finally consider what lay before her.

2

Hedda peered into the *Wintergarten*, letter in hand. She was trying to decide how best to frame this news for Lotte. It seemed their Fritz might be buried in a cemetery in Asheville, North Carolina. But then again, perhaps not.

She was still dithering when Lotte opened her eyes and blinked at her sleepily. "Hedda? Is that you? Is your lesson over so soon?"

Hedda clasped and unclasped her hands. "I have a letter. From America."

"Oh . . ." Lotte tried to compose herself, clearly muddled from her nap. "Well then. Come and sit so you can tell me this news."

Lotte finger-combed her short hair and rearranged the throw Hedda had placed over her legs, exposing her swollen ankles.

"Have you been putting your feet up?" Hedda asked.

"Of course, can you not see?" she huffed, then immediately softened. "Ach, *Liebling*. I'm sorry. It's only my breath comes hard, and as you have noticed . . ." She waved in the general direction of her feet.

Hedda tutted and grabbed a thick pillow. She lifted Lotte's feet one by one, raising them a bit higher. Lotte sighed deeply and let her head fall back. "It's good to have someone to look out for me. You are as dear as any daughter ever could have been."

Hedda sat beside Lotte and took her hand. "And you are as dear to me as my own mother was, God rest her soul."

Lotte squeezed her fingers. "We have both lost so much. Thank God, we have each other, yes?"

Hedda returned the squeeze. "Yes." She took a deep breath. "Now, let me tell you what this letter has to say."

Lotte closed her eyes. "Is it possible that we are to know what happened to my son? After all this time?"

"Perhaps," Hedda hedged. She read the letter, translating the English to German for her friend.

When Hedda finished, Lotte looked at her closely. "I see this leaves you with doubts. You're not certain it is our Fritz?"

Hedda realized she was twisting her hair with her free hand. She stopped. "There's much to suggest it is, but then again, there were several Fritzes on the ship, and who knows if there might not have been more in the camp? It's such a very common name. And the age—it's wrong."

Lotte nodded slowly. Hedda could hear a soft wheeze when the older woman inhaled. Lotte said it was her heart that caused her troubles—the swelling in her legs, the shortness of breath. Hedda feared her friend's heart might not have many more years in it, and the stress of this letter surely wasn't helping.

"You're right, I think, to be less than certain." She placed a hand over her chest. "My mother's heart isn't certain, either. I have always thought that I would know when my only child left this earth." She shrugged. "But then my heart isn't strong, so perhaps I shouldn't depend on it so much."

They sat in silence. Abruptly, Lotte lowered her feet to the floor and stood. She shuffled across the room to a small wooden chest tucked away on a bookshelf. Hedda knew Fritz had made it, shaping the wood and carefully fitting the pieces together before he painted it with incredibly detailed peonies, his mother's favorite flower. It was beautiful and demonstrated superior craftsmanship. Fritz had often joked that if he could have his way, he'd be an artist—a sculptor or a painter. But no, he always said, art doesn't bring in the Reichsmarks. Still, he sketched or painted whenever he had a free moment and a few coins for supplies.

Before he left on his first sea voyage, he'd presented Hedda with a portrait he'd done of her in charcoal. In 1913 they'd gone together to the new Galerie Der Sturm's *First German Salon d'Automne Exhibition* to see hundreds of works. Hedda remembered how taken Fritz had been with paintings by artists called Wassily Kandinsky, Marc Chagall, and Paul Klee. The portrait he'd done of her was in something called Cubism. At the time, she'd thought she would have preferred a painting of flowers but had treasured it simply because he'd made it. She wondered now where it had gotten to.

Lotte opened the box and drew something out. She returned to Hedda and dropped back down, her breathing heavy and face flushed. She took Hedda's hand and pressed some paper into it. Hedda frowned—what was this?

"You must go and see," Lotte said.

Hedda stared at the money in her hand. "Go and see?" she repeated faintly.

"Yes. I know someone. He can help get the papers you

need to travel to America. You'll go and see for yourself. If it is our Fritz, perhaps you can bring him home." She nodded to herself. "And if it isn't, then perhaps someone will know what became of him."

"But I can't." Hedda pushed the wad of bills back.

"No." Lotte shook her head slowly. "It is I who cannot." The words floated in the air between them like dandelion seeds—soft, ephemeral, not certain of where to land.

Finally, Hedda spoke. "It's true that I have a passport, but the newspapers say that with the current state of Germany, not to mention the world . . ." She let her words trail away. She knew Germany was in turmoil with more elections happening soon, but she generally skimmed over the more upsetting news in the papers.

"I have a cousin who can help. He's high up in the National Socialist German Workers' Party. They did very well in the July elections."

Hedda began to twist a strand of flaxen hair around and around her finger. She had never traveled farther than Austria, and that had been many years ago. Plus she didn't like getting involved in politics. Everyone seemed so angry since the end of the Great War and the hardships brought on by the Treaty of Versailles. Life was difficult enough without opening herself to the vagaries of politics and politicians.

"I don't know," she said at last. "What if it isn't our Fritz and I go to all this trouble for nothing? And even if it is him, I may not be able to bring . . . his remains home." She laughed—a nervous tittering that embarrassed her. "And then there are my students, my life here. I can't just step away without preparing."

But even as she spoke the words, she knew it wouldn't be difficult at all. Her few students would likely relish a break, and her friend Gretel—also a pianist—had been asking if Hedda might refer some students to her. She could easily send Liesl and the others to Gretel until she returned.

Lotte coughed, a dry hacking sound as though something deep inside her couldn't find its way out. She finally stopped, her breath coming in small gasps. She pressed a handkerchief to her mouth and closed her eyes. "I must know. I thought I had given up hope of ever knowing the truth." She opened her eyes, which were a faded blue just like Fritz's. "You have brought me hope. Don't take it away again."

Hedda stopped spinning her hair and pulled her hand free. She nodded once. "Very well. Tell me what to do to arrange the travel papers. I'll leave before Christmas if I can." If she delayed, she would lose her nerve.

The wide smile on Lotte's face did something to soothe the turmoil in Hedda's belly and the uncertainty in her heart. She returned the smile and was surprised to discover that she felt something else as well.

Excitement.

She'd been stuck, suspended in time since she'd lost Fritz. Finding him again, in whatever way, made her feel that she might, at long last, be more than the girl whose fiancé never came home.

Getting her nonimmigrant travel papers together hadn't been as simple as Lotte suggested. But it had been accomplished—perhaps at a cost Hedda dared not think about. It seemed some favors had been used, especially regarding her "legitimate" reason for traveling to America. And if she were to need future assistance, it most likely would not be forthcoming.

Nevertheless, she now stood at the rail of a ship on a frigid December day, watching her homeland recede and wondering what it would be like to spend Christmas at sea. She managed a wry smile. Surely no worse than the Christmases she'd spent alone with a book and a plate of *Pfeffernüsse*, making her miss her parents with an intensity she could barely endure.

Her mother had been a painter and her father an architect, who found places at the Bauhaus when it opened in Weimar, Germany, in 1919. Their home had been filled with color, laughter, and music. There had been guests from around the world on holidays and sometimes on regular days, too. Hedda had begun playing the piano when she was four and could manage pieces with some complexity by six. Her father loved to trot her out to play music that should have been beyond her years and her small hands. Hedda had loved every moment, including the inevitable point at which her mother would swoop in, scoop her up, and carry her to bed, singing as she went.

No, nothing could be worse than the misery of missing them.

Except there was something worse. On the second day at sea, they encountered rough waters, and Hedda soon joined the ranks of the seasick. Christmas Day was spent lying in her bunk, eyes tightly closed, willing her stomach to stop its roiling. Even when the seas finally calmed, allowing her to creep out onto deck to collapse onto a chair in the thin sunshine, she still felt even the slightest roll of the enormous vessel beneath her feet.

She squinted into the sun, praying that this horrible journey would soon be behind her. Someone took the chair beside her. Hedda ignored the woman, every fiber of her being focused on weathering the next wave passing beneath the ocean liner.

"It's a misery, isn't it?" The cheerful voice belied the comment.

Hedda nodded and risked a glance at her neighbor. "Are you ill, too?"

"No, it would seem I have a stomach of iron. But my husband . . ." She shook her head. "You would think he is the first man in all of history to lose his dinner over the side of a ship." She chuckled. "He's finally sleeping now that the seas are calmer."

Hedda sucked in her lower lip and groaned as a swell made the deck tilt and sway. "I keep telling myself the worst is past, but my stomach isn't inclined to agree."

"Poor chick." The simple words made tears sting Hedda's eyelids. She realized how desperately alone she'd been feeling in her illness.

The woman reached into a shapeless bag at her feet, withdrawing something wrapped in a square of linen. "Try this."

Hedda balked at the sight of a piece of bread—or perhaps some sort of cracker—in the woman's hand. "I can't possibly eat anything. I've barely been able to keep water down."

"Nibble it. It will help to settle your stomach. Eating a little something is what finally allowed my Amos to rest."

Hedda took the large square cracker, browned in spots, and placed a corner between her lips. It was plain and very bland. She was surprised to find her stomach didn't rebel. She took another small bite.

"Yes, good, good. You must eat to regain your strength." The woman seemed inordinately pleased with Hedda's pitiful appetite. "We'll be in America soon, and perhaps you are going there to find your future as we are."

"I'm going to try to find my past." Hedda spoke the words without thinking, but as soon as she said them, she realized how true they were. She needed to put her past to rest if she were ever going to have a future at all.

The woman nodded as though this made perfect sense. "The past can be a cruel taskmaster. Too many of us are slaves to our past." She smiled widely. "Which is why we're going to America. Germany is not a good place for people like us." Her smile dimmed. "And my Amos fears it will be much worse before it gets better. We were lucky to get visas." The smile brightened again. "And now we are going to a land of milk and honey, where Amos can teach in a university and I will continue my studies in botany. I understand the state of New Jersey has a wonderful diversity of flora."

Hedda was surprised to find she'd finished the cracker and felt almost as well as she had when she'd first boarded the ship. She was also surprised to learn that this woman was, what, a scientist? "So you are a student?"

"Not formally, but I enjoy dabbling. When Amos isn't retching on ships, he's actually a terribly clever physicist. We thought he would have a wonderful future in Berlin, but the government these days . . ." She trailed off. "No, let us not speak of hard things. Germany is changing, but perhaps it's only temporary and we will return home sooner than we think. Now, where are you going in America?"

Hedda drew in a deep draft of the invigorating sea air and felt, for the first time in days, that she might actually live to see a foreign shore. "North Carolina. I believe they call the area I'm traveling to the Blue Ridge Mountains."

"Oh, that sounds lovely. Perhaps Amos and I will find our way there one day. What is your purpose in going to these blue mountains?"

Hedda hadn't meant to, but she'd soon told her new friend her story of loss and the hope she had of learning what had happened to her fiancé. As she spoke, she found herself more and more resolved to unravel the mystery of what had happened to Fritz. And more and more confident that she could do so.

Her friend nodded. "We will say a prayer for your success and for you to find peace." She reached out and took Hedda's hand. "Wherever you go, know that Frieda and Amos wish you well." She stood. "Now, I must go and see if my husband is strong enough to dress himself and sit at the table for our evening meal." She chuckled. "He has been saying he was growing too stout. This trip has been a help for that!"

Hedda watched Frieda leave, half wishing she could go with her. Not just to the supper table but to New Jersey and a life of studying botany. To have such a meaningful purpose, wouldn't that be wonderful?

She realized she hadn't noticed the movement of the ship for some time now. She stood and gave her attention to the gentle swell and sway beneath her feet. It no longer felt foreign. Planting her feet wide, she took the motion into her body and felt the strength of the sea fill her with confidence and determination. She'd been living by rote long enough. The time had come to discover a new tune.

3

ASHEVILLE, NORTH CAROLINA
JANUARY 1933

The mountains were **indeed** blue. So many shades of blue.

Hedda had seen the Alps—great jutting mountains capped in white no matter the time of year. They had taken her breath and left her feeling immeasurably small. These mountains were different. They welcomed her even in the chill of winter. Where the Alps were insurmountable, the Blue Ridge Mountains invited her to explore, to find her way down into the valleys and up onto the rocky promontories. They were high, certainly, but not so very high. They made her think of a grandmother, still beautiful but careworn with the sharp edges and striving of youth worn away. They were comfortable mountains.

Hedda drew her attention from the mountain view as an automobile approached. A hatless man in a greatcoat got out and walked toward her. She had arrived at Riverside Cemetery early, fearing that she wouldn't be able to find it.

She was chilled now, but grateful that she'd given herself the extra time to take in the beautiful surroundings.

"Hedda Schlagel?" the man asked as he neared. Thomas Black had agreed to meet her at the cemetery where Fritz Meyer was buried. Hedda wasn't sure how it would help her discover the truth, but it seemed the obvious place to start. She'd spoken to Mr. Black on the telephone and thought that perhaps he was less than delighted to learn she'd traveled all this way in response to his letter.

She extended her hand. "Yes, are you Mr. Black? Thank you so much for your assistance in this matter."

He took her hand for the briefest of shakes. "Yes, well, you've come a great distance. It seemed the least I could do."

Yes, she decided. He was annoyed. But after traveling for a while, she found the annoyance of one man something she could bear. "I am grateful."

He frowned. "Your English is good." It sounded like an accusation.

"Thank you." What else was there to say to that? "Is the . . . uh, what is the word for *Grabstein*? Yes, gravestone. Is the gravestone near?"

"Not very. I can take you in my car if you like."

"That's most kind."

He led her back to his car and opened the passenger door for her. She slipped inside, tucking her overcoat beneath her as she sat. They drove in silence through the cemetery. Small talk was hard enough for Hedda when she attempted it in German. She didn't even try in English, and Thomas didn't seem to mind.

He finally came to a stop in a section of the cemetery that seemed near the edge. A tree barren of leaves cast a thin shadow over the large stone and the eighteen white crosses arranged in rows around it. The wreath Ambassador Von Prittwitz had placed there was gone, but she thought some of the scattered leaves might have been left by it.

Hedda got out of the automobile and picked her way between the crosses to the monument.

In Memory of the Eighteen German Sailors Who Died in the United States Army Hospital at Asheville, 1918–1919.

And then the names were listed, much as Fritz had described. Five Karls, two Wilhelms, two Johanns, and two Fritzes among others. She supposed the other three Fritzes had lived, or at least had not died here.

Mr. Black sneezed. "I beg your pardon." He blew his nose into a handkerchief before coming to stand beside her, gazing at the names chiseled into stone.

They stood in silence. Hedda heard some crows cackling among themselves in a nearby tree. She looked around. "Which cross belongs to Fritz Meyer?"

"This one." Thomas gestured and led the way.

Again, Hedda stared at the name in black letters. How was she to know if this was the correct Fritz Meyer?

"When I received your letter saying that you were coming, I took the liberty of digging a bit deeper. The hospital still has the personal belongings of each of these men. Of course, I couldn't claim them, but they did give me a list of Fritz Meyer's belongings."

He drew a piece of paper from his pocket and a pair of spectacles, which he slid onto his nose. "Let's see. There was a packet of letters. They didn't tell me who from, but perhaps they would tell you if you went there. He also had some pocket change—not much. A few clothing items and a small carving."

Hedda reached out a hand and braced herself against the tree. She focused on the feel of the rough bark under her palm, drew in a deep breath of the chill air, and squinted at the sun peeking out from behind a cloud. This was suddenly all too real. "What is this carving?"

Thomas peered at the list. "It doesn't say."

Hedda nodded. "Would I be able to claim his items?"

"Perhaps. If you can demonstrate that you're related to him." He squinted at her. "Are you?"

"We were to be married." She twisted the simple topaz ring he'd given her around her finger. It had belonged to Lotte once. She gave it to Fritz to use as an engagement ring when he couldn't afford one. "And I am here on behalf of his mother."

"That'll likely get you further than being engaged. Now if you were married . . ." Mr. Black shook his head. "It's a rotten deal either way. You have my condolences."

"*Danke.*" She decided to press her advantage. "Would you take me to where I can attempt to claim Fritz's belongings?"

He heaved a sigh. "Sure, sure. Why not? But I can't stick around. Will you be able to get back to where you're staying if I drop you off at the hospital?"

"Yes, I will find a way."

"Alright, let's go."

Hedda gave him a tight smile. She lagged as he strode back to his car. She walked slowly, pausing to lay a hand on the cross with Fritz's name on it. Surely her Fritz after all. She'd already inconvenienced Mr. Black. She supposed he would be even less pleased with her when he realized she was about to ask him what it would take to return Fritz's remains to Germany.

Thomas Black was every bit as annoyed as Hedda anticipated. And why wouldn't he be? A German woman had appeared out of nowhere, asking for the impossible: to remove a casket from an American cemetery and ship it across the Atlantic to Germany. Hedda marveled at her own audacity. She'd spent the past fourteen years living her life according to a predictable script. A series of chords and phrasing that she could easily anticipate. And now here she was on foreign soil, improvising a song she didn't recognize. She'd heard American jazz on the radio and hadn't much cared for it. But now she was beginning to think she might understand its appeal.

Her host stared through the windscreen, his jaw set like stone. Hedda pressed deeper into her seat, as though by appearing smaller she could avoid his ire. Finally, he spoke. "As it happens, there's talk of disinterring the remains of the Germans buried in Hot Springs." He glanced at her, frowning. "Apparently, the publicity our marker gained has spurred interest in removing the remains of other Germans who were buried in the Hot Springs Odd Fellows Cemetery. I suppose if it can be done there, it could be done at Riverside Cemetery." Hedda felt a surge of hope but kept her peace. "As to returning the remains to Germany, that is for the higher-ups to decide."

Mr. Black pulled up to a building with a sign that read *Appalachian Hall* and brought the automobile to a stop. It was a sprawling structure, five stories high, with architecture that would have been at home back in Germany. Hedda peered up at it, then held out her hand to Mr. Black.

"Thank you so much for bringing me here and for giving me hope that I might be able to return Fritz to his mother."

Mr. Black huffed and got out of the car instead of taking her hand. "I can take you in and introduce you at least. And I'll contact the team in charge of the Hot Springs disinterment to see what I can learn. But I make no promises."

"Certainly not, I understand," she said and offered him her brightest smile. He in turn managed to scowl a little less.

They walked inside, where Mr. Black asked to speak to Dr. Griffin.

"Which one?" the woman behind the desk asked.

"Whichever one is available," he said.

The woman with her nurse's cap and white uniform nodded and set off down the hall.

Mr. Black shifted his weight back and forth. Hedda simply stood, hands clasped, trying once again to appear small and of no consequence.

"This was U.S. General Hospital, number twelve, or simply Biltmore Hospital. And it's now the Appalachian Hall Psychiatric Hospital," he added in the voice of a tour guide. "It was the Kenilworth Inn before that." He barked a laugh. "The Germans kept ending up in fancy hotels that were leased by the government."

Hedda forced a smile. She supposed he thought Fritz and his fellow prisoners were lucky to have had such nice accommodations.

The nurse returned with a balding man wearing glasses and a flapping white coat. He strode forward with his hand out. "Thomas, what brings you here today?"

"Good to see you, William. This is Hedda Schlagel, the

young lady from Germany who's looking for her fiancé's, uh, remains." He tripped over the last word. "I called about the personal effects for Fritz Meyer."

The doctor stepped forward and clasped Hedda's hand in both of his. "I'm so sorry for your loss. This must be difficult for you."

Hedda was surprised to find tears pricking her eyes. Dr. William Griffin had a way about him that set her instantly at ease. "It is difficult. But at the same time, I'm grateful for this chance to finally know what happened to Fritz."

"Closure. Yes, my dear, closure is very important." He gave her hand a final squeeze. "Come right this way."

Mr. Black turned to go, but Dr. Griffin caught his arm. "You're joining us, aren't you, Thomas? For moral support?"

"Oh. Sure. Of course." Thomas Black flushed and trotted along behind them.

Dr. Griffin spoke as they walked along the quiet hall. "Of course, Appalachian Hall is no longer a medical hospital. James Chiles operated it as Kenilworth Inn until the economy took such a rotten turn in 1929. Ended up defaulting and selling the property on the steps of the courthouse. My brother Mark and I were fortunate to be able to step in and transform it into the health-restoring sanitorium you see today." He smiled kindly at Hedda. "All that to say we found remnants from the days when this was a military hospital. They were tucked away in the basement—records, patients' belongings, expired supplies, that sort of thing."

He opened a door to a spacious room with a large table in the center. "When Thomas contacted me, I had Fritz Meyer's items brought up from storage. There's probably some paperwork you're supposed to fill out, but I doubt anyone will ever come looking for this, so . . ." He waved his hand toward a pasteboard box.

Hedda moved deeper into the sunlit room. It hardly felt like a portal to the past. To her past when she was a girl of sixteen and newly engaged to a handsome young sailor. She would have preferred to do this alone, but the two men seemed intent on staying. And as kind as they'd been to her, she didn't want to shoo them away.

The pasteboard was dry and dusty as she removed the lid and set it aside. Inside lay the items Mr. Black had mentioned. A sailor's shirt neatly folded, its creases permanent after so many years. A pair of moldy shoes were next. There weren't any pants—which seemed odd. The handful of coins, a rough carving of a bird that didn't seem up to Fritz's skill level, and the real prize, a packet of letters tied with twine.

Her fingers turned clumsy as she tried to untie the twine. It finally slipped off, knot intact. She stared for a moment. How strange. She couldn't remember what paper she'd used to write to Fritz. Surely it hadn't been anything special. She flipped an envelope over and saw a familiar hand. Or was it? It was as though her eyes couldn't focus. She blinked rapidly and looked again, unfolding the page.

> *My darling Fritz,*
> *I am writing to tell you that our friendship must come to an end . . .*

She skipped to the bottom of the letter, which was signed, *With regret, Marta.*

She rushed to unfold another and another. There were earlier letters from Marta, some from *Your loving mother,* and one very short letter from *Friedrich,* whom she guessed was a brother. She carefully folded the page and replaced it in the stack.

Mind whirling, she looked up to see the two men watching her intently. She shook her head. A small movement that unsteadied her so that she needed to brace herself against the table. "This isn't my fiancé," she said. "It is some other Fritz Meyer."

4

ASHEVILLE, NORTH CAROLINA
JANUARY 1933

Hedda sat in her room at the Battery Park Hotel and studied a copy of the Asheville train schedule. She thought she should probably do some sightseeing while in America. The hotel concierge told her that there was a vast French-style château just to the south. He'd explained that it was a private residence that had recently opened to public tours to boost tourism. It would surely be a wonder to see, but she simply had no zest for it. Instead, she would purchase a ticket back to New York, book passage home to Germany, and that would be that.

But everything would have to wait until tomorrow. Today she would walk down to the Bon Marché department store. She had no thought of buying anything, yet it would be nice to look and perhaps she could find something to take home to Lotte. Small compensation for failing to bring her son home.

She was in the lobby when she saw Thomas Black come

barreling through the door, headed for the front desk. He changed his path when he saw her.

"Miss Schlagel," he puffed. "I'm so glad I caught you."

She stared wide-eyed, wondering what in the world could throw Thomas Black into such a tizzy. "Yes? What can I do for you?"

"There's another Fritz Meyer." The words stopped her cold. "I checked the records in Hot Springs, and two men by that name died. And"—he suddenly looked uncomfortable—"he is among those they plan to disinter."

Hedda felt a wave of dizziness. Could it be so simple? Could this be the right man whom she could return to his native soil? "What must I do?" she asked.

"If you're willing to go to Hot Springs, I can put you in touch with those in charge of the, um, process, and perhaps you can determine the likelihood of this being your fiancé."

"Yes, please, I would like to do that."

"Very good, I'll make the arrangements and let you know what to do next. You'll need to remain a bit longer. Is that possible?"

"Certainly. Thank you for all you've done." She marveled at how this man had gone from seeming to resent her presence to being eager to help her find Fritz.

He nodded once, slapped his hat back on his head, and hurried out the door. Hedda smiled. Perhaps she wouldn't need to purchase Lotte a consolation prize after all. She went back upstairs to write her friend a letter.

Two days later, Mr. Black informed Hedda that the graves in Hot Springs, including Fritz Meyer's, would be disinterred and sent to a "more suitable" site in Tennessee. But the process would take some time—weeks most likely. Thankfully, Mr. Black also recommended that Hedda move to a boardinghouse at 48 Spruce Street, where she would find more affordable accommodations. It was a rambling house, painted a dirty yellow, and called Old Kentucky Home for some reason she had yet to learn. She supposed the one who had named it must have been from the American state of Kentucky. The owner, a Mrs. Julia Wolfe, was gracious and hospitable, though apparently not from Kentucky.

Yet the boardinghouse was clean, the food tasty, and the other boarders genial. But to stay here for weeks on end? She had thought to stay a month at the longest. Perhaps that had been a foolish assumption. She'd feared this process would be difficult, and so it was turning out to be. She still had some of the funds Lotte had given her, but they wouldn't last forever. She wondered if she might use the piano in the parlor to give lessons to replenish her purse.

Her most recent letter from Lotte had been full of encouragement. Lotte wanted her to stay and recover Fritz if possible. And so she would, no matter how long it took. Perhaps she would travel to Hot Springs in the meantime to see if she could find anything left of this encampment where Germans were held fifteen years ago. Maybe someone there would remember Fritz.

"*Guten Morgen*," Julia chirped as Hedda entered the dining room. Some of the other boarders had asked her to teach them a few words of German and were eager to use them. Of course, not everyone embraced her nationality. An older gentleman called Clive Boldin had fought in the Great War and clearly had little use for Germans.

Each morning, he read the *Asheville Citizen* newspaper, peppering his fellow diners with comments and questions.

Blessedly, Hedda had yet to be on the receiving end of his queries. But now her luck seemed to have run out.

"Ah, Miss Schlagel, surely you'll want to weigh in on this bit of news." He thumped the paper with the back of his hand before turning it for her to read.

There at the top of the page, the headline read, ADOLF HITLER IS CHOSEN TO HIGH OFFICE. Hedda stepped closer to read more: *"Ex-Austrian corporal is named chancellor by von Hindenburg. Nazi urges care to his followers."*

She looked up at Clive, who quirked his eyebrows expectantly.

"I'm not certain what to think," she said. "Times have been difficult in Germany for several years now. I believe the people put a great deal of hope in Herr Hitler's plans." She hesitated. "I have never been entirely comfortable with him. He seems perhaps too passionate."

"Well, that's an understatement," Clive snorted. "And if that enabling act business goes through, your country could be in for some real trouble. It's never good when one party gets too much power. And this Hitler fellow has some ideas about racial purity that ought to make you uncomfortable."

Hedda frowned, taking her seat as Julia slid a plate of bacon and eggs with toast in front of her. The aroma of the food suddenly seemed heavy, and she found her appetite had fled. Even so, she ate her portion knowing she'd paid for it and shouldn't let it go to waste. Still, the news about her homeland troubled her greatly.

5

Hot Springs, North Carolina

Madison County Sheriff's Deputy Garland Jones couldn't believe the latest news going around the office in Marshall. "Why in the world would anyone want to disturb the dead?" he asked.

John, one of the other deputies, shrugged. "It's because of that memorial they put up down at Riverside Cemetery in Asheville. Got folks thinking about how there's still a bunch of Germans buried in Hot Springs. Guess they think they need to do right by them somehow after locking them up during the war."

"Seems like letting them rest in peace would be doing right," Garland groused. He'd helped dig some of those graves when he was a guard at the internment camp back in 1918. And he didn't relish the prospect of anyone digging them again. "I'm going over there today. Get the lay of the land in case they really do go through with this."

"Sure. Nothing else on the schedule today."

Garland lived in Hot Springs, had his whole life, as had

his father and grandfather before him. When the U.S. government turned the Hot Springs Hotel into an internment camp for enemy aliens during the Great War, pretty much the whole town got hired on. He'd been just a young pup then, unable to fight because of a bout with rheumatic fever. Being turned down by the Army was devastating, so when the chance came to be a guard, he'd jumped at it. After the camp closed, he'd gone on to a career as a deputy with some help from the camp superintendent, who'd put in a good word for him.

He'd long assumed what happened there was ancient history of the sort no one wanted to revisit. Least of all him. But here it came, cropping up again, because of some do-gooders who wanted to honor dead Germans. Not that he was against doing something nice to remember them—some of them had become friends. But why did they have to go disturbing the dead? There'd been some real characters at the camp, and he didn't necessarily mean the prisoners. Sometimes it was best to let the past stay buried.

Garland drove up to the Hot Springs Inn and sat for a moment, looking the property over. It was a far cry from the Mountain Park Hotel, where the German internees stayed. That building burned down in 1920, and Bessie Safford built the much smaller inn to be used as a retreat center, though it never really caught on. The building was pretty much abandoned this time of year, adding to the bleakness of the winter landscape.

He climbed out of the automobile and began rambling around the site. He half expected to see the whimsical village the Germans had built from driftwood, flattened cans, and other bits of debris. It had been a sight to see. Too good to last, like most things. Time and the flooding of the French

Broad River had erased everything except his memories. And truth be told, he'd be glad for some of those memories to be washed away as well.

While he didn't find even a scrap of the village, he did see another person walking his way, head down as though looking for something. He waited, seeing that their paths would likely intersect. It wasn't until she was perhaps twenty feet away that the approaching woman realized she wasn't alone.

"Oh, I didn't see you."

That accent. It was as though the scrap of Germany he hadn't expected to find had found him. "You're German?"

She flushed and ducked her head. "*Ja.* Am I in a place I should not be?"

"No, no, I don't see any reason why you shouldn't be here." He remembered he was in uniform. He was probably giving her a fright.

"That's good, thank you. I think perhaps I knew someone who died here. I wondered if I might find his grave, but I have not had the luck."

"That's because the ones who died were buried in the Odd Fellows Cemetery on the other side of Hot Springs. It's not far, maybe two miles. I can take you if you want. I was headed there anyway." He wasn't sure why he was offering to help. Or maybe he did. If a family member was around to protest the graves being dug up, that would suit him just fine.

"You are a policeman?"

"Sheriff's deputy." She tilted her head and furrowed her brow. "Yes, a policeman. My name's Garland Jones."

"Okay. I'll go with you to this . . . what did you call it?"

"Odd Fellows Cemetery. It's a fraternal order." He wasn't sure she understood what that meant, but she nodded and began walking with him toward his car. He stole glances from the corner of his eye. Flaxen-haired and neither tall nor short. He would guess her age to be a few years less than his own thirty-eight if he were the sort who dared to guess a woman's age. Maybe younger. If you did guess, it was always good to guess younger.

They rode across town in a silence that was oddly comfortable. Garland had never considered himself to be very good at talking to women. He got tongue-tied and uneasy, but this woman seemed different. Was it because she was German? "Say, I didn't get your name."

"I'm called Hedda Schlagel." She smiled. "I like your name, Garland. It's pretty."

She stretched his name out and added a little breath at the end. Garland swallowed a laugh and thanked her. Maybe that was what made him feel at ease around her. She was worse at conversation than he was.

They arrived at the cemetery, and he walked her to the section that was home to the Germans. Being here again after so long had him feeling anxious. His memory of coming here to help dig graves came rushing back, not to mention the nausea he'd felt the night he filled in the grave for Fritz Meyer. He still didn't know quite what happened that night. All he knew for certain was that Marie Spencer—who shouldn't have been in Hot Springs to begin with—had gone missing the same day his friend Fritz died. He'd convinced himself it was just a coincidence, but it had bothered him for a long time. And now it was worrying him all over again.

He pointed to the rows of graves near the back of the cemetery. "You'll find the Germans over here." She walked toward one of the few marked graves. "Not a lot was done to mark them at the time, but some of the families added stones later. That's a nice one." He read the name *Karl Gustav Engler*. Was that who she was looking for?

Apparently not. She laid a hand against the elaborate stone as she looked around. "How am I to know who else is buried here?"

"I was around back then. If you tell me the name, I might remember it." He smiled and stuck his chest out a little. "I have a good memory. Take Karl there. He was a wireless operator. I really thought that was something."

"It is good that we've found each other. The man I am searching for is Fritz Meyer. Not the one buried in Asheville, though. I've been told there were two men by that name who died here."

Garland barely heard anything she said after she spoke the name he'd just been remembering. He realized he was frozen in place—not moving, not blinking. Was he even breathing? He finally licked his lips and said, "Yeah, I remember. There were four or five Fritzes."

"Yes!" She perked up. "My Fritz was called *Fritz-zwei*, I think."

Garland didn't know about that. What he did know was precisely which grave she was looking for. He could feel the rough handle of a shovel against his palm. Could hear the thud of dirt hitting the plain box that held the big German who had been his friend. Felt the chill of a night when everything happened more quickly than it should have.

She stepped closer, and he smelled something nice, something spicy like cinnamon. It drew him back to the present. "So you remember that he was buried here?" she asked.

"Yeah, over there, near the fence. You wouldn't want him disturbed, I'll bet." Yes, this was the way to go. Get her on board with stopping this harebrained scheme to exhume the graves. "You know, folks are talking about doing just that. Desecration, I say. I'll sure be glad to back you in trying to make sure that doesn't happen. Maybe you could even put up a proper marker."

She clapped her hands and hurried over to the spot he'd indicated. "No, don't you see? I want to take him home!"

"You want to . . ." He was confused. "What do you mean?"

"For burial in the *Vaterland*. To return his remains to his *Mutter*. This is why I have come." She pressed her hands to her heart. "Thank you for letting me know that he is here. Surely, I have found my fiancé at last."

Garland thought he might throw up. First, this pretty lady had lost the man she was supposed to marry and had apparently been pining for him ever since. Second, she was in favor of digging up the past.

"You remember my Fritz? Can you tell me about him so I will know for certain?"

Shoulders drooping and head heavy, Garland nodded. What did it matter now? "Yeah. I can do that. But how about we head back to town, and I'll tell you over a cup of coffee. It's cold out here, and this might take a while."

Joy radiated from her face. He'd never seen someone so happy to have found someone who'd been dead for fifteen years. He sighed. So much for letting the past stay buried.

6

Hedda curled numb fingers around a steaming mug of coffee with plenty of good milk in it. Sugar was too dear, but it seemed there were plenty of cows around to indulge her taste for something rich. She could hardly believe her good luck in meeting this Garland Jones fellow. And she felt it in her bones that this was her own Fritz at last. She was eager to hear details about him that would make her more certain yet.

Garland slid into the seat across from her. The diner in Hot Springs was quiet with the breakfast crowd having moved on and the lunch rush yet to begin. Hedda was grateful for the peace as she studied her companion. He was tall. Very tall with a lean, lanky build that she could see now that he had removed his greatcoat and the hat that made her think of American cowboys. His face was all sharp angles with high cheekbones underlining eyes of rich, deep brown. His hair was a sooty black, cropped short on the sides in what she thought was a military style. He pushed the longer bit on top around as though conscious of the dent his hat had made in it.

He took a long swallow of his coffee, which he drank black. She thought it must burn on the way down, but he didn't even flinch. Just wiped his mouth with the back of his hand and gave a little sigh.

"So you were Fritz's sweetheart."

The look he gave her was so kind, so gentle, she felt tears spring to her eyes. "*Ja.* We were very young when he asked me to marry him. He wanted to earn some money to give us a good start, and my *Mutter* and *Vater* wanted me to be at least eighteen before we wed." She shrugged. "So Fritz got a good job on a very good ship, and he had already saved some money before . . ."

Garland was listening with his eyes, his ears, with his very presence. She noticed his ears were a little larger than was strictly proportional, but they suited him. He cocked his head toward her as though to hear even better. Now he nodded. "Before the United States extended its hospitality," he finished for her.

"Just so. We wrote letters to each other for a while, but then I stopped hearing from him. That was the spring of 1917." She took a deep breath, inhaling the bright aroma of the coffee. "And then I saw his name on a cross in Riverside Cemetery in a newspaper photograph. I thought that must be him, but it was not." She shook her head, still astonished that there were not only multiple Fritzes but multiple Fritz Meyers.

"Yeah. I remember. Lots of Fritzes. Lots of Hanses and Karls. Kind of like John or Joe around here." He tilted his head. "But it still seems like an awful lot to go through, traveling all the way here because you think you might have found the grave of the man you were engaged to a long time ago."

It wasn't a question, yet she sensed he was looking for an explanation. "His mother is not well. Maybe she is dying. She has long wished to know what happened to her only son. And when I thought I had found him, she begged me to come here and bring him home."

Garland nodded as though traveling halfway around the world for someone else's mother made perfect sense. "Got it. What do you want to know about Fritz?"

"What did he look like? Describe him to me so I can know it's really him."

Garland looked up at the ceiling as if the dead German's image might be found there. "Tall, but not quite so tall as me. Built solid, strong. I guess that was from working on a ship." He glanced back toward her. "Hair about the color of yours—maybe a little more yellow. Oh, and the prettiest blue eyes I've ever seen on a man. He used to get ribbed about his long eyelashes."

This time Hedda didn't try to check the tears. She couldn't. Garland pulled out a handkerchief and handed it to her without comment. She was grateful for that. He resumed speaking.

"Loved doing stuff with his hands. He was real artistic. I don't know if you've heard about the village they built out there, but it was something. Cottages with edged pathways and fences, stacked stone, a doozy of a church, shingled with Prince Albert tobacco cans they flattened out." He grinned now, clearly remembering well. "And a carousel, of all things, down there near the river." He shook his head. You know what they made all that out of?" Hedda shook her head. "Anything they could lay their hands on." Garland chuckled. "Driftwood, rocks, tin cans from the mess hall. There was even a log house two stories tall. Durndest thing I ever saw."

"And Fritz, he was part of this?"

"Front and center. He's the one who painted the pictures on the carousel. Did a layout with ships at sea. Looked so real he could've just about sailed away on one of 'em." Garland stopped talking and stared into his coffee. He lifted it to his lips and swallowed, then choked, pounding himself on the chest.

"Are you well, Mr. Garland?"

He spluttered and wiped his mouth with a napkin. "Went down wrong. Sorry about that. As I was saying, Fritz was a tall, blond fellow who was a pretty good artist."

Hedda nodded. "This is my Fritz. He always loved painting pictures, although he did not have much time for it. And supplies were scarce. Did he ever—" She cut herself off. If he had ever mentioned her, surely Garland would have said so before now. But he must have read her mind.

"He talked about a sweetheart back in Germany, but if he said your name, I don't remember it." Garland rubbed at a spot on the table. "Sorry about that."

"No, no, it would be too much after all this time." She turned the cup in her hand. "This is the Fritz I remember. He laughed much and had—what do you call it? He had the eye for beauty and liked to put it down on paper."

Garland smiled sadly. "Sounds like him. And looking at you, I can see he most definitely had an eye for beauty."

She frowned and glanced at her companion. Was this an idle compliment? He looked pleased with himself for having said it. She decided she wouldn't take his comment too seriously. She swallowed more coffee for fortitude.

"This plan to unearth the remains, when is it to happen?" she asked.

The tall man opposite her seemed to deflate. He sighed. "Within the next week or so. There's some red tape to get through, and I suppose the weather will have to be good. There's twenty-five or so men buried up there."

She noted a slight hesitation in his speaking, and it occurred to her he might be mourning these people as well. "You're sad about this? Some of these men were your friends?"

"Yeah. I guess they were. Fritz, he—" Garland paused and shook his head—"he was something else. Always ready for some fun, stirring up the other guys. But he was nice, too. Everyone liked him, I think."

Hedda nodded. "And how did he . . . come to be in the cemetery?"

Garland squirmed. Perhaps he was uneasy talking about death, too. "Typhoid broke out in the camp about the time they were shutting the place down. Some folks tried to say the Germans got sick on purpose because they had it so good here—" He cut himself off. "I don't guess it matters what the gossips had to say fifteen years ago. Anyhow, he just got sick and, you know, died."

"He was given a proper burial? Words were spoken?"

More fidgeting. Hedda was sorry to make Garland uncomfortable, but she wanted to know so much.

"Some of the burials happened on short notice. Maybe even at night when so many were sick and dying." He rubbed the back of his neck. "I was the one who took care of Fritz, but I think a preacher came around later."

She waved an airy hand. "That's alright. I don't suppose it matters now. I will begin working to see what needs to be done to return his remains to his mother right away." She laughed lightly. "This red tape you mentioned is something I will have to deal with, yes?"

"Oh, yeah," said Garland, and he sure sounded glum about it.

7

Today was the day they were going to start "digging up the Germans" in Hot Springs. Garland still didn't like it even though he hoped, for Hedda Schlagel's sake, that it all went smoothly. He and John had been sent to offer a police presence, although Sheriff Fitzsimmons grumbled that he hated wasting manpower on something so benign.

Funny, it didn't feel benign to Garland. Maybe it was the way it brought back memories of his friends who had died and how unsettled he'd been that night Camp Superintendent Harold White told him to bury Fritz's coffin and be quick about it. Something hadn't been right, and he'd long wondered if some dark secret was buried with all those bodies. He shook off the feeling and told himself that if nothing else, this was a good opportunity to put those old feelings to rest. He snorted softly. Yeah. He'd "lay his feelings to rest." Nothing like a little gallows humor.

There was an almost carnival atmosphere in Hot Springs

that morning. Elizabeth Lawson, the high school biology teacher, had even brought her class to what everyone was calling "the dig." She said she thought it would be an excellent supplement to their anatomy lessons. Garland shuddered to think. While some of the bodies had been buried in coffins, others were simply wrapped in tarps and buried. Could get grisly, although he was pretty sure fifteen years was long enough for the worst to be over with.

Work was already well underway by the time he arrived. It had been a couple of weeks since he'd shared a cup of coffee with Miss Schlagel. He saw her standing off to the side, hands clasped tightly in front of her, watching intently. She gave him a tight smile as he approached.

"This will likely take days, you know."

"I'm knowing this. But the good men with the shovels are beginning where Fritz Meyer is buried. I think he's not their first, but they'll reach him soon." She glanced at him as though it cost her something to look away from the work. "I've gained permission to return him home if I can demonstrate that he is the man I believe him to be." She spun a strand of hair. "He broke his right arm when he was a boy. About here." She indicated on her own arm. "I have been told that if the . . . the bones show such a break, that along with all the paperwork will be sufficient."

Now that the digging had begun in earnest, the crowd watched quietly with only occasional murmurs of conversation. When the diggers—some of whom Garland knew—brought up the first of the bones from a grave with no coffin, there was a collective gasp. They all knew what they were going to see, but the reality of it wasn't something you could prepare for, he supposed. The second round of gasps came with the production of a skull, short hair still clinging to it.

The first grave, thought to be August Proffe, was nearly complete. The men, wearing long rubber gloves, handed each bone up as though it were a sacred artifact. And Garland supposed to someone, it was. Others received each piece, numbered it, checked it against a list of bones to complete a full skeleton, and laid it in a wooden shipping box. Garland knew they had gathered records indicating if there was anything unusual to look for, such as a missing finger or broken bone, to guarantee they were identifying the remains correctly. They also pulled out some brass buttons—Proffe had been a steward—and a piece of a shoe. Everything went in the box.

Garland thought they might take a break after this first sally into gravedigging, but apparently everyone was eager to get the whole thing over with. They dug into the second grave—thought to be Fritz's—with efficiency and purpose.

He glanced at Hedda, who had closed her eyes and was murmuring softly to herself. Praying? A good idea, he thought. "I'll wait here with you," he said when she opened her eyes again. "You shouldn't be alone right now."

A tear streaked her cheek, and she let it. "*Danke.* I am nervous. It's a strange thing to see."

"It is." What else could he say? What else could he do but stand by her side and wait for whatever was left of Fritz to see the light of day once again?

Soon enough, they reached the simple box Garland remembered all too well. The top had rotted in, so they had to pick through the punky wood and soil. When they uncovered the first bones of the hands and arms, Hedda leaned forward. "Is there a break? Can you ask them if there is a break?"

"Let's let them finish. I know this is hard, but I think that would be best."

"*Ja*, you're right. Of course." Her accent was thicker than it had been.

Then from one of the diggers, "Hey, Joe, what do you make of this?" He lifted the skull, which was covered with hanks of long hair. "Any of them sailors have hair this long?"

Joe, someone Garland knew from around town, accepted the skull. "Wouldn't think so, but maybe things got lax in the camp." He shrugged, numbered the skull, checked it off his list, and placed it in the waiting box. Garland frowned. Fritz had kept his hair close-cut. Could he have gotten the location wrong?

"What the . . ." The first fellow reached down to retrieve something. "Did they bury a cat with this one?" He held up what appeared to be a piece of matted fur. Garland felt his blood turn to ice in his veins. Could that be? No, surely not.

Joe accepted the item and puzzled over it as others came closer. "What's that bit right there?" one of them asked, pointing.

Joe slipped off one of his gloves to brush at the spot. "Looks like jewelry. Some sort of brooch like my mum wears." He turned wondering eyes on the group around him. "What do you make of that?"

"What's happening?" Hedda asked Garland. "What are they finding?" She darted forward before he could catch her and pushed toward the group. She gasped. "It's a fur collar, I think," she said. "And that is to fasten it around the . . . the . . ." She motioned wildly to her neck.

"Throat?" Joe said at last.

"Yes, yes. This is a woman's item. And the hair." She exhaled sharply and let her head drop. "This isn't my Fritz." She glanced up quickly. "But perhaps he is near?"

Joe looked over Hedda's shoulder. "Garland, is this lady with you? Come fetch her, won't you?"

Garland nodded and took Hedda's arm. "Come back with me," he said. "Let the men do their work."

"But they'll look for Fritz next, yes?"

"Probably, but I think they may have a bit of a puzzle on their hands at the moment."

A little furrow formed between her brows. "I don't understand."

Garland blew out a breath, his mind in a confused whirl. "I think they just dug up the remains of a woman where we thought Fritz Meyer was buried. Where there should not have been a woman at all."

What he didn't say was that he was beginning to have some unnerving suspicions about a strange coincidence from his past. And the stomach-churning notion that he might have played an unwitting role in whatever was going on here was making him wish he were a hundred miles away.

Hedda stared out across the deepening layers of blue mountain peaks as the sun set and dusk wrapped its chilly darkness around them. They had not found Fritz. More bodies awaited removal, but she had little hope they would find him now. His remains were not where they should have been. No, there had been the remains of a mysterious woman instead. A woman whose coffin had been weighted with stones.

She was very upset but thought perhaps others here were even more upset than she was. There was much hushed conversation and many hooded glances. Garland had been called into action in his role as a person with authority and a badge.

She shivered, wondering how she was going to get back to Asheville this late in the day.

Garland appeared at her elbow as though materializing from the mist settling in as the day waned. "Can I give you a ride back down the mountain?" he asked. He nodded toward another man with a badge. "Sheriff Fitzsimmons wants me to ask you a few questions and seems like we could do that while getting you back to the boardinghouse."

"I would be most grateful," Hedda said and snugged her coat close to her chin. "I was wondering how to make my way back there."

Garland walked her to his police car. She had ridden in it briefly the day they met, but now riding in an official vehicle made her uneasy. In Germany, climbing into such an automobile would not bode anything good. She flinched when the door clicked shut behind her.

They drove in silence for a little while. The mist was thick, almost as if the air itself were turning to ice on this cold night. It bounced the light from the headlamps back into their eyes, making her squint. She caught herself holding on to the door handle with both hands. Fortunately, Garland's attention was so focused on the road that he didn't notice. She tried to relax.

After what seemed an hour but was probably only twenty minutes, the mist began to thin as they descended below it. Hedda took her first deep breath since seeing Joe hold up a skull with long hair still attached. "What is it you would like to know?"

Garland glanced at her, then back to lights bouncing from the road into the trees. "You said you had letters from your fiancé. Do you remember when the last one came?"

"It arrived in May 1917, but it was dated April ninth. Letters often took a long time to find their way to me."

"Anything special about that one?"

Hedda tried to remember. At one point, she'd had the letter very nearly memorized. But the words had faded over the years. "It was right after America declared war, so there was a mention of that and how he hoped his letter would still reach me. He wrote about eating something called a 'Nathan's hot dog.' He said that America was a wonderful land filled with opportunity and he wished he could stay. He also said he thought they would send him to North Carolina, and he was eager to see more of the country."

Garland nodded. "That's why it made sense to see his name on a memorial in Asheville?"

She nodded. "I was shocked when I saw the marker. It seemed like an answer to Lotte's prayers. She's not well, and so I've lived with her for some time now. My own parents are dead, and we are family to each other." She stopped talking. Perhaps she was saying too much.

Garland gave her a gentle smile. "Doesn't sound like there's anything there to help our investigation. I'll let the sheriff know he doesn't need to bother you about it."

They rode in silence for a few minutes longer. Finally, Hedda asked the question burning in her heart. "Is Fritz not dead after all?" Her voice sounded small, and she thought she might need to repeat the question for Garland to hear it.

"I doubt it," he said. "I'm betting it's just a mix-up, and it'll all be sorted out before long."

"But who is this woman?"

Garland thumped the steering wheel with the palm of his hand. "That right there would be the million-dollar question."

8

Hot Springs, North Carolina

Hedda had been asked to stay at the boardinghouse until they had anything new to tell her. Garland was pulling extra shifts at the cemetery as officials combed through the graves and accounted for everyone they expected to be there, other than Fritz Meyer. And the "headless *hausfrau*," as they were indelicately referring to the unknown remains.

Garland rubbed his gritty eyes. He was not sleeping well. No matter which way he looked at the situation, he kept circling back to Marie Spencer. And wondering if when he thought he was burying Fritz, he was actually covering up something more sinister. He stifled a curse. He'd known something wasn't right that night, but he'd been too timid to ask questions. Young and dumb, that's what he'd been. He should probably tell the sheriff everything, but what if he'd unwittingly assisted in foul play? He told himself he'd wait, see how things played out. Then he'd share what he knew. It'd been fifteen years—what was the hurry now?

Sheriff Fitzsimmons was on a tear. Demanding they focus all their attention and manpower on solving this mystery. Today, Garland was in line for his boss's ire as they watched a team remove the last of the boxed remains from the cemetery.

"You were there, weren't you? Back in 1918?" Fitzsimmons started in on him as soon as Garland drew near to the patch of earth where they'd lined up all the boxes.

"I was a guard, yeah."

"Well?"

"Well what?" Garland felt his temper rising, not to mention his heart rate.

"What on God's green earth happened here?"

"I don't know."

"You don't know. Well, that's just great." Fitzsimmons adjusted his hat over his close-cropped hair. "Stand right where you are and tell me what you do know. Don't leave anything out. If you went to the toilet the night a body went into the ground, I want a blow-by-blow account of it."

"I wasn't around for all the burials."

"Were you around the night Fritz Meyer got buried?"

Garland swallowed hard. "Yes, sir."

"Well, let's start there." The sheriff took a deep breath, clasped his hands behind his back, planted his feet wide, and settled in to listen.

Garland cleared his throat. "A bunch of the men had gotten sick. Some had already died. I hadn't seen Fritz all day. Maybe not the day before either. I don't remember for sure. Then I guess he got real sick, real fast. Died all of a sudden. The camp foreman, he called me in to take the body away." Garland licked his lips and tried to think. Had there been any clues he'd missed back then? "I'd helped dig a couple of

58

graves that week, what with how fast the men were dying, and so we put the body in one of those."

"We. Who else is part of this *we*?"

Garland scrambled. "I don't remember exactly. One of the internees, I guess."

"You guess." Fitzsimmons shook his head. "I hope when your time comes, someone pays more attention than you did." Garland flinched. "What do you remember about the body? Clothing? Markings? Anything special like that?"

Garland felt a bead of sweat slip down the side of his face, even though it was a cold day. "No, sir, nothing special. It was already in a coffin, so I didn't see any details."

"Any women around that night?"

Now Garland felt like someone had slipped ice down the back of his jacket. This was where the cheese could get binding. He was pretty sure Marie Spencer had been around earlier that day, but if he mentioned her, he'd have to confess that as a guard he'd looked the other way and that he hadn't cared enough to follow up on her disappearance. "It's hard to remember that long ago," he hedged.

Fitzsimmons narrowed his eyes. "Were there so many women around that it wouldn't have stood out to see one?"

"Some of the Germans had wives in the village."

"That's not in the camp, though, is it?" Fitzsimmons braced his fists on hips and glowered. "Deputy, I get the feeling you're dancing with me."

"N-no, sir. Not at all, sir. I guess women came around now and again, but, well, they shouldn't have been there."

"Right. So maybe there was a woman where she shouldn't have been the night Fritz Meyer died."

Garland flinched. "I guess it's possible."

"Possible. Well, you're not the only one who was around

in those days. I'll be asking some other folks these same questions. Maybe we can jog your memory yet."

Garland took a breath. Enough. It was time to come clean. He already looked a fool. Maybe being a helpful fool was his best bet at this juncture. "There was a lady— Marie Spencer—who came around the camp sometimes." He cleared his throat. "Now that I think about it, I didn't really see her anymore after Fritz died."

The sheriff's stare felt like it was boring a hole in Garland's forehead. "What else can you tell me about Marie Spencer?" He spoke slowly, enunciating each word as though Garland were simple or hard of hearing.

"I remember her wearing that fancy fur collar. And I think she . . . kept company . . . with some of the men."

"Did she keep company with you?" The sheriff's face was a study in controlled anger.

"No, sir." Garland flushed, grateful that he could answer that one honestly. Not that he would have minded, but he guessed Marie Spencer had her sights set higher up than a wet-behind-the-ears guard.

One of the men working in the cemetery stumbled and dropped an armload of tools with a clatter. "Hey!" another man hollered. "We could use some help up here if you're wanting this to be done anytime soon."

"Go help move those boxes," Fitzsimmons barked. "Then put everything you remember down on paper and get it to me by the end of the day." He looked like he was grinding his teeth. "First thing tomorrow I'll run the name Marie Spencer by that fiancée of Fritz's and see if she has anything to add." He jabbed a finger into Garland's chest. "You be thinking real hard about what else you have to add as well."

"Yes, sir," Garland barked back, nearly saluting. He

wanted to tell the sheriff to go easy on Hedda. Wanted to go with him so he could maybe help make this easier for her. But as he watched Sheriff Fitzsimmons stomp off, he guessed he was in enough hot water without making it worse.

Having finished breakfast, Hedda stared at the sheet of writing paper on the table in front of her in the shared parlor. What was she supposed to say to Lotte? *I'm so sorry to tell you an unidentified woman's remains were found in your son's grave?* She'd been so encouraging in her last letter, so certain she would be bringing Fritz home soon.

She dropped her pen and leaned back in the chair, staring at the ceiling. Since coming to America, she'd begun to feel like she might be shaking free from the years of regulating her life so that nothing could ever take her by surprise. Traveling, managing people, finding her way—it had all been exhilarating and oddly freeing. But now she just wanted to scurry back to Germany and a predictable life. This was all too difficult.

A tap at the door made her jump. She turned to see a squared-off fellow in a uniform like Garland's. "Miss Schlagel?"

"I am Miss Schlagel."

"May I come in? I'm Sheriff Wayne Fitzsimmons from up in Hot Springs."

"Yes. Please take a seat." She gestured toward an armchair.

The man held his peaked hat in his hands and rotated it as he sat. He seemed to be composing his thoughts. "I understand you were present when we failed to find your fiancé in the Odd Fellows Cemetery." She nodded, not certain what he might want with her. "Turns out we have a possible ID on the lady who *was* in that, um, grave."

She blinked rapidly. Could there be news after all? "Does she have something to do with Fritz?"

"Now that I don't know. Seems that fur collar was familiar to someone who was around back then. Most likely she was Marie Spencer, a lady who was known to . . . associate with gentlemen." The sheriff turned quite ruddy and tugged at his collar. "Can't say as I'm altogether comfortable having this conversation with you, but I thought you oughta know. And I wanted to see if you might could shed some light on the matter."

Hedda couldn't make these pieces fit. Perhaps it was her imperfect English. "And so you are telling me that she was Fritz's *Freundin* . . . girlfriend, I think you say?"

The sheriff's eyes narrowed. "That's what I wanted to ask you. Did you have any reason to wonder if he might have found someone in America?"

Hedda swallowed hard, questions coming at her from all sides. There was the sheriff's question, along with her own doubts over the years. "I did wonder why I didn't receive any more letters from him," she said in a small voice.

The sheriff ducked his head and shuffled his feet. "I'm sorry to have to be so blunt, miss. Was there anything other than the lack of communication with you? Did he mention anything in an earlier letter that gave you pause? Or did he maybe write to his mother? I understand you live with her."

Hedda shook her head. "No. Lotte received no more letters either. And Fritz's words to me were always good."

"Alright then. Sorry I had to ask. I can let you know that we believe Miss Spencer may have been spending time with one of the foremen there at the camp. And since she went missing around the time all those men were dying . . . we're thinking there was likely some sort of accident or maybe even a crime of passion. And then whoever was responsible used Fritz's death to hide what happened."

Hedda rubbed at a pain starting behind her eyes. "But then where is Fritz?"

"I'm sorry, miss. We're not any closer to learning that. I just thought you should know what we have learned since you came all this way." He placed his hat over one knee. "Plus I wanted to ask you a few follow-up questions, if that's alright."

He seemed more comfortable now, and that put Hedda more at ease. "Certainly. How can I help?"

"Can you tell me again when you last heard from Fritz?"

"His last letter to me was written in May 1917."

He nodded. "Right after the U.S. declared war. He never wrote to you from the Hot Springs camp?"

"He did not." She felt her heart plummet. "Do you think he and this lady met and he forgot all about me? That he may have had something to do with her death?"

"Now, miss, like I said, there's no reason to think that."

Hedda shook her head as though to clear it. "But Fritz, he died from the typhoid. What became of him if he is not in this cemetery?"

"I wish I knew, Miss Schlagel. But as of right now, there isn't anything to say he's even dead. Which is why I wanted to talk to you. Are you sure his mother hasn't heard anything in all these years? Might she have kept something like that from you?"

"No, I'm certain she would have told me. And she would not have sent me here to bring his body home if she thought he was alive." Hedda licked her lips. "Are you saying that this is what you think? Do you believe this could be true?" She felt her voice tighten and rise. Her breath stuck in her throat.

The sheriff stared at his feet a moment. "I don't know. But if, by some wild chance, he's still around, I'd have to wonder why he's been keeping his head down all this time." He looked up at her. "And I'm thinking that if he is still around and he gets wind that you're in town, he might try to contact you. If he does, will you promise to tell me?"

Hedda felt the words wash over and around her like the discordant sound of an orchestra warming up. Stars appeared in the corners of her eyes, the room slipped sideways, and darkness enfolded her.

9

M iss Schlagel, please sit up slowly."

The soft hand on her arm and the gentle voice soothed Hedda even as her head swam. She blinked up into a pair of warm hazel eyes in an unlined face that was both familiar and strange.

"Feeling better?" the woman asked.

Hedda raised a hand to her head as she tried to sort out where she was. Right. The sitting room of the boardinghouse. And the woman offering her a glass of water was Eleanor Martin—one of the other boarders. She noticed Sheriff Fitzsimmons was looking on with a sheepish expression.

"I've already taken the good sheriff to task for giving you such a shock," Eleanor said. "I understand he delivered an astonishing possibility without much finesse." She gave the sheriff a look that would make a tulip drop its petals. "Drink this." She pressed the cool glass into Hedda's hand.

After taking a sip of water, Hedda thought she could speak. "*Danke*, Eleanor. I'm glad you were nearby." Another swallow. "Sheriff, it seems that you suggested Fritz Meyer, my fiancé, might still be living. I would like to know more about that." There. She was handling this quite well.

The sheriff stepped forward, twisting his hat in his hands once more. "I'm real sorry I sprung that on you like that. I should have realized what a shock it would be. Just as there's nothing to say he's dead, there's also nothing to say he's alive. I don't want to give you false hope. The thing is, though, if Fritz is still around, hearing that his sweetheart is in America might flush him out. So I have to ask one more time. Are you sure you haven't heard anything out of him since you arrived?"

"*Nein.*" The word was sharp. Short. German. Hedda struggled to find what she wanted to say in English. "I've grieved for my fiancé. As has his mother. We hoped he would return to us for many years and then"—she shrugged—"that hope died. Just knowing what happened to him seemed like enough after all this time. I had thought, once I returned him home, I could finally continue with my life." She gulped the remaining water and wiped her mouth with the back of her hand. "And now this. You have, how do you say, thrown a spanner in my plans?"

"I reckon so," Fitzsimmons agreed, drawing his words out. "I guess I could say the same. There's plenty here for me to figure out yet."

"Yes. That is good. You will learn everything and tell me."

The sheriff heaved a sigh. "Would that it was that simple. I let the military authorities know what we'd found, and they seem awfully keen for it to 'remain a local issue handled by local authorities.' I get the sense nobody in Washington has the time or inclination to stick their nose in on the suspicious death of a civilian fifteen years ago."

He hove to his feet and settled his hat on his head, which

appeared to settle his frayed nerves as well. "Right. We'll keep investigating, and I'll let you know if we find anything. But I wouldn't be holding my breath if I were you." He left without giving Hedda a chance to say anything more.

Eleanor took Hedda's hand. "Well, I'd say this is rather more than you were expecting."

"It is." She leaned heavily into the sofa where she sat. She thought a moment and gave Eleanor a quizzical look. "What is this about holding my breath?"

Garland was none too popular with Sheriff Wayne Fitzsimmons. His failure to volunteer everything he knew about Marie Spencer as soon as a woman's body was discovered in a German prisoner's grave hadn't won him any points. Now he was determined to figure out what really happened that night Fritz died and Marie disappeared. Or wait. It was the night Marie died and Fritz disappeared. Garland groaned and rubbed his head. How he wished they'd never taken a notion to dig up those Germans. But now that the cat was out of the bag, so to speak, he planned to figure out how it ended up in there to begin with.

Garland shut himself away with records from the camp, hoping there might be a clue. He started with the records for German prisoners who'd died of typhoid. Yup. There was the form for Fritz showing the date of his death and giving the date for his interment. Just what you'd expect to find. Cause of death: typhoid. Additional details: blank. He checked the signature at the bottom and grimaced. *Harold White.* That made sense. Of course he'd be the one to sign off on the paperwork if he'd been the one covering up what really happened. Garland had been avoiding the obvious conclusion, but it was getting harder and harder to deny. It looked like someone had killed Marie Spencer. Most likely Harold White. The question was, how did Fritz get mixed up in it, and what happened to him?

Garland always thought better when he was doing something else. He picked up the newspaper and started trying to solve a crossword puzzle. In ink. He tapped his pen. "One down. Undermine. Three letters." He leaned his chair back on two legs and closed his eyes. Seemed like Harold and Fritz had undermined him all those years ago. But how? He didn't like having the wool pulled over his eyes, and the fact that he'd been all too willing to go along back then made him more determined than ever to figure this business out now.

The chair crashed back down when he heard a light tap on the door. He quickly slid the puzzle under a folder, straightened his jacket, and went and opened the door. Hedda Schlagel stood on the other side, wearing a navy-blue dress with polka dots and a wide white collar. One hand was near her face, seemingly caught in the pale hair hanging loose behind her ears in some half-up, half-down style. She froze when he opened the door. She tugged her hand loose and clasped her bag instead.

"Can I help you?" he asked.

"May I come in?"

Garland glanced at the mess of papers spread across the table. There wasn't anything shocking for her to see. "Sure. I guess. Just don't touch anything."

Hedda stepped lightly around the table and perched on a chair. "You are investigating what happened to Fritz, yes?"

"More like what happened to Marie Spencer, but yeah, Fritz might play into that."

"Then what I'm asking won't be so difficult." She smiled

like he'd given her a bouquet of flowers. "If you're already looking into what has happened."

Garland braced a hip against the table. He didn't want to get too comfortable, like he was planning for her to stick around. "The whole team's looking into it. Seems like the U.S. government ain't all that interested. Now what is it, exactly, that you're asking?"

"I would like your help in finding Fritz."

Garland held up both hands. "Whoa now. What's this you mean about 'finding' him?"

"Perhaps he's still alive. I'm certain he had nothing to do with this poor Miss Spencer's death, but since his body is not here, it must be somewhere. And perhaps that somewhere is still alive."

Garland wasn't so sure that sentence worked, but English wasn't the lady's first language, and he sure as shootin' wasn't going to try and talk German. Although he had learned a few words of it back when he was a guard. Taught by Fritz Meyer, as it happened. Not that he was going to mention that to Miss Schlagel.

"I don't think there's anything I can do for you." He raised his chin and squared his shoulders. "This is an open investigation after all."

"But as you have said, you knew him. Yes?"

"Yeah, I knew him."

"Tell me." She leaned back in the chair, crossed her slim ankles in snazzy T-strap shoes, and settled in as though for a good story.

Garland rubbed the back of his neck. "Look, I've told you what I can. It was all a long time ago, and like I said, this is an open investigation. You'll have to get somebody else to help you out." She looked like she might burst into tears. He softened his tone. "Seems to me, if he is still alive, he's not worth your time and effort. If he's willing to give up on a woman like you, well, I guess you're better off without him."

She swallowed as if trying to get something big down. She gave a small nod. "Yes. I see. Thank you for what you're doing to solve this problem." She stood, then hesitated. "Maybe, if you find some truth, you'll let me know?"

"Yeah. Yeah, I can do that. Just don't get your hopes up."

"Right. No holding my breath."

He started to laugh but caught himself. He didn't want her to think he was making fun. He liked her. He just couldn't help her. "Right," he agreed.

She smiled bravely like she was doing it for him. And the look of her nearly did him in. But no. There was too much he still didn't know. As much as he wanted to console her, he didn't have anything concrete to offer yet. He watched her walk away, shoulders back, head high, with that hand reaching for her hair again. He felt something unexpected surge in his chest and was surprised that he wanted to solve this mystery as much for her as for himself.

If Fritz Meyer was still alive, he was a fool indeed.

10

ASHEVILLE, NORTH CAROLINA

Hedda was surprised to receive a second letter from Lotte in one week. She'd been back to visit Hot Springs, talking to everyone she could find who had any recollection of the German camp. She'd met lovely people, many with wonderful stories to share, but had yet to learn anything about what had become of Fritz. She was giving herself until the end of the month and then she'd "call it quits" as the Americans said. She'd return to Germany and try to carry on as if nothing had changed.

Even though she felt as if *everything* had changed.

She settled into a cozy armchair to read her letter. Lotte wasn't given to sentiment. She generally shared a few specifics of her daily life and reported any "news" from home she thought was worth sharing. This ranged from the price of lamb at the butcher's shop to her neighbor's gout. Hedda assumed there must be something exciting to warrant another letter so soon.

Lotte didn't disappoint. After a few preliminaries, she got straight to her news.

Do you remember Josef and Anni Albers? Josef teaches at the Bauhaus, where Anni received her diploma not so long ago. And that is what is so terrible. The Nazi Party claims the school is a hotbed of communist intellectualism, so those in charge have decided to close. Can you believe this?

The city is becoming less and less like itself every day. Anni, of course, is a Jew. And our new chancellor does not care for Jews. A law was passed earlier this month requiring that non-Aryans leave civil service. Frau Vogel, my Jewish friend two doors down, has lost her teaching position as a result. Life is growing more difficult for those who don't agree with the Party. There are rumors that the Alberses will immigrate to the American state where you are staying. There is a school in a town called Black Mountain where they can work as teachers.

I'm glad you are far from Berlin right now. Perhaps everything will calm down again soon, but until it does, it would be no bad thing for you to remain in America. And while I hope you learn what became of our Fritz, perhaps it is better that he is not with us to see what is happening to our homeland.

My heart continues to trouble me at times, but I think I am a little better. That, too, is something that should not cause you distress. Even if I never learn what became of my son in this world, I will know soon enough in the next and am not sorry to think about it.

I hope you can play sometimes. Does your boarding-

*house have a piano? I know it cannot be so fine as your
own, but making music is what you were created to do.
Don't let your shine tarnish from neglect.*

With much love,
Lotte

Hedda looked up from the letter but didn't see the room around her. Instead, she was picturing the cozy parlor where she'd spent many an afternoon in Lotte's company. She had fine antiques, passed down through her family, but preferred to ensconce herself in one corner of a sagging sofa, where she could reach her bookcase and the table that held her cup of tea. The table also held a photo of Fritz as a boy in a heavy silver frame. Hedda had often gazed at the image, wishing she could have known this lively, passionate young man even then.

She reread the letter. She did remember the Alberses. Josef had been a good friend of her father at the Bauhaus. Her parents had known so many interesting people before they succumbed to influenza, one after the other, in 1925. In those days, Hedda had still been hoping that Fritz might come home. It had been blow upon blow, the worst days of her life.

A few years before her parents died, the Bauhaus moved to Dessau, and there Josef married Anni—a student who was quite a bit younger, close in age to Hedda herself. She remembered the vibrant young woman with the dark, piercing eyes that seemed to see into your very soul. She thought that Anni had written a letter of condolence but couldn't remember for certain. She had packed everything from those days away in a box that she supposed was even now in a closet gathering dust on a shelf at Lotte's. She would look for it when she returned home.

Home. She thought of it with a sudden pang. Lotte's descriptions of the changes just in the short time she'd been gone seemed dramatic. Maybe the older woman was exaggerating. She didn't get out much, relying on her sister and a few friends for news. Hedda remembered Frau Vogel. A difficult woman, it was just as likely she lost her job for some shortcoming as for being Jewish. Lotte was surely overreacting.

She folded the letter and tucked it into her copy of a book titled *Look Homeward, Angel*, written by Julia's son. She preferred reading in German but had made an exception since the book was about the place she was staying. She wasn't sure she understood it. The main character, Eugene Gant, seemed to have a very difficult time with the world, and she wasn't sure she wanted to tag along with him while he did. Her life was challenging enough.

She looked around the room, allowing her gaze to settle on the upright piano against one wall. She'd noted it the day she arrived and had taken comfort in knowing it was there, thinking that it might even come into service if she could find some students to teach. But she'd had no urge to play it for pleasure. Until now. Lotte's letter reminded her that music had been her comfort and her stay for as long as she could remember. In the joy of Fritz's proposal. In the bittersweet days after he first went to sea. And in the darkest days after she stopped hearing from him even as the war raged all around. Germany had gone from finding "our place under the sun" to times of privation and near starvation. And in those times, music had sustained her.

And now, if she was to remain in America much longer, it might need to sustain her again. Both as a source of comfort and to earn a few American dollars so that she would not have to depend on Lotte or anyone else to pay her way.

She moved to the instrument and pushed the fallboard back, lightly touching the cool ivory with her fingertips. It was as if an electrical charge traveled from the keys up her arm to her heart. Now that she'd taken the first step, there was no stopping. She sat and lifted both hands, pausing a moment with eyes closed before launching into Strauss's Piano Concerto in B Minor. It began emphatically, full of the sort of passion she'd never been able to express any other way, before softening and soothing. Hedda adored Richard Strauss. In 1924, she attended his opera *Intermezzo* at the Dresden Semperoper. It had been quite possibly the greatest artistic moment of her life.

She played the piece through to the end, losing herself in time and music. It was as though she'd been thirsty for a long time and had not known it until someone handed her a glass of cool water. She let her hands hover as the last notes faded away. She had not played it perfectly, but she was the only one to know that. And she was refreshed.

Soft clapping startled her from her world of music. Turning, she saw Eleanor seated on the sofa behind her. She hadn't heard the younger woman enter the room, but that wasn't surprising. She often lost herself in music. She gave a slight bow from her seat on the piano bench.

"I had no idea you were such a gifted pianist."

"Gifted? I don't think so. But the music passes through me happily enough."

Eleanor laughed. "I should say so. I wish I was a conduit like that." She stood and moved to the piano. "Why have you not played for us before?"

Hedda shrugged, folding her hands in her lap. "I teach students in Germany. Perhaps I needed a rest from playing every day." She flexed her fingers. "Although rest can produce *Rost*."

"Rust? Yes, I know what you mean. My art is photography,

75

and if I go too long without using the equipment, I feel as though I've grown clumsy."

"You take photographs? Of people?"

"Sometimes. Do you know the work of Albert Renger-Patzsch?"

Hedda blinked. "But he is a German."

"Yes, his book *Die Welt ist schön* is a favorite of mine."

"The world is beautiful," Hedda translated. "I've seen his photographs of nature and industry. They're wonderfully simple and direct."

"Yes, exactly," Eleanor said, brightening. "I like to capture things just as they are without trying to make them more or less beautiful." She smiled. "But I also take photographs for businesses to use in advertising and for people who want to sit for portraits. One must earn a living while pursuing one's art."

"Art." Hedda rolled the word around in her mind. "Fritz wanted to be an artist."

"The man you're trying to find?"

"Yes. I suppose everyone knows why I am here and the troubles I've had." Hedda felt relieved to not have to explain, even if it did mean people were gossiping about her.

"Not everyone, I don't guess, but your story is a doozy."

"I like the sound of this word," Hedda said. "A big deal, I think you must mean."

"Exactly. So what'll you do now?" Eleanor, rather than prying, seemed to be genuinely interested.

"I hope to learn what happened to Fritz, but I cannot find this out on my own. If no one will help me, I suppose I'll have to return to Germany." She shrugged. "Even though it is not what I want."

"Germany is in a bit of an uproar these days, isn't it?"

"Yes, but it's my home. Where else can I go?"

Eleanor nodded at the piano. "Playing like that, I'd say you could go on tour. Seems like you're awfully good, and folks will gladly pay to listen to music like that."

Hedda laughed. "It's very kind of you to say. I once dreamed of performing for an audience, yet it's too late for that now. No, teaching is what I prefer."

Eleanor tapped her chin with her index finger. "I wonder . . . what are you doing later this week?"

Hedda had planned to return to Hot Springs to try to find someone new to talk to, but the idea was wearying in its futility. "I have no set plans."

"Want to come with me? My pal Fred Georgia told me there's this fella named John Andrew Rice who's starting a liberal arts college in Black Mountain. I'm not sure yet if I want to be a student, but I figure it's worth heading over there to see what I can find out. Who knows, maybe they need a piano instructor? I have an auto and can drive us. Mom and Dad may have packed me off to 'find my own way in the world,' but they did send me in style. I'm betting they'll think more highly of my photography if I can tell them I'm going to school for it."

Hedda laughed. "I'm more suited to learning than teaching, I think. But yes, I'll go with you. This sounds interesting." She thought of Lotte's mention of Josef and Anni coming to America to teach at a place called Black Mountain. Could it be the same?

Maybe it was simply a hunger for something to do that wasn't searching for Fritz. Whatever it was, Hedda found herself looking forward to her outing with Eleanor.

11

MARSHALL, NORTH CAROLINA

Garland, I'm thinking it's about time you gave me an update on Marie Spencer and Fritz Meyer." The sheriff pushed into the room, where Garland sat surrounded by files. He thumped into a chair, stretched his legs out, crossed his ankles, and settled in like he was planning to hang around awhile. Wayne Fitzsimmons tended to get right to the point and didn't like to waste time. "First, tell me everything you know about Miss Spencer, including anything you've already shared. Act like this is the first time we've talked about this."

"What do you want me to start with?"

"Everything. If you remember the color of her hair, I want to know it."

Garland heaved a sigh and tidied papers into stacks. "Brown."

"What's that?"

"Her hair was brown. So were her eyes. I think. She was pretty."

"Go on." Wayne folded his hands across his belly and looked expectant.

"Guess she was what you might call a 'camp follower.'" Garland spoke slowly, trying to think through what he remembered and how honest he wanted to be about looking the other way all those years ago.

"You mentioned that before. Seems like you hinted she was following a particular camper."

Garland wet his lips. "There was a foreman. Harold White. I think they might've been . . . partial to each other."

Wayne nodded. "Were they partial to each other at the camp?"

Garland hesitated but couldn't see any harm in the truth. "I'm pretty sure they were."

"And did you help facilitate those meetings?"

Now sweat began popping out on Garland's upper lip, and his collar felt tight. "That would've been against the rules."

"Sure enough. Did you do it?"

"I, uh, no. Not exactly."

Wayne lifted one bushy eyebrow. "Elaborate."

"I guess I looked the other way, but I didn't, you know, didn't directly—"

"You helped by omission rather than commission. I get it. You were young, trying to get ahead. Didn't want to upset the foreman. How often did you 'look the other way'?"

Garland flung his hands in the air. "I don't remember. It was a long time ago. Like you say, I was young and didn't halfway know what was going on."

"Being a fool isn't much of an excuse, but I'll let that slide for the moment. Any idea where this Harold White is now?"

Garland relaxed. Finally, an easy one. He riffled through a stack of papers near his elbow as he spoke. "I looked into that. Turns out he's dead. Word is his heart gave out a few years back. There was a wife once, but she must've taken off before he got sick. No other family that I could find." He slid the paper over. "There's his last known address and the cemetery where he's buried."

"Well, that's awfully convenient."

Garland frowned, feeling almost as if Wayne was suggesting he'd arranged for Harold's demise. "Not for Harold," he said.

Wayne snorted. "Don't know about that. Considering he'd be a murder suspect if he were still around."

The knot in Garland's stomach tightened. "Are we sure about that?"

"Yup. That's why I'm here today. Coroner's results are in, and there's evidence of blunt force trauma to Miss Spencer's skull. Not to mention a dislocated left shoulder. Like someone grabbed her arm and twisted it right out of the socket. Coroner said it's highly unlikely she died of natural causes."

Garland fought back a wave of panic. What had he helped do all those years ago? "You think Harold did it?" He'd known, even as a young pup, that something wasn't right about Marie's disappearance. But outright murder? And he'd buried the body! His chest felt tight. He fought to keep his breathing even.

"Durn if I know, but everywhere I look, I run into a dead end." Wayne waved at the files spread out around Garland. "You turn up anything here?"

"Harold signed off on the forms recording Fritz's death. The camp doctor should've been the one to sign those, so I guess that's further evidence that he was up to no good. The rest of it is run-of-the-mill. Transfer papers to the camp in Georgia. Employee files about the workers. Boring stuff."

Wayne sat up and rubbed his temple. "We don't even have a next of kin to confirm the remains are Marie Spencer's. Seems hard—somebody dying all those years ago and no one to care."

"Wait." Garland closed his eyes and thought hard. "Seems like there was a sister. She came to visit once. Got mad about how Marie was sneaking around and left in a snit." He drummed his fingers on the table, trying to remember. He'd been there when she let Marie have a piece of her mind. "Lucy. Her name was Lucy Spencer. She lived over in Black Mountain, I think."

"Why didn't you mention this sooner?" Wayne demanded.

"I forgot until just now. She only came that once and didn't stay long. Seems like Marie thought she'd be impressed by Harold. She wasn't, and as I recall, the feeling was mutual."

"Find her." Sheriff Fitzsimmons stood and slapped his leg. "You just volunteered to speak to the next of kin."

Garland watched his boss leave the room, then sagged in his chair. As he let his head fall back, he pondered what to do. Maybe finding Lucy was just the break he needed. Maybe then he could figure out what had happened to Marie. He'd ignored his suspicions that night he'd been called on to hustle Fritz's body into a grave. Now that he knew it had been Marie rather than Fritz, he understood why. But what happened to Fritz? Had his friend been party to murder? He couldn't imagine the jovial German doing such a thing. Then again he'd been imprisoned for nothing more than being in the wrong place at the wrong time. That could make anybody bow up with resentment and do something desperate.

Sitting up and stretching his neck, Garland came to a decision. He would find Lucy, give her the news about Marie, and make it his personal mission to figure out what all happened that night. And if it turned up the truth about Fritz, well, he'd be glad to set Hedda's mind at ease as well. He just hoped whatever he learned wasn't too awful.

Lucy Spencer turned out to be surprisingly easy to track down. Seemed she'd lived in the same place all her adult life. Now Garland stood outside her house on Church Street, trying to convince himself to knock.

He'd just raised his fist when the door popped open and a sharp-faced woman with black hair shot through with strands of gray glared at him. "Why are you loitering outside my door?"

His hand went to his badge involuntarily as though that would tell her all she needed to know.

"What does a policeman want with me? I've done nothing wrong."

"No, ma'am, that's not it. I'm just here to . . . to tell you something. You're Lucy Spencer, aren't you?" Good grief, he sounded like a tongue-tied ten-year-old.

She crossed her arms over her thin bosom. He considered that she might be pretty if she smiled. "I am. Now what do you have to tell me?"

"Can I come inside? Maybe sit down? This might be upsetting."

"You standing there is upsetting. I can't imagine letting you in to get dirt on my good rug would make it less so."

Garland felt a bubble of nervous laughter form in his chest. The way she was going on, he was feeling less and less sorry for her. Maybe this wouldn't be so hard after all. "I'm here about your sister, Marie Spencer."

She frowned deeply, grooves at the corners of her mouth making her look older. "My sister ran off fifteen years ago, and I said good riddance then. If she's turned up in trouble now, I don't know what she thinks I'll do about it."

"The thing is, ma'am, we think we've found her, and she's . . . well, if we're right about this being her, she's deceased."

Lucy stared at him. "Dead? She's dead? Isn't that just like her. No word from her for all these years and then a stranger turns up to tell me she's finally met her demise. What was it? Too much drink? Too many men?"

Garland took half a step back. The anger rolling off this woman made it hard to stand his ground. "Are you sure I can't come inside to talk about this?"

Lucy huffed a breath. "Fine. Seems you have a story, and there's no need to tell it out here where the neighbors are watching." She turned and walked inside, clearly expecting Garland to follow. He wiped his boots on the mat even though he was pretty sure they were as clean as could be expected and pulled the door closed behind him.

The house was small but beautifully decorated. Even he noticed how nice it was. The furniture looked like good quality pieces, and it was arranged in an inviting way—as though intended for comfortable conversations and quiet afternoons. It didn't fit the woman glaring at him with her arms wrapped tightly around her as though she were cold. She didn't sit, so neither did he. But he did find himself shifting uneasily from foot to foot.

"Well? Spit it out!"

"I don't guess you've heard about the German enemy aliens buried up at Hot Springs being disinterred and relocated?"

She stared at him as though *he* were speaking German.

"So, yeah, the thing is, they found a woman's, uh, remains in one of the graves, and it looks like it was . . . is Marie."

"How in the world would they be able to tell that?"

Garland fished a wrapped item out of his pocket. "Actually, we're hoping you can help us out there. We found long brown hair, which I recall is the right shade for Marie, and we found this on a fur collar." He pulled back the cloth in his hand to reveal the brooch that had since been cleaned.

Lucy froze. She stared at the jewelry, then reached out a tentative hand. Her eyes flicked to Garland's as though asking permission to touch it. He nodded, and she gingerly lifted the brooch from his hand.

"This was Mother's," she said. She turned the brooch over and peered at the back of it. "See, here?" She pointed, and Garland stepped closer to see what was scratched on the back.

"We thought those might be initials," he said.

Lucy nodded. "K. M. E. Katherine Marie Evans. That was her name before she married Papa. Katie Marie is what he called her. Marie was the eldest, so she got this when Mother died." She wrapped her fingers around the brooch and closed her eyes. "Marie didn't care for much in this world, but she treasured this brooch." She hung her head. "Do you know how she died?"

Garland opened and then closed his mouth, thinking how to answer that. "We're not sure."

Lucy's eyes flew open. "But it's suspicious, isn't it? Her being buried with those Germans? Especially since she was messing around with that awful Harold White." Her eyes flew to his. "This means she's been dead for, what, fifteen years?"

Garland saw something raw in her dark eyes. "Yes, ma'am.

Do you know anything that makes you think we should suspect foul play?"

"I do not." She snapped the words out. "Only that Marie was determined to make a mess of her life and seems to have succeeded. I hope you plan to question Harold closely."

"He died a few years ago," Garland said.

"What about the Germans? Could one of them have done it? They're a cold, calculating people, not to be trusted." She narrowed her eyes. "You say she was found when they were disinterring the prisoners? Who was supposed to have been buried in that grave?"

Garland stiffened. That question was far too perceptive. "I'm not at liberty to say." He didn't know if that was true; there were certainly plenty of people who knew the answer, but it seemed the best response for now. He tried to steer the conversation in a different direction. "If you want to claim the . . . the remains and arrange for proper burial, I can help you do that."

"Yes, I suppose I should." She held up the brooch. "Can I keep this?"

"We'll return it to you once the investigation is closed, but I need to take it back for now." He held out his hand, and she reluctantly dropped the piece onto his palm.

"Don't lose it," she chided. "It's valuable."

"Yes, ma'am."

"What will you do next to discover who murdered my sister?"

Garland's eyes widened before he could school his expression. "No one's mentioned murder."

"Well, what then? She tripped and fell into an empty grave in a cemetery full of foreigners? I should think not. Can I count on you to provide regular updates? Or should I seek out your superior?"

For half a beat, Garland was tempted to turn her loose on Sheriff Fitzsimmons, but he thought better of it. "Yes, ma'am. I mean . . . no, ma'am, that won't be necessary. I'll check in with you in the next week or two to let you know if there have been any developments."

She nodded and herded him toward the door. The next thing he knew he was standing on her front sidewalk staring at his car, feeling dazed. He snapped his fingers. That's what she reminded him of, one of those collie dogs with the dark fur and long pointed nose. Good-looking animals, but they could worry a sheep to death. And right now he felt almighty sheepish.

12

April proved to be a breathtaking time to visit Blue Ridge Assembly near Black Mountain, North Carolina. Eleanor, vivacious and full of life, told Hedda the names of the flowers they saw along the way. Great drifts of rosy redbud trees were punctuated by white dogwoods with plenty of azaleas and mountain laurel to underscore their beauty. Hedda felt her spirit lift and brighten with the glory of the day.

At their destination, they pulled up in front of a grand building with white columns rising three stories high. They climbed the steps to the porch and, as if they'd planned it, turned together to take in the view.

Hedda gasped. The mountains were a soft, fresh green, their peaks rolling into valleys that made her wish she could visit each one. Billowy clouds framed mountain crests with a robin's-egg blue sky for contrast.

"*Wunderschonen*," she whispered.

"I'm guessing that means something like . . ." Eleanor gave a low whistle.

Hedda laughed. "Yes. Beautiful, spectacular, wow!"

"I don't know if this college will ever get off the ground, but they sure picked a good spot to give it a go." Eleanor slipped her arm through Hedda's, and the two of them stood there soaking in the beauty and the gentle April sunshine.

"Can I help you, ladies?" They turned to see a Negro man wearing round glasses, standing at the door.

"I hope so," Eleanor said. "We're here to find out about the college that's supposed to start here this fall. My pal Fred Georgia told me about it."

The man nodded. "I know some about that. Come on in." He held the door open for them as they passed into a cavernous lobby with a huge stone fireplace in the back. It was echoingly empty. "Have a seat," the man said, waving toward a group of rocking chairs. "My name's Jack."

"I'm Eleanor, and this is Hedda. She's a pianist, while I'm a photographer."

Jack smiled. "And I'm a cook. Been cooking for the summer conferences for a long time now. It's seasonal work. But if this college business works out, me and Rubye might get work year-round. And with times like they are, that'd sure be fine."

"What do you know about the college?" Eleanor asked.

"That Mr. Rice, he's been here to look things over. Said the rent sounds right, and the place is just what he's been wantin'. Guess it's a question of raising enough money to get started."

"They'd start this fall, though, wouldn't they?" Eleanor asked.

"Far as I know. Been some other folks out to see what's what. Some young go-getters who want to take the classes. I'm sure hoping they work it all out. Say, how about I show you ladies around the place?"

"Thank you, we'd like that." Hedda jumped in for the first time. Something about this place spoke to her. There was a piano in the lobby, and she longed to throw the windows and doors open to play to the mountains all around. But not today. Today she'd simply take in what she could. Later, when she was alone, she'd dare to dream about what her future might hold.

The next morning, Hedda entered the dining room with a smile for everyone. Something about her visit to the Blue Ridge Assembly had inspired a lightness of spirit that she hadn't felt in years. Alone in her room, she'd pondered what it would be like to find work and a place where she'd be welcomed as a musician. If she did, maybe she could stay in America at least until she'd learned the truth about Fritz. The idea made her feel freer than she had since she was a girl.

"Have you been keeping up with the news of your homeland?" Clive folded his newspaper and slapped it against the table.

Hedda stopped short. Why did his question make her feel as if she were being chastised? "What do you mean?"

Clive thumped the paper with his fist. "That Hitler fellow. Have you heard what he's up to now?"

Hedda struggled to give a lucid answer. "He is perhaps making things difficult for the people he disagrees with," she said at last. Truth be told, other than the news Lotte had shared with her, she hadn't paid a great deal of attention.

"Difficult? I'll say. That Enabling Act passed in March, and now Adolf Hitler can make whatever laws he wants. And what he wants is to run everyone who isn't what he calls 'Aryan' out of the country. Did you read about this business of dismissing all civil servants with Jewish blood? And they've built a Nazi concentration camp outside of Dachau. They're claiming it's for political prisoners—communists, trade unionists, and the like—but just you wait and see. They'll soon be tossing anyone in there who doesn't go along with what they want. Firing tenured employees is only the tip of the iceberg."

Hedda felt fingers of ice travel along her spine, making her scalp prickle. "Is it really so bad?" she asked lightly. "The Great Depression has been very hard on Germans. Perhaps Chancellor Hitler is only trying to make the situation better."

"By boycotting Jewish businesses? By firing government employees with even a hint of their being Jewish? You think that will make the situation better?"

Hedda cringed. She thought of Lotte's friend Frau Vogel. She had nothing against the Jews and didn't understand why Herr Hitler did. Some people claimed that their blood was different from hers, but she didn't believe that. Surely it would all come to nothing in the end. The situation in Germany Clive mentioned wasn't good, yet she had so much to worry about here in the United States. What was happening back home seemed distant to her, even a bit unreal.

"It's true I don't understand what's happening or why," she said, "but we must put our trust in our elected officials. That's what they are there for."

Clive snorted. "They're there to take care of the people. And your Chancellor Hitler is only taking care of *some* of the people."

Hedda bristled. "He isn't my Chancellor Hitler. I wasn't there when he was appointed."

"Right. You didn't vote for him. No one did. He was appointed. That right there ought to give you pause."

Hedda pressed her lips together firmly as though to stop

any more words from coming out. But she didn't have any more words. She feared Clive was right. She feared trouble was brewing in her homeland. And it made her more determined than ever to find a way to remain in America. If all went well, perhaps she could persuade Lotte to join her here. Now, wouldn't that be fine?

13

ASHEVILLE, NORTH CAROLINA

Waves of sound poured out of the open windows of the Old Kentucky Home boardinghouse as Garland stepped onto the porch. He stopped and stood there for a moment, letting it wash over him. It was unlike anything he'd heard before. There was a rolling, distant thunder sound punctuated by single notes that climbed to a crash of lightning. It stirred him, caused his spine to straighten. He glanced upward, almost expecting some sort of heavenly announcement.

He stood there awestruck before realizing that a woman was watching him through the open window. She beckoned for him to come inside.

Hedda sat at the piano in the parlor, her back to the room. She was completely absorbed in the music she drew from the instrument. Garland was smitten. It was as if the music were light entering a prism. Each note entered him and then exploded in a rainbow of color and joy. He hardly dared breathe for the pleasure it brought.

The woman who'd waved him in smiled and pointed at a chair. Garland moved forward, distracted, and caught his toe on a throw rug. He stumbled and knocked a framed photo to the floor, breaking the glass. Hedda's hands froze at the sound of the crash, and she turned to look at him. Her cheeks were flushed, her eyes shining with the light she'd been spilling into the room.

"I'm so sorry," he blurted.

"It's just a bit of glass. Easily remedied," the first woman said.

Garland realized it wasn't the photo he was sorry about. It was interrupting the performance. But he didn't clarify.

"Ach, have you been there long?" Hedda asked. Did she sound like she was accusing him?

"Long enough to wish I hadn't interrupted your playing."

"Oh." Her color deepened. "It's nothing."

"What's the name of that song?"

"*Sprach Zarathustra*. It's by Richard Strauss."

"That's a funny name." He immediately wished he'd said something more intelligent.

"That first bit I played is titled 'Sunrise.' Perhaps that's more to your liking."

"Well now, that does seem to fit it better."

Hedda pushed her silvery hair back from her face before folding her hands in her lap. "I'm assuming you didn't come to hear me play. Do you have news about Fritz?"

Right. That's why he was here. "Not exactly. We're still investigating, and I was hoping you could answer a few more questions for me."

"Certainly. I'm happy to help." She glanced at the other woman. "Is it alright if Eleanor stays with us?"

"Of course." He nodded to the woman, who looked quite a bit younger than Hedda. "I'm Deputy Garland Jones."

"Eleanor Plum," she responded. "I room down the hall from Hedda."

He nodded, then turned back to Hedda. "We're considering the possibility that Fritz might've escaped from the camp somehow. Did he ever mention wanting to go somewhere else in the United States?"

Hedda reached up and began twisting a strand of hair around and around her finger. "He used to talk about American cowboys and how he would like to learn to throw a . . ." She twirled one hand in the air. "What is it called?"

"A lasso?"

"Yes, as you say, a lasso. He also wrote to say that California sounded like heaven on earth."

"You think he might've gone out west?"

Hedda shrugged. "Who is to say? Now I wonder if I knew him at all."

"But you're still looking for him."

"Yes. But perhaps it's for Lotte—his mother. Perhaps it's for her sake that I continue to try to know what happened." Hedda frowned. "She's very ill. It would mean a great deal to her."

Garland chose not to examine too closely the fact that this explanation pleased him. "I'm trying to track down any of the other enemy aliens who might still be around, to see if any of them know anything. I considered him a friend when I knew him at the camp, but maybe, like you, I didn't know as much as I thought." He flushed. Might the comparison offend her? He hurried on. "Did he mention anyone as a particular friend in his letters?"

"Yes, I brought them with me for sentimental reasons

that seem silly now. Wait here and I'll get them." She darted from the room and returned in moments with a small stack of letters, tied with frayed blue ribbon. She quickly sorted through the envelopes.

"Ah, yes, Here it is." She pulled out a sheet of paper. "There was Hans Koestler, who he called his bunkmate. And a passenger on the ship, Johann Hoffman, who also liked to make things and was, I think, a teacher." She pulled out another letter and scanned it. "Yes, Johann worked with wood but was also a—I'm not sure what the English is—a *Chemiker*."

"Chemist?" The other woman offered. "A chemistry teacher?"

"I think so," Hedda agreed.

"I remember him," Garland said. "Tall fellow with hair he was always pushing back off his face. He and Fritz worked on the carousel together." He jotted the names down, making sure he had the spelling right. "It's a long shot, but the federal boys might have records of where the prisoners ended up."

Garland shoved his notebook into his pocket. He'd gotten what he came for—a promising lead—but found himself lingering, looking for an excuse to stay.

"Are you enjoying your time in America?" he asked, then flinched. What a ridiculous question to ask a woman who'd come to fetch a dead man home.

Hedda tilted her head to one side with a soft smile. "You know, I am. The reason I'm here isn't a happy one, and not finding Fritz has been difficult, but this place . . . it lets me feel free." She ducked her head. "That sounds strange, I suppose."

"Not at all," chimed in Eleanor. "It's the mountains and

the fresh air. Folks come from all over to take the air around here."

Hedda nodded. "And my home, Germany, things are very difficult there now."

Garland sobered. He'd read the newspapers. "Will you go back anytime soon?"

She sighed deeply. "My papers to come to America say that I am here only for a short time. If I am to stay longer, I must have a 'legitimate purpose' for remaining." She flipped a hand in the air. "Eleanor and I visited Black Mountain. There's a school starting there. If I could get a position or could become a student, perhaps I might be able to stay longer. It's an idea, but of course it may come to nothing."

Garland found he liked the idea. "If there's anything I can do to help, just let me know."

A smile warmed Hedda's face, putting roses in her cheeks. "You are very kind. Thank you, but you're doing enough in trying to find Fritz. You will let me know if you learn something new?" She stood from the piano bench, and Garland took that as his cue to leave.

"You'll be the first to know," he said, then flushed. "Well, the second, that is, after I tell the sheriff."

Eleanor laughed lustily. "Right you are, Deputy Jones. Don't go getting your cart before your horse."

He shot her a look, suspicious that she meant more than she was saying. Was his interest in Hedda so obvious? He was just getting used to the idea himself. She winked at him, confirming his suspicion. He cleared his throat. "Thank you for your help." He gave Hedda a slight bow and hurried from the room.

14

There's a message for you." Julia Wolfe spoke as soon as Hedda entered the dining room for supper.

Hedda frowned. "A message? Is it a letter?"

"No, a telephone message."

Hedda was nothing short of stunned. Who in the world would place a telephone call to her in Asheville, North Carolina? "I don't understand."

Julia sighed. "Here, I wrote it down. If you want to call her back, that'll be extra." She handed Hedda a folded slip of paper.

Sliding into a chair at the table, Hedda flipped the paper open to read the cryptic note, followed by a telephone number. *Anni Albers – Black Mountain College – Wants to see you.*

"They're here?" Hedda asked the question as if Julia would be informed about the arrival of her parents' friends.

"All I know is what I wrote down on that paper. Like I say, there's a charge to use the telephone."

"Is it very much?"

Julia shook her head. "No, not so much if you keep the call short."

Hedda had never used a telephone before. She didn't have one in Germany, and there had never been an occasion to use one in America. "Will you show me how?"

"Yes, yes, after we eat."

Hedda found she could barely swallow a bite with the anticipation of talking to someone from home. Someone who had known *Mutter* and *Vater*. She pushed food around on her plate, earning a frown from Julia, who hated to see good food go to waste. She forced down a few bites to appease her landlady.

Finally, the dishes had been cleared, the leftovers put away. Julia led Hedda to the telephone and made a great production of spinning the rotary dial, which made the most marvelous clicking sound. She spoke into a handset before giving it to Hedda to cradle against her ear, cold and hard.

"*Hallo?*" The voice seemed to materialize in Hedda's ear. She nearly dropped the handset as she glanced over her shoulder, realizing as she did so how silly that was.

"Say something," Julia admonished her.

"*Hallo*. Is this Anni?"

"*Ja*. Is this Hedda Schlagel?"

"It is, and I'm so very glad to speak to you."

"Will you come see Josef and me?"

"I will. Where are you?" Hedda realized they were both hurrying as though the connection might be lost at any moment.

"We are in Black Mountain, staying in a cottage so we may

visit this place that may soon be a college. You will come to see us while we are here?"

"I'll come tomorrow if you like." Hedda hoped she didn't sound too eager.

"*Ja.* That will be good. Josef, his English is not good, and he will like to speak to you. Come in the afternoon for *Kaffee.*" Anni gave the address, and Hedda jotted it down.

"*Gut.* I'm very glad to see you." Hedda wasn't sure how to end the conversation over this instrument. "Tomorrow then."

"*Ja, gut.* Tomorrow." The voice was replaced by a buzzing sound. Hedda gave the handset to Julia.

"I hope that didn't take too long," she said.

"No, that was fine. Just don't go making a habit of it."

Hedda grinned, the joy of getting to see Josef and Anni surging through her. "I won't," she said and returned to her room with a skip in her step.

The next morning stretched on and on for Hedda. Finally, it was time to catch the bus to Black Mountain. She tried to take in the beauty of the mountains flashing by her window but kept getting lost in her thoughts. She clasped her hands in her lap to keep from twisting her hair. She wanted to arrive looking her best and loosening her carefully coiffed chignon wasn't going to help.

She arrived in Black Mountain and walked the short distance to the address Anni had given her. It had been at least ten years since she'd seen Josef and Anni, but she felt certain they would know her. She couldn't stop the smile spreading across her face as she knocked on the door of a little white house with a massive azalea spilling white blossoms across the yard. The door flew open, and Anni covered her mouth with both hands as tears sprang to her eyes. Josef appeared over her shoulder. He took out his handkerchief to swipe at his own eyes and blow his nose lustily. Hedda fought tears as well.

"*Mein Schatz*," Anni said, holding her arms open wide.

Hedda sank into the embrace, trying to remember the last time someone had called her their treasure. Too long. Much, much too long. "Oh, it's so good to see you!" Hedda exclaimed. "People here are very kind, but to see someone from home . . ."

Josef clapped her on the back and spoke in German. "Home is not what it used to be." He glanced at Anni. "Especially if you are *Juden*."

"Is it really so terrible?" Hedda asked. She'd begun reading the newspapers that Clive left lying about, pages folded back to stories of Hitler and the Nazi Party, but hearing from someone who had so recently been in Germany made if feel more real.

"*Ja*. First the closing of the Bauhaus, then dismissing anyone Jewish working for the government, and now students burning books in the *Opernplatz* in Berlin."

"Burning books? But why?"

Anni turned away as Josef answered. "Only the Jewish books. They said they were un-German." He spat the words. "It seems 'German' now means something other than what I have always known."

Anni's eyes sparked. "It is good that we have this opportunity in America. We will see where John Andrew Rice says he is going to start a school, and if he does, well, this place seems good. Although we have yet to meet Dr. Rice. He is out raising the funds to make it all possible."

"I've been there," Hedda said. "It's quite remarkable. A friend at the boardinghouse where I'm staying took me to see it. She's a photographer and thought I might go there to study or perhaps teach music."

"Ah, this would be very good," Josef said. "We are in need of good news. Come, sit, and we will talk all about it."

"Yes, I have the *Kaffee* ready and some of these treats the Americans call 'oatmeal cookies.' They are quite delicious." Anni gestured toward a small table covered with a bright cloth that Hedda suspected she'd woven herself. Hedda remembered that although Anni had initially resisted weaving at the Bauhaus, she'd warmed up to it and was now passionate about the fabric arts.

"Will you teach weaving at this new college?" she asked.

Anni shrugged. "I think so. And Josef will oversee the painting program. He has some very exciting ideas about color, don't you, *Liebling*?"

Josef brightened and began talking about color theory and chromatic interactions. It was interesting, but Hedda found herself distracted. Eventually, Anni shooed Josef off to his books and invited Hedda outside for a stroll around Black Mountain. They walked in silence for a time, enjoying the warm spring afternoon and the busy hum of the town.

Finally, Anni spoke. "I understand you have come in search of the man you hoped to marry. Has this brought you much sorrow?"

Hedda considered the question. "Sorrow strangely mixed with the joy that is America. First, I believed Fritz was dead but that I could, at least, return his body home. Then I discovered that he has disappeared without a trace." She explained about failing to find Fritz's remains and the mystery of the woman they found in his place. "I grieved Fritz for so many years, I didn't think I had any grieving left in me. But this . . . this is all so confusing. I think he must have died some other way, but not knowing for certain . . ." She squinted up at the blue sky and let the breeze wash over her. "And here I am, enjoying America so very much."

Anni looped her arm through Hedda's as they strolled past a livery stable and approached the train depot at the bottom of a hill. Passersby nodded and smiled. Men tipped their hats. It felt so free and relaxed. Hedda tried to put her finger on what was so very different from Berlin. And then it came to her.

"Anni, you know how it was in Germany, especially in places like Berlin. Everyone was nervous. Being a little bit afraid all the time was ordinary." She inhaled the fresh mountain air and let it out slowly. "I think losing Fritz had already made me afraid, and then times were so hard, money so tight, and the government . . . but here I can breathe at last."

Anni squeezed her arm. "I know. I felt such fear in Germany. I tried not to. For a long time, Josef and I told each other it would not last, this upheaval. But each day we lost a little more. And since I am from a Jewish family . . ." She trailed off. "But now we are here, and I think I like this land. Tomorrow we go to the place where the college will meet, if Dr. Rice can raise the money. He tells us it is beautiful, and the accommodations are good." She shrugged. "So we will see what is in store."

"It *is* beautiful. I hope I'll have reason to come see you there. When would you begin teaching?"

"I am not certain. In the fall but perhaps not right away. So much is, how have I heard it said in America, up in the air?"

Hedda laughed as they turned and started back to the cottage, where Josef would be lost in his books and ideas about color. "I've always preferred to keep my feet on the ground, but lately 'up in the air' doesn't seem so bad."

15

Garland felt like he was finally making some progress. As did Sheriff Fitzsimmons, thank goodness. He'd tracked down Johann Hoffman, one of the enemy aliens who'd been at the German camp. And, get this, he was living in a small community called Riceville not far from Black Mountain while working at a hospital there for veterans suffering from tuberculosis.

As he drove east toward the hospital, Garland tried to dredge up anything he could remember about Johann. He'd gotten close to a few of the prisoners—Fritz chief among them—but he didn't recall much about the chemist with an affinity for building things. He thought he'd built one of the driftwood cottages with a garden out front, but other than that, he was drawing a blank. Which made him anxious. He needed to think carefully about what he should ask this fellow.

At the hospital, he found the correct building and asked the receptionist to point him toward Dr. Hoffman. She gave him directions, and he made his way up the stairs and down a corridor. As he pushed a door open, the acrid odor of chemicals stung his nostrils. The room was clearly some sort of laboratory, with glass beakers and Bunsen burners on black counters. A man wearing a white coat and safety glasses hunched over a microscope in the back of the room.

Garland cleared his throat.

Nothing. Clearly, this fellow was focused on his task. "Excuse me," he said. Still nothing. He walked closer. "Pardon me, are you Johann Hoffman?"

The man held one bony finger up in the air without lifting his head from the microscope. Garland shifted from one foot to the other. Should he assert himself as a police officer? No, he decided, he wanted to keep this as friendly as possible.

"And there we have it!" the man crowed and lifted his head. "Negative!"

Garland almost felt as though he should offer congratulations but opted to cut straight to the business at hand. "Johann Hoffman?"

"*Ja*, that's me." He shoved unruly hair from his face and blinked a few times, peering more closely at Garland. "I think I know you. Do I know you?"

"I was a guard at the camp for enemy aliens in Hot Springs."

"*Ja*, I remember. This is a surprise. I have not thought about those days in a long time. You were very young then."

Garland bristled. "Not so young."

"It's good, being young. I'm getting older, but not so old that I don't want to try something new. This is why I like science—there is always something new to try and discover."

Garland had the feeling Johann would run off with the conversation if he didn't jump in. "Did Fritz Meyer want to try something new back in 1918?"

Johann frowned and tilted his head to the side. "Fritz

Meyer. How do I know this name? Ah, yes. We made the carousel together." The man's lean features softened, and his eyes lost their focus. "How strange, to have such happy memories of such difficult days." He shook his head. "But how do you mean about 1918? *Mein Freund* Fritz, he died that year. In the outbreak of typhoid. One day he is fine and the next . . . *pfft*." He made a flitting motion with his fingers.

"Maybe not," Garland said. "His fiancée has come here from Germany to claim his body, and, well, his body isn't where it's supposed to be."

Johann straightened up and stared. "How strange. I remember visiting his grave, along with so many others in those terrible days."

Garland leaned in. "Do you remember anything else that happened around the time Fritz died? Anything out of the ordinary?"

Johann scrunched his face like he was thinking hard. "Now that you remind me, here is the strange part." He closed his eyes and drummed his fingers on the counter. "The night Fritz died I remember seeing two men carry a body into the morgue." He nodded. "This is right, I think. Do you remember that we had to make a morgue because so many were dying with the typhoid?"

"I do remember," said Garland, hardly daring to breathe.

"Yes. So that night, I see two men, and one looks very much like Fritz." He held his arms out and flexed his muscles. "He was a big man, very strong. But when I hear it is Fritz who is dead, I think it was me only wishing I had seen my friend."

Garland tried to think. "What time was it?"

"Oh, late, I think. After ten of the night. I was in need of relief." His face turned red. "The latrine, it was not close, so I made my own." He laughed. "I suppose that does not matter now."

"No, I guess it doesn't. But it's helpful to hear that you think you saw Fritz that night. Could help explain why his body wasn't found at the cemetery."

Johann shook his head slowly. "I remember how sad I was because he had such big plans."

Garland cocked his head. "Big plans? What do you mean by that?"

"He said he would stay in America after the war ended. That he would become a great artist and would send for the woman he loved."

"Stay? Here in North Carolina?"

"*Nein.*" Johann shook his head. "Let me think." He tapped his chin. "Ah, yes! New Mexico. Fritz read about a woman who hosted what she called 'salons' in New York City before moving west. Fritz said he could be an artist and meet cowboys. He was very much excited by this idea." Light dawned in his eyes. "Do you think he only pretended to die so he could slip away and go there?"

"His fiancée mentioned that he was interested in cowboys. If he did escape, that could fit. I don't suppose you've ever heard from him?"

Johann shook his head, clearly lost in thought. "Fritz, he wasn't happy with his life in Germany. I can see that he might want to find a new life. One where he could be himself."

Garland frowned. "Be himself? What do you mean by that?"

"He was an artist who must work on a ship to earn enough money to marry his sweetheart. And then he was made to stay in America, behind a fence, even though he never lifted a weapon against anyone. He only wanted to paint. To make beauty out of the troubles of the world." Johann spread his hands wide. "Is that not enough? Perhaps I would have run away, too. It was something I thought about many times."

"But what about Hedda?"

Johann furrowed his brow. "Who is this?"

"His fiancée."

"Ah, yes, I had forgotten her name." He shrugged. "Perhaps he meant to send for her. Perhaps he didn't love her as much as he thought. Who knows? These were difficult days." Johann grew serious. "Or perhaps he did not survive. It would have been very hard to travel so far, and America was not so welcoming of Germans." He shook his head. "It could have ended very badly for Fritz."

Garland's stomach knotted. The thought had occurred to him that if Fritz had run away, he might have died some other way. Which would be worse for Hedda? Finding out that Fritz had escaped and never contacted her or never knowing one way or the other?

"Wait. I remember something." Johann held up a finger. "The river. Fritz liked to sit and watch the water go by. He said he thought he could swim across it. There was no fence there." He began laughing. "I remember a joke we made. A piece of driftwood looked like a . . . what is the big lizard with a long nose?"

"An alligator," Garland filled in mechanically. He'd forgotten about the driftwood carving. But Johann's guess about the river sounded right. If Fritz had been involved in Marie's death, maybe he'd escaped by swimming across the French Broad River. But then who put Marie's body in Fritz's coffin? It had to have been Harold. The foreman had instructed Garland—who'd just come in from night watch at midnight—to bury the coffin that he now knew held Marie Spencer. Which made Garland inclined to think the two men had been in cahoots.

Johann was still talking. "*Ja*, an alligator. Adolph Thierbach was detained with us. He was a photographer, and we took a photograph as if we were being attacked. It was very funny."

"Was Fritz in the photograph?" Garland also remembered Adolph, a quiet man who'd been allowed to document the daily life of the camp with his camera.

Johann thought a moment. "No, not that one, but there were others. I think he must have been in some of those."

Garland thanked Johann for his time and headed back to Asheville. He wasn't sure if it would help, but he was determined to track down those photographs in case they might offer a clue.

16

ASHEVILLE, NORTH CAROLINA

The hair at the nape of Hedda's neck was an impossible tangle. She tried desperately to work a brush through it. Why couldn't she break this nervous habit? And today of all days. She had an appointment to meet with John Andrew Rice to discuss how she might participate at Black Mountain College. Anni had arranged the meeting. She and Josef had agreed to teach at the college with classes starting in September. Hedda needed a reason to stay in America, and she thought this was her best chance.

Her original travel papers said that she was coming to America to bring home the body of her deceased fiancé. In addition, they stated that she would travel to western North Carolina, including Asheville and Hot Springs, where she would spend up to six months. At the time, this sounded like an unnecessary abundance, but now her six months were nearly up. She didn't know how these things were tracked, but she feared someone would soon ask her why she wasn't preparing to return to Germany. She understood that people with important jobs were sometimes given work papers. If she could say that she was a teacher at a college, perhaps that would be reason enough to let her stay.

Because she was determined to stay.

In Germany there had been a muddled uprising—so the newspapers said—against Hitler that had ended in the deaths or suicides of several key government leaders, all of whom seemed to have one thing in common: they had threatened the new order. Rumors suggested that soon the Nazis would become the sole legal political party. And they weren't wasting any time making changes. Naturalized German Jews had seen their citizenship repealed, and more frightening still, new laws had been passed to allow the sterilization of "undesirables." This included people with physical or mental disabilities, Gypsies, and Afro-Germans.

Hedda thought of sweet Liesl, who perched beside her on the piano bench week after week for her lessons, the stump of her left leg swinging in time to the music. Would Liesl be prevented from ever having children? She shuddered to consider the possibility.

After dragging the brush through the snarls she'd twisted, Hedda pinned her hair up so that she couldn't tangle it anymore. Eleanor offered to drive her to Black Mountain. She was grateful not only for the ride but for the support of a friend. She'd gotten out of the habit of having friends in Germany. Her simple, structured life had made it easy to remain solitary with only her students and Lotte to populate her days. But now she was finding friendship—even with someone fifteen years her junior—refreshing and engaging in a way she'd forgotten was possible.

"Don't you look smart," Eleanor said when Hedda came down the stairs. "They'll hire you without a doubt."

Hedda clenched her hands to keep from reaching for her hair. "I'm glad you think so, but I'm not so certain. My credentials . . . they may not be sufficient."

"Then play for them. That should be credential enough."

Eleanor hustled Hedda out to her automobile and whisked her off to Blue Ridge Assembly. Dr. Rice met them on the porch of Lee Hall. He was a stout man with a round face and equally round glasses. He wore a small bristle of a mustache, and his tie was askew.

"Miss Schlagel, I presume." He took Hedda's hand for a brisk shake. He glanced at Eleanor but didn't acknowledge her. "Josef and Anni suggested I speak to you, but I'm not at all certain that this is the right place for you. Do you have any teaching experience?"

Hedda fought the urge to spin around and flee down the steps. "I've been teaching for more than a decade." She wanted to add more but found herself short of words.

"At the college level?" Before Hedda could answer, he continued, "We're a bit different here. Our goal is to educate the full person, both in mind and in body. In addition to the usual classes in science, philosophy, history and so on, we place the arts at the center of our work. That's why I hired the Alberses. Someone must oversee the arts curriculum, and they say you could contribute. There will also be a strong focus on physical work, exercise, and active entertainments such as trekking and dancing." He looked at her in a long moment of silence. "Well. We shall see. Come inside." He turned and entered the hall.

Eleanor caught Hedda's eye and pointed to a rocking chair as she made a shooing motion. Hedda nodded in understanding, although she wished her friend would come inside for moral support. She trailed Dr. Rice through the door, clasping her hands together to keep them out of her hair.

"Jack told me you visited in the spring. Even before the college was a certainty."

Hedda hoped he wasn't angry about that. "Eleanor, my friend outside, is a photographer. She thought she might find a place here."

"As a student, I hope. There isn't money for teachers."

Hedda felt the knot in her stomach tighten. "But I thought—"

"Yes, yes." Dr. Rice waved a dismissive hand. "Room and board, perhaps a small stipend." He gestured toward a pair of chairs placed haphazardly in the middle of the space. Hedda sat, feeling as if she were trying to play a familiar piece of music in the wrong key. "Now, tell me your credentials." He pulled a pipe from his pocket and clamped it between his teeth.

"I have been playing since I could sit at a piano and teaching since I was twenty, sixteen years. Some of my students have gone on to study at the Royal Conservatory of Music of Leipzig, as well as at the universities in Berlin and Cologne. I am classically trained and particularly enjoy the music of Richard Strauss." She saw an upright piano placed against the far wall. "I would be happy to play for you."

She began to rise, but Dr. Rice waved her back. "But your training—where were you trained?"

Hedda flushed. "At home. My mother taught me at first, and then friends of my parents from the Bauhaus would come and give me lessons. Or sometimes I went there." She felt her cheeks grow hotter. "It seems I have always had a natural affinity for music."

"So no formal credentials." He removed the pipe and cradled it as he spoke, as though talking mostly to himself. "Which is not always a bad thing. Still, in the beginning it would be best if our teachers were of the highest caliber." He stood. "No, I don't think we have a place for you here."

Hedda froze as if rooted to her chair. "But you haven't even heard me play," she offered in a low voice.

"Not necessary. I'm sure you play very well. Once we're more established, you'd likely do quite well. But this first year I must be selective."

Hedda surged to her feet. "I'll teach at no cost. I can even play for entertainment. You mentioned dancing. I could play for dancing." She bit her lip to keep from saying more.

John Andrew Rice looked at her steadily, making a low, humming sound. "Hmmm. Perhaps we could find room for you as a translator for Josef and allow you to exercise your musical talents as well." He dropped the cold pipe into his pocket. "The man's English is terrible, and I fear he doesn't have much interest in improving it." He nodded once, emphatically. "Very well. We'll try this on a temporary basis until the end of the year. You'll have a room in the faculty wing. Come back next Monday and I'll introduce you to the others. You won't be paid, but you'll have plenty to eat, and if some of the students want to take private lessons, I will leave that up to you." With that, he strode out of the room and disappeared into the depths of what Hedda presumed was the faculty wing. Where she would soon be living.

Hedda stumbled back out onto the porch, where Eleanor sat with her head thrown back and eyes closed, rocking gently in the cool afternoon breeze. She opened one eye and then the other. "Well? I didn't hear you playing."

"He didn't ask me to. And I don't think he really wants me here, but he agreed that I could translate for Josef and perhaps play for entertainment. And I'll live here. If I take on a few private students, I think it will be enough."

"Well, that's aces! I didn't want to say anything until after your meeting, but I'm planning to apply as a student just as soon as there's anything like registration in place." She laughed. "I think they're kind of making it up as they go. Which suits me just fine." She stood. "What say we go have a soda to celebrate?"

Hedda laughed, letting all her nerves bubble up and out. She realized her hands were shaking. "I think I can manage that."

Eleanor skipped down the steps. Hedda watched her go, then lifted her eyes to the view. She'd admired the soft green of spring leaves the last time she'd stood here. Today, summer was maturing into a more verdant tapestry, like velvet draped over the bones of the mountains. She watched billowy white clouds drift across the worn blue of the summer sky and whispered a prayer that her home country would find its way back to a peace like this.

17

Finally. Garland had tracked down Adolph Thierbach's photographs at the Marshall Library. Somewhere along the line, the photographer had placed his images in an album with captions and entrusted it to the library. Now, on a breezy June morning, Garland had an appointment with librarian Martin Noth to look at the photos.

When he arrived at the library, he was greeted warmly by Martin, who seemed thrilled that someone wanted to see the album. "Herr Thierbach didn't know if anyone would ever care to see his photographs, but I felt certain they would be important one day. Did you know the village the internees built was demolished?" He made a *tsk*ing sound. "Such a shame, but I suppose that is the price of progress."

He ushered Garland into a small room with a table and four chairs as well as bookshelves lining the walls. "Our historical room. I hope to continue growing it for as long as I'm able." Martin's chest puffed out. "History is so very important, especially in these difficult days." He laid a hand on Garland's arm. "I've heard it said that each generation thinks their time is the worst, but truly the times we live in . . ." He shook his head. "I fear 'the war to end all wars' may have been misnamed." He moved to the table, where an album lay. "But you didn't come to hear me preach. This is Herr Thierbach's work. Please, take your time. I'll leave you to it." He gave a small bow and exited the room.

Garland was grateful Martin had left him alone. The librarian seemed a decent fellow, but he didn't want to socialize. All he wanted to do was find out what happened to Fritz. In part to satisfy himself, but also so that he could offer Hedda the truth she'd waited much too long to learn.

He settled in one of the creaking wooden chairs and drew the album closer. He flipped it open and began turning the pages. He worked slowly, examining each face in each image, hoping he would recognize Fritz after all these years. Some of the images were of buildings: the camp, the hotel, the railway station. He flipped by those quickly. Images of the German village slowed him down. He'd forgotten how beautiful the log and driftwood structures were. Some even had fences and stone-lined paths. There were gardens and curtains at the windows. A few of the images showed men standing about. He thought he spotted Fritz in one but couldn't be sure.

He stopped cold when he reached a photo titled *Kirche im Dorf in Bau*. Under the German words, someone had written, *Church in Village Under Construction*. And there was Fritz, perched high atop the steeple in the bell tower, along with several other men. He remembered the church well but had forgotten just how artfully it was crafted. The men began with a stone base, then used scrap lumber and salvaged pieces of tin for the roof. It was hard to tell in the photo, but what resembled cedar shakes had been flattened Prince Albert tobacco tins.

Garland sat back in his chair and stared at the far wall. It was almost as if he could hear the men laughing and talking in German, could smell cut lumber, and could see the intensity with which Fritz focused on his craft. Although younger than many of the men, he often guided the work with patience and vision. Fritz had been the sort of fellow who always had a smile on his face. Even when he was most serious, his mouth was in a perpetual curve.

He turned another page and there was Fritz again. This time he stood in the background of a photo of the carousel Johann had mentioned making with him. Garland remembered it as a remarkable piece of engineering, with four hanging gondolas and detailed paintings of ships at sea on the center column. Fritz's detailed paintings.

What if he really had escaped across the French Broad River? Would he have swum? Built a raft? Simply grabbed on to a floating bit of debris and let it carry him wherever it would? Garland made a mental note to check a map of the river before he left the library.

Returning to the album, he found images of more buildings, some group photographs, and then the clincher—a photo titled *Lagerauto*. The camp vehicle. And who should be standing beside the truck other than Fritz, wearing gauntlet gloves and a tweed cap with his pants tucked into tall boots. For once, he looked serious. And just like that, Garland remembered.

All the men wanted to drive the shiny black truck with its tufted seat and perfect windscreen. The flatbed was ideal for moving everything from lumber and supplies to men. Fritz, who had worked in the engine room on the ship, took to the truck like a duck to water. He seemed to understand how it worked without needing any explanation and kept it running in tip-top shape. Which earned him the honor of being one of the few internees who were allowed to drive. Mostly, the truck was driven by guards—although not Garland. He'd attempted it once and had done such a bad job, grinding gears and stalling it, that he'd never been asked to try again. Of course, now he could drive beautifully.

A notion began to form in Garland's mind. There had been plenty of coming and going between the camp and the town. The enemy aliens were sometimes driven out to work in the community. He could remember them building a gazebo for the Gentry family, and there had been other work projects, building roads and bridges or clearing land.

What if Fritz hadn't crossed the river? What if he'd used his familiarity with the camp truck to make his escape? He could have crouched on the floorboard or hidden under a tarp on the back. Would one of the other guards have allowed that?

The knot that had been in Garland's stomach since the day they found Marie's body in Fritz's grave drew tighter. Harold White had been one of the drivers. Harold who'd persuaded Garland that it was in his best interests to look the other way every time Marie visited. Harold who'd given him the task of burying the coffin he had thought held Fritz's body.

Garland remembered the piercing grief he'd felt that night. He'd really cared about Fritz, and he'd seen him just the day before, seemingly fine. On top of the grief, he'd been afraid he might catch typhoid, too. For the first time in his life, he'd realized how close death could be. He remembered hurrying to bury the coffin so he could leave the cemetery. He hadn't even said a prayer.

As he stared at the image of Fritz standing beside the truck, he wished he could go back and do it all over again. That he could slow down, think everything through, and maybe save several people—Hedda, Lucy, himself—a world of trouble.

The next morning, Garland knocked on Wayne's office door. "Got another update for you, Sheriff."

Wayne grunted and waved him in. "Your timing couldn't be better. Hope this is good."

Garland wasn't sure what that meant. He slid a copy of the photo of Fritz across the desk. "Found some photos of our missing man and talked to one of his pals from the camp. Seems like Fritz had it in mind to either be an artist or a cowboy, but either way he talked about heading out west. New Mexico, to be specific. He knew how to drive and was on good terms with the guards who drove this truck. Maybe he snuck out that way."

Wayne stared at him. "That's it?"

Garland felt his face go hot. "Uh, his pal also suggested he might've swum the river, which also points to a possible escape."

The sheriff sighed gustily and looked over Garland's shoulder. "Come in, Miss Spencer," he said. Then he glared at Garland. "Deputy Jones was just updating me on your sister's case."

If he thought it would help, Garland would have bolted from the room and never looked back. Instead, he stood and gave Lucy Spencer a slight bow as she sailed into the room and planted herself solidly in a chair in front of Sheriff Fitzsimmons's desk. Garland resumed his own seat. "Excellent," she said in a tone that suggested the situation was anything but.

Wayne turned his cool gaze on Garland. "Go ahead, Deputy."

Garland closed his eyes for just a moment and dug deep. What else did he have? Pictures. He had more pictures. "As I was saying, I found several photos from the camp with Fritz in them. I think learning what happened to him is our strongest lead in learning what happened to Marie Spencer. And I'm hoping these images might offer some clues."

He spread the photos on the desk where they could all see them. The librarian had allowed him to borrow these few, as well as a handful of others that he said were "spares." Garland pointed out Fritz on the church steeple and behind the carousel. He pushed the spare photos aside, reaching for the one of Fritz beside the camp truck.

"Oh, my word." Lucy's voice was barely audible. She stared at the photos, then reached a shaking hand out to draw one closer.

Garland had skimmed past it because it didn't show Fritz. It was a fuzzy image of one of the more elaborate houses in the German village. The building was in the chalet style with an octagonal tower on one corner. There was a slim woman standing at the door—an oddity in a camp populated by men. And while the image was poor, Garland realized with a jolt that this woman looked an awful lot like Harold White's paramour.

"It's Marie. This is a picture of my sister." A tear traced Lucy's cheek, and she swiped it away. "We'd fallen out over her continuing to see a married man she swore was going to leave his wife for her. Harold White, of course. I always thought she'd gone to St. Louis. She threatened to run off to St. Louis more than once. Whose house is this?"

Garland felt a terrible sinking in his gut. He gripped his knees as though bracing himself for a sudden impact.

"Well?" Lucy looked at him expectantly. "Sheriff Fitzsimmons has shared that you were a guard there. Surely you know who stayed in this . . . this structure."

Garland did remember. "Fritz Meyer," he murmured, wondering just how involved Fritz had been in assisting Harold with his liaisons, perhaps even helping him end one when it became inconvenient. Could he have been so wrong about the man he'd considered his friend?

"Who?" Lucy sounded shrill, a little unhinged.

"Fritz Meyer. The man who was supposed to be in your sister's grave."

Lucy closed her eyes, her pale face a study in tightly reigned emotion. "Was he her lover?" Her words were low but clear.

Garland was pretty certain that wasn't so but couldn't say for sure one way or the other. It seemed Fritz was becoming more and more of a stranger to him. "I-I don't know. I don't think so."

Lucy's eyes grew wide. "It appears there's a great deal you don't know." Her words were sharp, meant to cut. Garland let them slice through him without flinching. "Do you even remember my sister? She invited me to visit her in Hot Springs just that once. She introduced me to that awful man she was seeing. The one you say is conveniently dead now. I suppose she thought I'd be impressed. I wasn't."

"I, uh . . ." Garland scrambled for a coherent response. He darted a look at Wayne, who was watching him through narrowed eyes. "I guess I do remember seeing her around a few times. But it wasn't my business as to why she was there."

Lucy leveled steely gray eyes on him. "It wasn't the business of a guard to ascertain why a woman was coming and going from a camp where men were detained?"

Garland dared a glance at Wayne, who looked like he was enjoying himself. "She wasn't my guest. She . . . well, I thought Harold had asked her to come. Maybe as a teacher or something like that. He was the foreman. He was in charge."

"My sister was no more a teacher than I am a brain surgeon. Did Harold kill her, then? Or maybe it was this Fritz Meyer fellow. He was a German, wasn't he? Violent? The last war demonstrated to us how we ought to think of the German people."

Why didn't Wayne say something? Garland shot his boss a desperate look, but Wayne just gave him a slow grin. "We're still looking into all the possibilities," he said at last. Then he hurriedly added, "But we don't have any direct evidence beyond the coroner's report that your sister was murdered."

She gave him a look that suggested she'd met fence posts with a higher IQ. "Except for her body being found in the grave of a German prisoner who is strangely missing."

The sheriff finally leaned forward in his creaking chair and addressed Miss Spencer. "Harold White has been gone for a good while now. Although we're actively looking for Fritz Meyer, it's difficult when so much time has passed." He tapped the photo. "That said, your identification of your sister is very helpful. Thank you."

Lucy was like a ruffled hen finally allowing its feathers to settle. "Yes, well, someone needs to be making progress in this case, and it seems to me your deputy could be doing more."

Wayne nodded. "Yes, ma'am, I'll keep after him. I appreciate your being willing to stop by today, and we'll be keeping you apprised of what's happening in the case."

"That's what your deputy promised me the first time he came to speak to me. And as you can see, I had to come all this way to get an update for myself."

Wayne got a wicked gleam in his eye. "Right you are. As it happens, I'm assigning Deputy Jones here to check in with you weekly. How's that sound?"

Lucy smoothed her dress over her knees and nodded. "That's the least you can do. I'll look forward to hearing from him regularly." She glared at Garland, stood, tilted her chin in the air, and sailed out of the room without another word.

Garland stared at Wayne, who looked like he wanted to laugh but instead composed himself and leaned back in his chair. "I'm thinking she's right to have concerns about you. I'm thinking this case is stirring up some old memories that are making you uncomfortable. I debated giving it to someone else." He let that sink in a moment. "But you being there gives you a leg up." He nodded at the photos on the desk. "This is good work. Can I trust you to continue giving this case your full attention?"

"Yes, sir," Garland said before gathering up the photos. And he meant it, too. At first he'd been embarrassed about his gullibility coming to light, but the more he dug into that night, the more he wanted to know what happened. If Fritz Meyer had been a murderer who'd fooled him and Hedda so completely, he needed to be found and brought to justice. A man like that—a German like that—shouldn't be running around free. Especially not these days. And Hedda, sweet Hedda, needed to be free from the past.

18

ASHEVILLE, NORTH CAROLINA

Hedda waved goodbye to Jimmy Thompson as he jogged down the steps of the boardinghouse, folding and then jamming the page of sheet music she'd given him into his back pocket. She strongly suspected Jimmy's mother was more invested in him playing the piano than he was. Still, she wasn't about to get picky about paying students. Especially since she would lose this one when she moved into the faculty housing at Black Mountain College.

She turned as someone approached from the opposite direction. "Garland." She whispered his name before she could catch herself. Why was her heart doing a stutter-step? Speaking louder, she said, "Deputy Jones, it's good to see you. Do you have news for me?"

"Of a sort," he said and joined her on the porch. He looked up at the blue summer sky. "Sure is pretty out here. Maybe not as pretty as Hot Springs, but it'll do." He slanted a look her way. "Teaching piano, huh? I also heard you'll be doing that out at Black Mountain College come fall."

Hedda sighed. "Yes, but Dr. Rice has made me to understand that it's unofficial since I don't have the desired credentials. I'm to provide lessons in a purely extracurricular way. And for entertainment, dancing, that sort of thing."

"Still, sounds perfect for you."

She smiled. "Yes, but I'm not certain it will be enough to keep me in America." Even as she spoke, she remembered that as a policeman he might be the sort of person who would want to check her travel papers. She had nearly told him that soon she would have overstayed her welcome. She forced a bright smile.

"Oh. That's tough." He shuffled his feet. "If there's anything I can do to help, let me know."

"I'll do that," she said. "But what is this 'sort' of news you have for me?" Best to shift the conversation, she decided.

"Right. I found some pictures of Fritz. Not sure it helps us figure out what happened to him, but I thought you'd like to see them."

"Oh, yes, very much. Come, let's sit in these chairs where the breeze will keep us cool."

Garland trailed after her and settled his lanky frame in a rocking chair. "Here you go." He handed her three photos.

She took them, feeling a buzz of, what, excitement? Dread? She really didn't know what to think or feel about Fritz anymore. She glanced at Garland. Or what to think of the deputy for that matter. Perhaps he was the one confusing her thoughts.

She turned to the photos but didn't see Fritz in the first one until Garland pointed him out standing in the background. Then she couldn't unsee him. It was as though his eyes were boring into hers with a message she couldn't understand. She covered her mouth with one hand, her feelings now a roiling mess she couldn't begin to sort through.

"The next one shows him better." Garland's voice was gentle.

Shifting to the next photograph, Hedda stared, then laughed. There he was, perched high atop a church. "He was not a religious person," she said. "But I think he must have enjoyed building something so fine." This was the Fritz she remembered. Strong, fun-loving, artistic.

She flipped to the final image and gasped. It was by far the plainest image of him, standing beside a truck and looking very handsome in some sort of driving uniform. She touched his face with her fingertips. Then touched her own face. "So long ago. He wouldn't look the same anymore, I think. I certainly don't." She shook her head. "Time is not kind to any of us."

"I can hardly imagine you being any prettier than you are now," Garland said.

She jerked and stared at him, but he ducked his head, hiding his eyes beneath the brim of his ever-present hat. From what she could see of his expression, he was sorry he'd spoken.

"I shouldn't have said that. I just . . . well, if he's still alive, he's a fool for not going home to you." The words came out in a rush. "I don't mean to be forward; I'm just speaking my mind. My mother always said I should do less of that."

Hedda looked back at the image. Fritz was so young, so handsome, and so much a stranger to her. "I think it's good, this speaking of the mind. Thank you for what you have said to me." She flipped back through the photos, pausing at the church. "This reminds me. Fritz told me how when he was a boy, he would climb into the steeple of the local *Kirche* so he could see as far as possible. Even then he dreamed of where he might go one day."

Garland frowned. "Do you think he might have climbed up there to look for a way to escape?"

"Oh. I wouldn't think of this." She frowned at the picture. "And once I would have said Fritz would not think that way either, but now?" She shrugged and handed the photos back. "Now I think I did not know him at all."

"Do you want to keep one?" Garland asked.

She hesitated, then shook her head. "*Nein.* I will keep my memories of him." She swallowed hard. "Even if they are not perhaps how he really was."

Garland took the photos back, his eyes boring into hers. He was about to speak when the door opened and Eleanor popped out with two glasses of lemonade.

"Well, hello there, Deputy Jones. I was just bringing Hedda a cool drink now that her lesson is over. Can I get one for you?"

Garland stood. "Thanks, but I'd better be going." He smiled down at Hedda. "If there's anything new to report, I'll let you know." He made a face like tasting something sour. "I've been sentenced to give a report to Marie Spencer's sister every week. She's in Black Mountain, so even when you're out at the college, it won't be any trouble." He flushed. "I mean, if that's alright."

Hedda stood as well, more gracefully than he had. "I'd like that," she said, and the simple words felt freighted with more meaning than even she understood.

19

BLACK MOUNTAIN, NORTH CAROLINA

The day came for Josef and Anni to return to Black Mountain after spending some time in New York City. Hedda was excited to see them. Now that she was staying at the college, her days had fallen into new routines, more varied than she'd experienced in Berlin. She gave lessons to several students, including Eleanor, who wasn't terribly promising but who enjoyed herself immensely.

Lively meals in the dining room had become a delight. Especially now that she didn't have to listen to Clive peppering them with upsetting headlines from his newspapers. And every week Garland would come by on his way to see Lucy Spencer. Sometimes Hedda went with him. He never had much to tell Lucy about the investigation into her sister's death, but Hedda suspected she looked forward to the visits and had softened toward Garland. Perhaps she was simply lonely. Hedda knew a great deal about lonely.

She'd also found her place among the faculty and students. She played almost every evening, sometimes rollicking tunes and other times quiet, pensive pieces. She and Eleanor were together often, although she was forming other friendships as well. And while Hedda's position there sometimes felt tenuous, she was enjoying sitting in on classes, trying her hand at painting, and helping with work in the gardens. Funds were tight, so everyone pitched in whether it was maintaining the grounds, doing laundry, or helping Jack and Rubye in the kitchen.

Hedda couldn't remember being so happy.

Every now and then she had the niggling thought that she should contact someone in the government to share that she was gainfully employed so she could renew her papers. But she didn't know where to begin, and since no one seemed to care, she was content to push the troubling thought away each time it reared its head.

She went with Dr. Rice to meet Josef and Anni at the train station in Black Mountain. She adored the neat station with its overhanging roof and bright yellow paint. Dr. Rice was his usual taciturn self, though she didn't mind since she would soon see her friends.

Anni was first off the train. She wrapped Hedda in a huge embrace, calling her *Mein Schatz* once more. Josef soon appeared carrying luggage. He and Dr. Rice shook hands and exchanged a few words in English, but it was obvious Josef was uncomfortable speaking anything but German. Hedda stepped easily into the conversation and was soon translating at such a pace that it hardly slowed down the two men's communication. They mostly exchanged pleasantries and some details about where the Alberses would be staying and how the faculty was coming along. When they finally climbed into Dr. Rice's automobile for the rattling drive back to the college, Hedda was grateful for the respite.

She sat in the back with Anni, who laid her hand over Hedda's. "It is so good to be coming to rest at last. These past months have been difficult. The news from Germany is terrible." She let her head fall back against the seat. "The National Socialist Party formed chambers for literature, fine arts, music and so on." She sighed heavily. "They have banned anyone who is Jewish from membership. Which means even if we could return, I would not be able to work—though I was baptized in a Protestant church and am only Jewish in Hitler's estimation. Josef believes things will get better, and we will go home again. But I do not think so. The hate, it is too strong."

Hedda nodded. "Yes, I've had a letter from Lotte. A neighbor married a man from Roma—a Gypsy. Recently their daughter was taken from school. They didn't know where. Two days later, she was returned to them having had a procedure to ensure she wouldn't pass on what they called her 'mixed blood.'" Hedda paused, overcome by the horror of it. "She will never bear children."

Anni gripped Hedda's arm. "She is lucky they left her with her life. It is not the Germany we once knew." She hesitated. "I do not expect ever to return." She stared out the window for a moment, then turned back to Hedda. "But enough of this. Let us be glad we are together and trouble is far away. When we arrive, you will play for us, yes?"

Hedda managed a smile. "Nothing would please me more." And as she spoke the words, she realized they were true. She was happy to be in America with friends eager to hear her play. She had once dreamed of being a concert pianist, and this was as close as she'd ever come to such a thing. And yet there were moments when she missed Lotte, her students, and the coffee shop around the corner with its aroma of roasting beans and baking pastries. She thought of the *Kirche* she had gone to in those difficult days when she lost Fritz and then her parents. She should have continued going. She had found comfort in the beauty and peace of the sanctuary, but it had been so hard for her to connect with people. She glanced at Anni. Perhaps if she did have to return, it would be easier now.

Her friend stared pensively out the window. These days weren't easy for any of them. Hedda had been waiting so long for something to change—to either be released from her promise to Fritz or to see it fulfilled. And strangely, failing to find him, realizing that she might never know what had happened to him, was freeing. She felt as though she'd been given permission to stop waiting. She looked out the windscreen at the road ahead, winding between the hills and forests, until Blue Ridge Assembly came into view. While she wasn't certain what the future held, she was positive it would look much different from the past.

The day after the Alberses arrived, Garland picked Hedda up for a visit to Lucy. While he dreaded seeing Lucy, the pleasure of seeing Hedda did much to lighten his spirits, especially when, like today, she came along with him to the tidy little house in Black Mountain.

Hedda sprang into Garland's Studebaker and bounced on the seat. Did he dare to hope her lightness of spirit had anything to do with him?

"What news do you have for Miss Spencer?" she chirped.

"No news really, but I've been given permission to return the brooch we found when we discovered Marie's remains."

"I think this will make her happy and sad together."

Garland gave a rueful laugh. "I don't think I've ever seen Lucy happy. Seems like she's always in a foul mood when I'm around."

"You bring the sorrow of losing her sister back to her each time. Of course she isn't cheerful."

Garland glanced at Hedda. He hadn't thought of it that way. "I suppose you have a point there."

They rode in silence for a few moments. "May I see this brooch?" she asked.

"Go ahead. It's in the glove box."

She opened the compartment and found the pin inside, wrapped in an old rag. "Oh, you can't give it to her like this." She dug into her pocket and pulled out a clean handkerchief. She stuffed the rag back in the glove box and laid the brooch on the square of cream linen. "*Besser*," she breathed, admiring the bauble. And Garland knew that word meant *better*.

When they arrived at Lucy's house, Garland asked Hedda to present the jewelry. "I think you might be onto something about me bringing sorrow. Maybe you can bring a bit of joy."

"I would like that," she said as she folded the soft cloth around the oval brooch. Her gentle smile gave him all the courage he needed to raise a fist to rap on the door.

After a few moments, the door eased open a crack, its hinges squawking. "Who's there?"

"It's Deputy Jones, and I am with him," Hedda said. The door inched open a little further, and the sour pucker of Lucy's lips relaxed into, well, not a smile exactly, but something a bit more like it.

"Come in then. Maybe this week you'll have something of use to say to me." Lucy turned and disappeared inside.

As they followed, Garland took more than a cursory look around for once. He shoved the door closed behind him, noticing that it didn't latch properly. He also noticed that some blinds were hanging askew, and if he wasn't mistaken, the sofa was propped up with books where a leg should be.

"Come into the kitchen and I'll pour you some coffee," Lucy said.

Garland nearly missed a step. This was the first time Lucy had offered any sort of refreshment. Hedda's presence really did work wonders.

He held a chair out for Hedda to sit at the kitchen table, then sat beside her. Lucy fussed at the stove, lighting the gas burner and placing a percolator over the flame. The sulfurous smell of the match made Garland think briefly of fire and brimstone, but he quickly pushed such unkind thoughts aside.

Lucy clattered some chipped china onto the table and sat while the smell of the brewing coffee made the room feel cozy, warm, and dare he say, welcoming?

"Well then, what have you come to say? Is it hard news and you've brought Hedda to soften the blow?"

Garland was about to reply when Hedda spoke before he could get the words out. "Deputy Jones continues his work on the case, but in the meantime, we've brought you this." She placed the handkerchief in front of Lucy as though tucked inside were the Crown Jewels. And Lucy unwrapped it in like manner.

Once the brooch was revealed, Lucy just sat looking at it for a few beats. Garland wanted to jump in and fill the silence, but Hedda cast him a look that kept his lips sealed.

A tear slid down Lucy's cheek. "Mother knew it was foolish, giving this to Marie, but it was tradition for it to go to the eldest. She was thirty-four the last time I saw her. Now I'm forty-six. Older than she'll ever be." She laid the brooch in her palm. "I suppose my having it won't break tradition in that sense."

"It's a lovely piece," Hedda said. "Did your mother wear it often?"

"Do you see this?" Lucy pointed to a loop on the back of the pin. "This is so it can be worn as a pendant as well. That's how Mother wore it, around her neck. She mostly wore this brooch on holidays or for special occasions."

She suddenly laughed, and Garland, who had been surprised to hear her age, realized she wasn't quite the old crone he'd taken her for.

"I remember one Christmas," Lucy went on, "we'd gone to church and Mother was wearing it pinned to her blouse. Aunt Ida gave her a big hug, and the brooch snagged in Ida's shawl. They couldn't get it untangled, and Mother finally had to unfasten the brooch and let Ida take it home to work it free. Oh, how she grumbled. She said if it hadn't been so cold, she would have insisted on taking Ida's shawl home with her."

Lucy's smile faded, her countenance taking on a softness Garland hadn't seen before. "I really am the last of the Spencers, aren't I? So long as there's no proof, one can hold out hope. But now . . ." She clutched the pin and looked imploringly at Hedda. "You understand, don't you?"

A tear streaked Hedda's cheek. "*Ja*, I do. I, too, am the last of my family. My parents died from the influenza, leaving only an old aunt who never writes. She married a Dane and now lives in Saeby on the northern coast of Denmark."

Garland, fighting a knot in his throat, stood. "I noticed a blind that needed fixing in the front room," he choked out. "Why don't you ladies continue chatting while I take care of that?"

A cloud began to form on Lucy's face, but Hedda spoke quickly. "What a good idea. We will, how do you say, remember? No, *reminisce* is the right word, yes?" She covered Lucy's hand with her own.

"Alright." Lucy nodded. She shot Garland a sharp look. "Just don't expect me to keep your coffee hot."

"Yes, ma'am. I mean, no, ma'am." Garland hurried from the room and began to set Lucy's parlor to rights. He could hear the murmur of voices in the kitchen and the clinking of cups in their saucers. He was surprised to find himself humming as he worked.

20

Black Mountain, North Carolina

The peace Garland had been surprised to find at Lucy Spencer's house stayed with him as he drove Hedda back to the college. He drove slowly, not wanting their time together to end.

"It was good of you to fix Lucy's house." Hedda tucked a strand of silvery hair behind her ear.

"It was nothing," Garland said with a shrug.

"*Nein.* I think it was something to a woman who is alone in the world. I know how this is, being alone. It's good to have someone care for you, even if you don't know them well."

Garland shifted, feeling uncomfortable. Was it the praise? Surely not. He wanted Hedda to admire him. Maybe it was the fact that he knew all too well that he didn't deserve her praise.

"Are you still waiting for him?" he asked.

"For who?"

"For Fritz. Are you still hoping he's out there somewhere?" Garland stared straight ahead, afraid to look at Hedda.

She was silent for what felt like a long time but was probably only a few moments. Finally, she spoke. "There is this word in German, *Sehnsucht*. You don't have anything like it in English, I think." Now he risked a glance. Her head was tilted, her brow furrowed. She was far too lovely, so he kept his eyes on the road ahead. "It's when you want something very badly but cannot have it because it is out of reach in some way. It's a hunger that can't be satisfied, a hole that can't be filled. I've felt this about Fritz for a long time. And when I learned that he was dead, it was a relief because without hope I could stop feeling this way."

Garland glanced her way again, afraid he would see tears. But she was only pensive. He'd learned that she twisted her hair when she was anxious or upset. Now her hands remained folded in her lap. He returned his focus to the road, thinking he might have some idea of what *Sehnsucht* felt like.

"And now," she continued, "perhaps he is still alive. But if so, why has he never written me a letter? Why has he not comforted his mother? I think probably he is dead after all. So I will mourn him and tell him goodbye."

Garland couldn't think what to say. He pulled into the entrance of Blue Ridge Assembly and stopped the Studebaker in a wide spot beside the road. He felt strongly that he needed a moment alone with Hedda and didn't think he'd get that at the college.

He turned to her and reached for her hand. She let him take it, which made his heart glad. "I'm very sorry," he finally said. It seemed the right place to start.

"*Danke*," she answered, her pale lashes dropping, then rising again, those brown eyes boring into his.

"I'm sorry you've waited so long, not knowing what happened to Fritz. Even now you still don't know for certain."

He hoped she didn't feel the tremor in his hand. "But at least I can tell you everything I know." Her eyes widened, and she gripped his hand—involuntarily, he thought. "I'm the one who buried the coffin that was supposed to hold Fritz."

Once he started, the words came more easily. "I hadn't seen him all day, and it was after midnight when Harold White, one of the foremen, brought me a cart with a coffin in it and said that Fritz had been struck down by typhoid like so many others. He said to hurry and get the body in the ground." He took a deep breath. The memory of that day stirred up feelings he'd hoped to leave behind him. "I didn't know what to think. Fritz was a friend, and hearing that he'd died was like a punch to the gut. I wanted to look inside the coffin, to see him one last time, but Harold said the lid was nailed down and there wasn't time for sentimentality." He hung his head. "And if I'm being honest, I didn't push because I was afraid of catching typhoid."

He risked another glance at Hedda. She was hanging on his every word. "It's tough now that I know I was hiding the body of Marie Spencer. Maybe helping a murderer cover up his crime. You see, Harold and Marie were an item, and I believe maybe Fritz was helping them meet." He paused, catching himself before sharing anything that wasn't fact. "I'm not sure the sheriff would like me telling you this, but I think you deserve to know."

Hedda exhaled long and slow, as though she'd been holding her breath. "*Danke* for telling me. Do you think . . . was Fritz . . . did he have something to do with Marie dying?"

"I don't know, but it sure doesn't look good. Her body in his coffin, and him never being seen again?"

She startled, grabbing his hand. "Oh, but what if this

foreman killed them both? What if Fritz tried to help and
. . . and . . ." She ran out of steam.

"Maybe," Garland agreed slowly. "But then where's his
body? Why not two coffins?" *Or two in one*, he thought,
but didn't say it.

"It's very confusing, is it not?" Hedda stared out the window as light, shining through the leaves, danced across her
features. Finally, she said in a small voice, "Do you think he
ran away because of this woman's death? That he was so
frightened, he dared not contact his mother? Or me?"

"It could have happened like that. Maybe he helped, or
maybe he witnessed it and Harold killed him in some other
place. Maybe he'd been planning to escape all along and it
just happened to be the same night." Garland ran a hand
through his hair. "I just don't know."

He glanced at Hedda and saw tears welling in her eyes. He
needed to do something to make this better. "Here's what
I do know. He spoke of you with great love, to me and to
others who were around back then. The fact that he didn't
return or write makes me think that whatever happened,
something stopped him from returning to you."

Now tears flowed freely, and she did nothing to stop them.
"You will not be in difficulty for telling me all of this?"

He blinked back his own tears. "I don't think so, no. And
it's past time you knew what little there is to know." He
took a deep, cleansing breath. "You were so kind to Lucy, so
understanding of what she's gone through the past fifteen
years, it made me realize how hard this has been for you. I-I
thought it was the least I could do." He wanted to add *And
I like you very much*, but he kept that bit to himself.

Hedda released his hand and sank back into the seat. "So
if he did escape and he has not died in some other way, he

may still be living in fear somewhere." She darted a look at Garland. "He was very smart. I think if he were still alive, he would have found a way to contact us by now."

Garland held his breath. Had he been a fool to tell her? Would this make things worse for her and for him? "This country wasn't very kind to Germans at the end of the war. If he did escape, he could have run into all sorts of trouble."

She began to dry her eyes with her sleeve. Garland fumbled to fish out his handkerchief, remembering that she'd given hers to Lucy. She took the cloth and dabbed her eyes. "I'm thinking that you don't want me to tell others about this."

He gulped. "I can't see any harm in it, but Sheriff Fitzsimmons might disagree with me."

Her silence left him quaking. Was this all a terrible mistake?

"In my country, lies are being told. Terrible lies for terrible reasons." She seemed to be searching for words. Maybe for the English from her German. "I think I will not need to hide anything. Who would ask me about such things?" She smiled through her tears, and it was as though a burden had lifted. "And who would I tell without being asked?" This time it was Garland who felt a weight—a fifteen-year-old chain of regret—slide from his shoulders.

Hedda sat alone in her room that night, ghostly in her white nightgown with her hair in a single braid over her shoulder. She touched the braid but didn't twirl it. Instead, she admired how her hair and the moonlight were almost the same color. She wondered if Garland admired girls who were fair, or would he prefer someone dark like Anni with her ebony locks and expressive eyes?

As she gazed out at the lawn and mountains, she noticed that the first of the autumn leaves were drifting down even in the dark. She smiled. She'd never thought about how the leaves would continue falling after the sun set. But of course they did. Just as life was even now going on in Germany without her.

Were leaves falling in Germany? Was Lotte sitting at her window, too? Her dear friend who was like a second mother to her continued to urge her to stay in America. Back home there was political upheaval with many goods in short supply. While the economy had improved somewhat, times were still hard, and Herr Hitler was making many uneasy.

And what point was there in returning without Fritz? She would always wonder where he had come to rest. Hedda was glad Garland had told her what he knew of the truth. Now she could finish mourning Fritz and let him go for good. Perhaps she would never know for sure, but that he had died long ago felt like a certainty. She supposed it was something she'd known for the past decade, but now it finally felt real.

As real as her new life in America. As real as the music she played each day and the people she'd come to care for and spend time with. How had her life gone from the grays of her existence in Germany to this multihued happiness she'd found on a fledgling college campus?

She laughed and startled at the sound ringing out with such contagious joy. A voice, tired but not unkind, floated through the thin walls. "Either share the joke or pack it up and go to bed."

Hedda clapped a hand over her mouth, stifling a giggle. Then she eased her window shut and slipped into bed, where she could snuggle under her American quilt and dream her American dreams.

21

Fritz Meyer stretched his arms wide as he woke on the train that was pulling into the station in Black Mountain, North Carolina. This spot was precariously close to where he'd been interned in 1918. Imprisoned more like, but Americans were always finding ways to make things sound better than they were. And it had been nearly sixteen years since he'd made his escape from the camp in Hot Springs. Surely, Harold White and all his threats had moved on, and it was safe to return now.

His friend Giovanni told him he was foolish to seek out fellow Germans, to travel so close to the place where his old life died and the new began. But what did an old man nearing the end of his own life know? Sometimes it was good to look backward.

When Fritz heard that Josef Albers had come to lead the art department of a new college within his reach, how could he resist? It was as though he'd found the dreams he'd had as a young man in the bottom of a dusty trunk. He had to take them out and hold them to the light to see if they still shone the way they once had. He'd built a good life for himself, filled with people he loved. He'd held the two choices in his hands. He could stay in Bethania and put his dreams behind him once and for all. Give in to the fear that Harold White was still out there somewhere, waiting to make good on his threats. Or he could trust God and step out of the safe life he'd built. He could take a chance to see if the life he'd once dreamed of might be possible after all.

As he considered the two options, he knew the risk was worth it. God had planted this seed in his heart long ago. Surely this was a gift from heaven. Harold White probably hadn't stuck around after the camp closed. And if he had, he wouldn't want to drag back up what happened there any more than Fritz did. He would have faith.

As soon as the decision was made, he arranged for Denis to stay with his aunt and uncle. The boy wanted to come with him, and Fritz promised that if all went according to plan, he would send for him before too long.

Once his plans were finalized, he felt almost giddy. An artist. That's what he was meant to be. Not a worker of wood and a builder of simple houses, but a painter. Someone whose work would be inspired by Bauhaus luminaries like Wassily Kandinsky and Paul Klee. Fritz had no illusions about his art rivaling that of his heroes, but the hunger to create was strong—had always been. And while he did make art for himself and his friends in Bethania, it was a small part of what he did. Mostly he built houses and crafted useful items for his adopted community. The occasional mural or portrait was a pleasure but hardly a living.

Fritz passed through the station and stepped out onto the street. His English was good enough after all these years, and he soon learned that the college was only a few miles outside of town. An easy walk for someone used to manual labor. He shouldered his rucksack and set off to follow the directions he'd been given. He whistled as he went, feeling a deep sense of rightness. At long last he would meet a German artist, one who had worked alongside his heroes. He allowed himself the luxury of imagining that Josef Albers would one day introduce him to Herr Kandinsky. Fritz would tell him how much he loved *Couple Riding*. Yes, it was an older work, but it foreshadowed the coming shift toward Impressionism. And the way Kandinsky painted the town and the trees and the sky . . . the work emanated light. It sparkled.

Fritz smiled and walked more briskly, filling his lungs with crisp air and feeling like a new man—a creature reborn. He'd begun his life anew once before. Perhaps now it was time to go back to the beginning, to a time when being a painter seemed possible. His smile dimmed. A time before he'd fallen in love and had become a sailor so that he might wed. Such a long time ago and yet he remembered the expression on Hedda's face as she'd waved goodbye the last time he saw her. She'd been so lovely with her pale hair and a blue dress that he could still pick out in the crowd as the ship sailed out of view. Light and dark, like Kandinsky's painting.

When he arrived at Black Mountain College, it was nearing the dinner hour. Fritz hoped he would be welcome at the table. He'd eaten some bread and cheese on the train, but that had been a long time ago.

An immense white building with tall columns across the central portion and wings extending to each side greeted him. For the first time, Fritz hesitated, wondering if he would be welcome here. As he considered this, a lanky young man loped across the lawn toward him.

"Hey there. You looking for someone in particular?"

"I am hoping to find Josef Albers."

"He's around here someplace. Might be teaching now. But everybody'll be along for supper soon. You can catch him then." The man waved toward the imposing white building. "C'mon, I'll show you the way."

A wave of excitement coursed through Fritz. Could it be this simple? Could meeting Josef Albers require nothing more than train fare and a decent stretch of the legs? He trotted after the young man, his blood fizzing in his veins.

Hedda finished her bowl of beef stew with Rubye. They were eating ahead of the supper crowd so that Rubye could serve and Hedda could play. While Hedda had adjusted to being much more social, she sometimes preferred spending the meal hour at the piano to engaging in the endless banter over cups and plates. And on this evening when dusk had fallen, she simply didn't feel like talking. Thankfully, Rubye was an easy companion who didn't mind a quiet meal.

After carrying her dishes to the sink, Hedda went out and began playing the piano softly. She stuck to soothing, classical pieces as meals began in the belief that they were good for the digestive system. And perhaps good for keeping conversation to a dull roar.

As she played, she saw Pete Stone, one of the students, ushering in a broad-shouldered, blond stranger. She didn't get a good look at him but guessed he must be a new student arriving late for the semester. She hoped that was the case at any rate. She knew Dr. Rice and the other founders had struggled to raise enough funds to open the college and would need every penny they could scrounge up to keep it going. Most of the professors were working for room and board with little to no pay just as she was.

Mealtime was ending as she concluded the final piece she had planned for the evening. On her way to the kitchen, she saw the stranger seated on the far side of the room and craned her neck to get a better look. Joe Martin, a professor of English, stood and approached her, blocking her view.

"We missed dining with you this evening," he said.

"I ate early with Rubye. Sometimes I don't feel up to the tumult of the communal table."

He nodded. "I know what you mean. It can be overwhelming. But tomorrow you'll join us again?"

"No. I'm sorry. I'll be preparing for the evening salon." She wiggled her fingers to indicate that she'd be playing. She took a step and peered back over her shoulder, trying to see the stranger once more. Again, Joe blocked her view.

"Are you headed for the kitchen? I offered to help with cleanup this evening. We can go together."

Hedda agreed and allowed Joe to escort her into the warm clatter of the kitchen. She looked back once more, just in time to see the blond man passing through the front door with Josef and Anni. Good, Anni could tell her all about the newcomer.

22

Garland tied the small package of peppermints with red ribbon. He was clumsy about it but decided it looked better than the plain brown paper. Hedda had invited him to some sort of performance that evening. He wasn't altogether clear on what it was about, but apparently the students would act out scenes from Shakespeare's plays, and there would be recitations of poetry, and then Hedda would play something new she'd been practicing all week. Regardless, he took it as a good sign that she welcomed—maybe even sought out—his company.

It had been more than a week since he'd told her what he knew about Fritz and nothing terrible had happened as a result. He hadn't seriously pursued a woman in a very long time and felt uncertain about how it was done these days. Especially when you met someone because their dead fiancé's body failed to turn up. Nonetheless, he was ready to give it a try.

By the time he arrived at Black Mountain College and Lee Hall, he'd sweated through his undershirt and was having second thoughts. His reservations evaporated, though, when he saw Hedda standing near the piano and chatting with someone he assumed was one of the teachers. He bristled at the way the man was standing close, inclining his head to catch her every word, and smiling.

He was headed for the pair when a dark-haired woman caught his arm. "Pardon me," she said in a thick German accent. "You are the policeman who has been helping our Hedda, are you not?"

"That'd be me," Garland said.

"I must speak with you."

Garland cast a longing look in Hedda's direction. "Can it wait?"

"*Nein.*" The German word was sharp and urgent. Something told Garland this was indeed important.

"Right then. Let's step outside."

The evening air made his skin tingle with the crispness of fall, like biting into a tart apple. Garland drew it into his lungs deeply, grateful for a moment to steady his nerves. They moved to the far end of the porch, where a man waited for them. The woman spoke. "I am Anni Albers, and this is my husband, Josef. We knew Hedda and her family in Germany. We have been very happy to see her here." Anni's harried expression softened. "She has been through so much."

"I'm glad to meet any friends of Hedda's."

Anni became serious again. "My husband, he oversees the art department here. He taught at the Bauhaus in Germany—a well-respected school for art and design. And it seems someone who admired his work in Germany has sought him out."

Garland nodded along, uncertain as to why this woman was telling him all of this. "That's good," he offered. "But I'd like to get inside and speak to Hedda before the concert or whatever it is starts." He tried to turn back, but Josef laid a restraining hand on his arm.

"*Mein Frau*—my wife—hear her."

Anni smiled. "Josef, his English is not so good. But yes, please listen to me." She seemed to be struggling, perhaps wondering how to express what she needed to say in English. "Hedda's betrothed—the one you did not find?" Garland nodded, growing impatient. "We have found him."

Now Garland was confused. "Found him? What do you mean?"

"He is here," Josef offered.

"What? Here? Fritz Meyer is here? How . . . what do you mean?" His head spun. He reached out to brace himself against the rough wall of the building.

Anni spoke again. "He has come to find my Josef. He would like to be an artist, and I think believed enough time had passed that he would not be harassed. He did not know that Hedda was here, did not realize that Hedda is dear to us. He—"

Whatever she was about to say was cut off by a scream and then a great commotion inside the hall. Garland didn't wait to learn more but ran back inside. Eleanor knelt beside Hedda, who was slumped in a chair, her face ashen and a handkerchief pressed to her mouth. A brawny fellow with a shock of blond hair stood with his back to Garland, speaking and gesticulating. Hedda held up a hand as though to fend him off.

"What's going on here?" Garland bellowed in his most authoritative voice. Every face turned toward him, except for the blond man. "You, what business do you have with Hedda?"

The man turned, and Garland immediately knew it was

Hedda who had screamed. And he knew why. Screaming was the appropriate response to seeing a ghost.

John Andrew Rice insisted on continuing the evening's entertainment without Hedda. He packed Garland, Hedda, Fritz, and the Alberses off to the college's makeshift library while the rest of the campus enjoyed their show. Although Garland got the feeling plenty of them thought the return of a dead man offered more entertainment. He fingered the package of peppermints in his pocket and wished he could go back to the moment when tying a ribbon properly had seemed his biggest problem.

Dr. Rice closed the door, leaving a palpable silence. It hung in the room like dusty old curtains you hated to move lest you release a storm of dirt and who knew what else. Josef and Anni sat close together, their elbows touching. Hedda sat a little apart, still pale and clearly shaken. Fritz stood near a table, his gaze bouncing from face to face, never quite coming to rest.

Garland stationed himself beside Hedda and cleared his throat. "Guess I'd better get this conversation started." His voice seemed too loud and his word choice all wrong, but what else was there to do but keep going? "Am I correct in thinking you're Fritz Meyer?"

The big man shifted from foot to foot. "*Ja.* This is my name." His eyes darted to Hedda again but danced away upon seeing her stricken face. "Josef and Anni, they say I am to stay hidden, but I heard the music and so . . ." He shrugged.

Garland wanted to take Fritz by the shoulders, shake him, and demand to know what happened all those years ago.

Should he go ahead and arrest him and haul him off to jail for questioning? Garland was so astonished by Fritz just turning up out of the blue that he couldn't quite think what to do next.

Fritz's gaze stopped on Garland. "I think I know you from the camp," he said. "It has been a very long time, but you are Garland, *ja*? I think it is good to tell my story to you and these others." Fritz seemed to be asking permission.

"Hold on there." Garland held his hand up. "You're someone of interest in what may very well be a crime. I'm not sure you should be telling your story to a roomful of people. Probably I should haul you up to the courthouse in Madison County and take your statement there."

Fritz's eyes widened. "You will take me to jail?"

"I didn't say that—"

Garland was interrupted by a hand wrapping around his arm. He glanced down at Hedda, who looked at him with pleading eyes. "Please, let me hear this story."

Garland frowned. Of course she wanted to hear what Fritz had to say. And didn't she deserve to hear it after all these years? He wrestled with his conscience, trying to think what the sheriff would want him to do. Finally, he turned back to Fritz. "Are you going to incriminate yourself in a crime? If you're going to confess to something, it'd be good to know that going in."

Fritz shrugged. "Is it a crime to have run away? I don't know." He rubbed his hands on his pants. "*Sprechen sie Deutsch?*" he asked, looking at Garland with hope in his eyes.

"No. Speak English."

Fritz sighed. "At home we speak mostly *Deutsch*. My English is just okay."

"Home?" Hedda choked out the word. "I thought home was in Berlin. Where have you been?"

Fritz looked at her, appearing on the edge of tears. "*Es tut mir leid.*"

"English," Garland barked.

Fritz tugged his jacket into place and ran a hand over his hair as though looking dignified was important to his story. "*Ja.* As you say." He took a deep breath and composed himself. "The night I run away, I am driving Mr. White's *Freundin*. She is not supposed to be where she is, but I am a prisoner who must do what I am told. I am waiting outside when Mr. White, he comes out with *Blut* on his shirt and tells me I must help him." Fritz paused, drew in a breath, and blew it out slowly.

"I go in and see his *Freundin*—Marie is her name—is very still, and I try to leave. He tells me if I do not help, he will say I do this thing. Then Mr. White, he says if I help him, he helps me. So we put the woman in a box for burying with some rocks to make it heavy and say it is me inside." He was speaking faster now as though eager to get it all out. "Then I swim in the river. But I cannot take things with me. I hide in the woods, and next day Harold White, he bring me clothes and money."

He took another breath and slowed back down. "And then I am alone. How to make my way in America where my English is worse than now and Germans, they are not smiled at?" He stared at the floor, clearly deep in thought. Lifting his head, he continued, "There is too much and the English too hard. I will go to the end. I get on a train to go west, but it is wrong and I go east. When I see the sun come up in front of me instead of behind, I jump off the train in a place called Bethania."

"In North Carolina?" Garland burst out. "Down near Winston-Salem?" He still found it odd to combine the names of the two cities, but they'd merged a decade earlier and had agreed on the compound name.

"*Ja*, this is the place. Like the hand of God has led me there. The people, they speak German. They are good people—Moravians—who only want to worship as they like. I am very welcome there and find a place where I fit." He stopped then as if that were enough. Garland doubted very much that it would be enough to satisfy Hedda. He certainly wanted to know more. Had to know more.

Hedda twisted a handkerchief in her lap. She seemed to be searching for the right words when Anni jumped in. "But why did you not return to Germany? To your mother and betrothed?"

It was a question that was surely on their minds—most of all Hedda, who shot Anni a grateful look.

Fritz moved to a chair and sagged into it, his wide shoulders slumping. "When he gives me money and clothes, Mr. White says I must disappear or I will go to jail for killing his *Freundin*. He says no one will believe a German prisoner if I say it is different. And now that I have run away, it will be worse." He heaved a great sigh. "I have much fear so I do as he say. And then time is gone and I become a builder of houses. A doctor, Edward Strickland, he wants a house and so I make him one. And then I make others. I save the money in case the time comes when I can return. But then I think maybe you would find another man to love. I think maybe it is better you and *Mutter* think I am dead so I cannot bring you trouble with Harold White." His eyes glistened. "And I think it is better if I leave the past where it is." He pressed a hand to his heart. "It gives me much pain, but I make a new life, make a new family . . ." He looked at Hedda, his voice catching. "I hope you are happy without me."

Garland watched Hedda, who was no longer trying to hide her tears. He wasn't sure where to take this interview from here. Fritz's story sounded credible, but there was no statute of limitations on murder, and they were still going to have to resolve Marie's demise to the law's satisfaction.

"Are you saying Harold White killed Marie Spencer?" The words sounded cold and harsh after Fritz's heart-wrenching story. But that was the meat of the matter, wasn't it? How did Marie die?

Fritz's eyes widened. "I only know that she is dead. Not how she becomes that way. You must ask Mr. White."

Garland grimaced. "He's been dead for some time now."

The change that came over Fritz was palpable in the dimly lit room. He sat up straighter, color returned to his cheeks, and his eyes brightened. "I can fear him no more? This is good news to me."

Garland shook his head. What a mess. "Yeah, well, maybe not. Without him around to tell us he did what you say he did, we're going to have ask more questions, investigate this further."

The big man's ruddy face paled. "You will put me in jail like Mr. White said you would?"

"I . . . no, I don't think we need to do that. I'll talk to the sheriff and see what he wants to do. Where are you staying?"

"Here. I am a student now."

Garland blinked. "You're a what?"

"A student at the college." Fritz puffed his chest out and turned to Josef. "I will study art with you. As I have dreamed of doing."

Josef looked surprised and spoke in German. Fritz replied in kind, and they had a brief, rapid-fire conversation.

"English!" Garland yelled.

"*Es tut mir leid*," Fritz said. "I am sorry. German is much easier."

"Okay, here's what we're going to do," said Garland, praying he wasn't digging the hole he was already in any deeper. "I'm going to let you stay here with the Alberses and Dr. Rice. They'll keep an eye on you. No leaving the college, no wandering off on your own. Just stay put until we can figure out what to do next."

Fritz released a deep breath. "I can do this. *Danke*."

Garland exhaled as well, feeling that he'd done a pretty good job of handling this first interview with a man they'd all given up for dead. He looked at Hedda and saw that she was just staring, cheeks wet but tears no longer falling. How was she handling this? All he had to do was sort out a mysterious death. She had to process the return from the dead of the man she'd once planned to marry.

Fritz turned toward her. "Hedda, it . . . it is good to see you. You have found an American man, *ja*? This is why you are here and not in Germany? You maybe have children now, and I am right that you are happier without me."

Garland wanted to step between Fritz and Hedda as though to protect her from the painful darts Fritz didn't even know he was throwing. His heart ached to see this man she had put her life on hold for try to untangle a web of time and deceit with a few easy words.

Hedda surged to her feet, fists clenched at her sides. "*Nein! Nein, nein, nein.* I have not found another man. I do not have children. You did not write because you were afraid of Harold White? Well, I was afraid of everything because

I did not know what became of you." She shook her finger at him. "I waited for you. I longed to know what happened to you. And I'm here now because I came to claim your body and return it to the *Vaterland*, to your mother, who is mourning you even now." She sucked in a great breath of air. "But now I see I should not have waited. Whatever I felt for you was only here." She banged a fist against her forehead. "And you are no longer welcome here." She dropped her fist to her breast. "I don't care what you do now beyond writing a letter to your mother this very night. Do that and we will be done." She turned and ran out of the room, slamming the door behind her.

Once again silence reigned, only heavier and grubbier than before. Garland suppressed an urge to applaud for several reasons, chief among them the fact that seeing such fire and passion in a woman he'd come to admire only made him admire her more.

Anni walked to a desk, where she extracted several sheets of paper and a pen. She motioned to Fritz. "Come. You will do as Hedda has said, and I will post the letter myself."

Fritz nodded and moved to the desk, where he sat and picked up the pen. He remained motionless for a few moments before Garland realized tears were dripping from his chin. He said something in German. Anni nodded.

"Josef, Mr. Garland, you will please to leave us alone now. Fritz must think, and you do not help this process."

Garland followed Josef out into the cool, starry night. They stood there a moment, staring at stars against the velvet of the sky. Finally, Josef spoke. "This is trouble, *ja?*"

Garland fished out the package of peppermints and offered his companion one. "*Ja*," he answered.

23

BLACK MOUNTAIN, NORTH CAROLINA

Hedda couldn't cry another drop. She held up the topaz ring Fritz had given her as a promise so many years ago. She'd worn it ever since, sometimes thinking of it as a talisman that would return him to her and sometimes as a touchstone that simply kept his memory fresh. Now she dropped it in a dish on her bedside table. She would not wear it ever again.

She let her head fall back against the pillow propped at the top of her narrow bed. She was thirsty. That she could register any sensation beyond a broken heart came as a surprise.

Someone knocked softly on her door. She didn't have the wherewithal to even speak. The door creaked open, and Eleanor peered inside. "I brought you water, and Rubye said I should bring this wet cloth." She held up the items as though they were tickets to gain her entry. Hedda waved her friend inside and gladly took a long swallow from the glass.

"I don't get what this is for," Eleanor said, offering the

cloth. Hedda took it and laid it across her burning eyes. It felt wonderful. "Oh. Guess you've been crying."

"I have," Hedda said, her voice low and raspy.

"So Fritz isn't dead, then." Eleanor's voice was soft, rueful.

"It would seem he is very much alive."

"Are you going to turn him in?"

Hedda removed the cloth and looked at her friend. "What do you mean?"

"Tell the authorities—the army or whoever. I guess he's been in hiding all this time because he's on the lam."

Hedda shook her head. "I don't think anyone cares about a man who ran away from a place that no longer exists."

"Then he's not in trouble?"

"With me he is. And with his mother, too, I think."

"But I mean, if he's not hiding out, why didn't he get in touch?"

Hedda sighed heavily and adjusted the cool cloth, scrunching back against her pillow. "He was afraid. This terrible man called Harold White said Fritz would be blamed for Marie Spencer's death if he ever spoke of it." She shrugged. "I think he was more afraid of jail than caring about me or his *Mutter*. We were very young and hurrying too much. It was a bad plan from the start."

Eleanor took her hand, and they sat in silence. Hedda was beginning to feel drowsy when Eleanor asked, "What will you tell his mother?"

"*He* will tell his mother the truth. After that, I don't know."

Eleanor squeezed her hand. "I'm sorry you had to find out like this. I'll leave you alone now." As she began to pull away, Hedda grasped her hand more tightly.

"Eleanor, will you stay a little longer? It's good to sit here like this. I think you must be helping to carry my burden."

"Yeah, I can do that," she answered, her voice tight with emotion. "I know what it's like to be alone when times are hard. My parents, they give me money and stuff, but not much time. It's good to have a pal."

"*Ja.* I forgot how important pals are for a long time. But now I remember."

"Hey," Eleanor said, sounding brighter now, "did I tell you about the time we taught our St. Bernard to pull our sled?"

"No, please tell me." Hedda relaxed, letting Rubye's cool compress and Eleanor's voice soothe the sting of being left behind by Fritz Meyer.

Garland finally had Fritz alone. He'd written his letter and given it to Anni to post first thing in the morning. Now it was just the two of them in the library.

"They dug up the grave you were supposed to be in and found Marie's body," Garland began.

Fritz's head jerked up. "What is this?"

"Yeah, the government decided to relocate the Germans who'd died in the typhoid outbreak to another cemetery. Which looked like it would work out great for Hedda, who came to America to take your remains back to Germany for a proper burial there."

"How does she know where I am buried?"

"A monument was dedicated—your name was on it, and she saw it in a magazine or something. Of course, that was the other Fritz Meyer from the camp. Remember him? Anyhow, Hedda put the pieces together and figured out you were supposed to have been buried in Hot Springs. She's smart as a whip."

"And the body, how do they know it is Marie and not me?"

Garland grimaced. "The remains had long hair, and there was a fur collar with a fancy brooch still pinned on it. Plus they could tell it was a woman. Which means the police—that'd be me included—are investigating the death of Marie Spencer."

Now it was Fritz's turn to make a face. "But now you know what happened because I have told you the truth of the matter."

"That you helped cover up a murder? Is that the truth?"

"Murder? But we do not know that this is murder. Perhaps Harold did not mean for her to die."

"Murder or a terrible accident that Harold never told anyone about, which would be manslaughter at best. Either way, you helped hide the evidence and then you escaped. I buried the body, even if I didn't know it at the time. Harold made sure I got a good job in the sheriff's office after the war, and it appears as though he made sure you were taken care of, too, what with bringing you clothes and money. Even if it was just an accident, neither one of us spoke up about some seriously shady dealings."

Fritz frowned. "So we stay quiet. I will return to Bethania, and this is the end of it."

"Are you kidding me? You just turned up in a place where five or six people know who you are. And Marie Spencer's sister, Lucy, is pressing us hard for answers." He thumped a bookcase hard enough to make a book tumble to the floor. "Why couldn't you have just stayed where you were?"

Apparently Fritz thought this was a serious question. "All my life I dream of being a *Maler*, a painter. I want to go to

160

school for this when I am younger, but my *Vater* thinks this is a waste of money. When I read in the newspaper that Josef Albers is here, so close to me, I must come to see him. To learn from him. Another sign from God."

Garland dropped into a chair. He braced his elbows on a table and cradled his head in his hands. "Yeah, well, bully for you. Now we've got to figure out what to do next."

"I think I must make this right with Hedda. She does not understand why I did not return to her."

"That's what you're worried about? I'd think being an accomplice to murder carries a little more weight than that."

Fritz's ruddy cheeks paled. "But I have not made a crime. I have only acted foolishly."

Garland shook his head. "If Harold murdered Marie, what you did is called being an accessory after the fact. And since you were also an enemy alien at the time, it could get sticky."

Fritz seemed to shrink in his chair. He squeezed his eyes shut and scratched his head. "So we will continue to tell the truth. I have learned that the truth will set you free."

"How's that?" Garland's mind was reeling. Was he dealing with a simpleton?

Fritz shrugged his big shoulders. "I do not try to understand, but it is true. I have done it before, and it has worked."

"Good grief, you're no help at all. Let me think." Garland began pacing the room, head down, pondering the situation.

He'd been so determined to figure out what happened to Fritz, and now that the answer had been dropped in his lap, he didn't know what to do next. While he guessed there was still the possibility that Fritz had been directly involved in Marie's death, he felt certain the German had simply been in the wrong place at the wrong time. And had suffered for it. He was going to have to report Fritz's sudden reappearance to the sheriff and most likely to the federal government. What then?

He rubbed the back of his neck, thinking. What if he did take Fritz into custody? Now there was an idea. It would make him look good for apprehending the missing man and he could keep tabs on Fritz, who didn't seem to understand just how serious this all was.

"I know I said I wasn't going to put you in jail, but I think I'd better take you back to the office with me. Sheriff Fitzsimmons will want to hear 'the truth' from your own lips. Then we can figure out what to do next."

Fritz looked worried. "You are promising that you will not put me behind a fence again?"

Garland wasn't sure he could promise that but figured reassuring Fritz was the best way to keep things moving. "Yeah. Yeah, sure."

"*Gut.* I will make this right with Hedda tomorrow." The big man stood and slapped his hands together. "And then I will learn much about art, *ja*?"

Garland just shook his head. "Right. Come on then. Let's get this over with."

24

Fritz tucked his hands under his thighs in the policeman's car. He was grateful he was not made to sit in the back like a prisoner. He was grateful he was not a prisoner. Although, depending on what this sheriff had to say, he supposed that he still might be. Again.

Garland didn't speak, seemingly lost in thought. Fritz looked forward to telling the truth about Harold White to this sheriff. Since joining the Moravians, he'd learned that the truth was the most important thing. Like the truth of why he'd been willing to give up his old life and start a new one. Why, even with Harold White dead, he could no longer risk returning to Germany without endangering his mother and perhaps his very life. Why he'd come to believe it might be better for Hedda and *Mutter* to think he was dead. Leaving them behind had been a terrible sacrifice but one he'd thought he must make. And then when he made a life for himself, formed a new family among new people . . . well, if he was telling himself the truth as well, it would be that he'd eventually come to think of his former life—of his mother and his fiancée—with a fond distance that allowed him to carry on happily. He shifted in the seat, wondering how such choices—good and bad—had brought him to this place.

Of course, his new family had also taught him that mistakes could be forgiven. Sometimes they could even be corrected. He hoped this was one of those times. In his mind he asked God to guide him.

When they walked into the office, he thought Sheriff Fitzsimmons looked like someone who laughed often. Although he wasn't laughing now. Garland must have sent word that they were coming because the sheriff appeared to be waiting for them. He shook Fritz's hand and offered him a chair.

"You're the best-looking dead man I've ever seen."

Fritz froze, not sure how to answer that.

"Sorry. This isn't the time to make jokes."

Fritz let out the breath he was holding. American humor. It often eluded him.

"Alright then." Sheriff Fitzsimmons sat down behind a desk and folded his hands on top. "Let's hear it."

Once again, in his halting English, Fritz went through what happened that night years ago. When he'd finished, the sheriff turned to Garland. "Anything in that account change since he told it the first time?"

"No, that's what he told us back at the college."

"I'm still not altogether sure you should have allowed anyone else to be part of that initial interview, but I understand why you thought Hedda deserved an explanation and some moral support." The sheriff leaned back in his chair and stared at Fritz. Then he shifted his gaze to his deputy. "Now you tell me your version of that night one more time."

Garland closed his eyes and rubbed his face. He took a

deep breath and walked the sheriff through that fateful night from his perspective.

Fritz listened closely. He had never stopped to think what happened after he'd helped Harold carry poor Marie's body to the makeshift morgue. His focus had been entirely on getting away. The river was cold and swift, and at one point he'd thought his life would end right there. Finally emerging on the other side, wet and exhausted, had been like crossing from one life to another. A rebirth of sorts. And then Harold brought him clothes and a little money. He'd threatened him again, told him as far as everyone was concerned, he was dead. And if he ever showed his face again, Harold would make sure he either spent his life in prison or lost it at the end of a hangman's noose.

Even now, a shudder of fear passed through him.

"I guess I was pretty dumb not to ask more questions," Garland said. "Harold had always been pushy and didn't mind making trouble for anyone he didn't like. I should have checked that coffin, should have paid more attention to how strange Harold was acting."

The sheriff snorted. "While I wish you had, I can see how a young guard eager to finish an upsetting detail might be in a hurry to take things at face value." He tilted his head to one side. "Say, how about you go grab those files you've been poring over for way too long. Bring me anything that mentions Fritz here."

Garland frowned. "I can do that after we're finished."

"Now."

Even Fritz could tell there was no more room for talking about this. Garland nodded, said, "Yes, sir," and left the room.

Once they were alone, Sheriff Fitzsimmons leaned back

in his chair and drummed the fingers of his left hand on the desktop. "Guess you were pretty scared back then."

"I . . . yes."

"You were how old?"

"I had twenty-two years."

"Not all that young, then. Still, it must have been hard for you, so far from home and being treated as an enemy alien."

"*Ja.* Very hard."

"Did you ever try to go back to Germany once the war was over? After enough time had passed? It's not like Harold White was continuing to threaten you."

"No. The threat he made, it was strong in my mind."

"Really? I met Hedda. Seems like she'd be pretty strong in your mind as well."

Fritz heaved a sigh. "I am sorry about Hedda. In the beginning, I think of her often. I miss her very much. *Mein Mutter* too. But I am afraid I will be sent back to a camp or the jail if Mr. White tells the wrong story. He tells me I will be hanged for killing Marie. And I think I am in trouble for running away." He shrugged. "Soon my life is good in Bethania and so I do not, how do you say, risk it?"

"That must have been a tough decision for you."

Fritz leaned forward and thought hard. He wanted to say this right. There was something about the sheriff, maybe the way he really listened, that made Fritz want him to understand. "Hair." He tugged at a lock of his hair. "It grows and you must . . ." He made a scissoring motion with his fingers.

"Get a haircut," Sheriff Fitzsimmons filled in.

"*Ja.* But then you wait. You think *Morgen.* Morrow."

The sheriff laughed and nodded. "Right, you'll do it tomorrow."

"*Ja*. And then you think so again the next day. And then your hair is too much."

"I think I get what you're saying. You kept waiting, kept putting off the decision until too much time had passed. Maybe until you it felt like it was too late to even try."

"This is what I am saying. And the family I came to have—maybe they would not understand." Fritz felt such a sense of relief. He'd never had a chance to explain himself like this before. "It is a sorrow for me that I have made pain for Hedda and *Mutter*. I hope they will forgive me this."

"So that night when you escaped, you didn't really think that through either?"

"There is no time to think. Only I see my chance for a new life. Maybe one where I can make art, and I want to be free so much. I do not want to be punished for something I did not do." He smiled. "And I have made the art in my new home. It is good. But still I long for being taught the right way. So I come to Black Mountain College. Josef Albers, he teaches me."

The sheriff nodded and pressed both hands to his desk. "Okay. I think that's everything I need to know for now." He stood and clapped Fritz on the shoulder. "This isn't settled, though. We're still going to have to deal with Marie Spencer's death, and while I believe you didn't do it, there's going to be some paperwork involved in tying everything up. Hopefully the federal boys won't want to draw too much attention to this with what's happening in the world these days. Where are you staying?"

Fritz nodded, standing as well. He liked this sheriff and was happy to trust him. "I will stay at the college with Josef Albers. I have much to learn from him."

"That'll work. I'll have Deputy Jones take you back there.

Don't go anywhere else, though. You aren't under arrest, but you also aren't free to come and go. Do you understand?"

"*Ja, das ist gut*," Fritz said, feeling a little bit lighter even though he knew he still had many sins in need of forgiveness.

Garland gripped the steering wheel hard. What had Wayne asked Fritz after he left the room? "So you just talked about what happened that night? About Harold and Marie?" He stopped before adding *and me*.

"*Ja*. And he asks why I do not go back to Deutschland." Fritz thought a minute. "He is good at hearing me. Too bad he does not talk *Deutsch*."

Garland frowned. Wayne was good at listening and often heard things other people missed. That's what made Garland uneasy. And grateful for the language barrier. If Fritz said something amiss, he could always claim it had been a misunderstanding. Of course, now that everything was out in the open, there was nothing to misunderstand. Right?

Fritz interrupted his thoughts. "You have a *Frau*?"

Garland knew that word. "A wife? No."

"What about—how do you say—a woman friend?"

"A sweetheart? Nope, don't have one of those either."

"Why is this?" Fritz asked.

Garland considered the question. "Guess I haven't found the right girl." He let silence fall again, then added, "There was a girl once. Sister of a good buddy of mine. My friend went off to fight in the war, and I promised him I'd take care of her. Betty."

"You did not go to the war?"

"I had rheumatic fever when I was a tyke." He tapped his chest. "They said it damaged my heart and wouldn't take me." He shook his head. "Bunch of rot if you ask me. I wanted to go more than anything."

"It is good you did not go, and I did not go. We would be *Feinde.*"

"What's that mean?"

Fritz shut his eyes and tapped his fingers on his thigh. "Ah, yes, *enemies.* We would be enemies."

"Yeah," Garland agreed. "I guess we would at that."

"This is why it is good I am in America now. I think maybe our countries will battle again." He turned in his seat to better see Garland. "But there is Betty. Where is she?"

"She died." Garland hated talking about Betty.

"I am sad."

Garland glanced at Fritz. "Yeah, me too. That's why I looked the other way when Harold snuck Marie in, you know. Harold paid me under the table, and I used that to try and help Betty when she got sick. For all the good it did."

Fritz laid a large meaty hand on Garland's shoulder. "It is always good to try to help. God, He will take the bad things and make them good." He dropped his hand and sighed. "He is slow at times, but He will do it."

Garland wasn't sure how he felt about being preached to by a German who'd helped cover up a murder, escaped from an internment camp, then ran off and left his mother and fiancée to wonder what happened to him for fifteen years. Then again, he wasn't exactly an angel, was he? And at least Fritz had a good reason for his actions.

"Thanks, Fritz. I appreciate that."

"*Es ist nichts,*" Fritz murmured while staring out the window. His mind was clearly somewhere far away.

25

Hedda had been surprised to learn that Dr. Rice was letting Fritz stay on at the college. As a student of all things. *"He paid tuition,"* Dr. Rice said with a shrug. *"We need the money."* She'd avoided Fritz as much as possible the first week but soon realized he was becoming part of the fabric of their little community. Josef was delighted to have someone to speak German with, especially since Fritz's whole purpose in coming had been to study with the professor. Anni kept Fritz at arm's length out of loyalty to Hedda, but the brawny German was charming, and Hedda could see that soon even Anni would give in. She was beginning to remember why she fell in love with him all those years ago.

"Guten Morgen."

Of course, Fritz would be the person to greet her on this chilly morning. "Good morning." She nodded and kept her chin high. She assumed that by now, most of the staff and students would know that this was her former fiancé.

She saw Anni and Josef leaving their breakfast table, heads together, deep in conversation. Her eyes darted about the space, trying to find someone who would give her a reason to abandon Fritz without appearing rude to those around them.

"*Willst du hier sitzen?*" He motioned toward a nearby table with food already arranged on it.

She frowned. "I prefer to speak English. And it would serve you well to practice."

Fritz's smile faltered, but then he recovered it. "*Ja*. You are right. Will you sit here?" He pulled out a chair. Hedda gave a curt nod and sat. "I have food for two. You see? I am hoping to find you."

"Well, here I am." Hedda unfolded a napkin and sipped from a mug of coffee that was, thankfully, still hot and quite delicious. She was grateful to have something to do with her hands as she cradled the warm mug and considered him over its rim. "Why did you hope to find me?"

"I must make this up to you."

Hedda started to ask him what he meant by that, but she knew and it seemed like needless torture to drag this out. "I'm not sure you can," she said at last.

Fritz chuckled. "*Ja*, this is very true. I am not sure either."

The warmth of his smile and the honesty of his admission were disarming, though she wished they weren't. "I suppose we should make a truce," she said, "if you plan to stay here much longer." She took a sip of her coffee. "Do you plan to stay?"

"I hope to, *ja*. The sheriff, the one Garland takes me to, I think I must stay until he says I can go. I do not mind. This is different from the camp in Hot Springs. There are no fences, no guards, only one man asking another to do what is right."

Hedda nodded and nibbled a type of bread they called a biscuit. She was very fond of these with butter from a nearby farm and jam Rubye had made the summer before. She had been determined not to eat with Fritz but couldn't resist the golden, fluffy treat.

"Fritz, did you at least think about me after you escaped?" She groaned inwardly. She hadn't meant to ask that question. Now he knew that it mattered to her.

Fritz set down his mug and ran a hand over his cropped hair. "So much. In the beginning I think about you so much." He looked at the table as though composing his thoughts. Or perhaps he was trying to think how to put them in English.

"When I escape, I am afraid of what Harold White tells me he will do. I think I must never return to a place where people know who I am, or he will say I am the one to kill Marie Spencer." He sighed. "When I get off the train in Bethania, there are people like me. They speak *Deutsch*. They welcome me like family." He pushed his plate away, the food half-eaten. "I think of you, but the fear of what will happen is strong. I have no papers, and I think I will be in trouble for running away even if Harold White does not condemn me. So I do as Harold tells me. I think old Fritz is dead and new Fritz, he will make this new life. I build houses. I make pictures. I-I learn about *Gott* . . ." He hesitated, darted a look at her, then ducked his head. "And I find a family and . . . and I am happy like I did not think possible." He sighed. "The years, they go away so fast."

Hedda felt the sting of tears. While he'd been finding a new kind of freedom, she'd been trapped by not knowing what had happened to him. He'd moved into the future while she was left mired in the past. And what did he mean by "family"? Was he talking about the Moravian community, or did he . . . ?

He leaned forward and took her hand. "*Verzeih mir*. Forgive me."

172

The words pierced her. Such a simple request. Could she do it? "I-I want to forgive you, but it's very difficult." She attempted to smile. "I'm barely used to you not being dead. It might take me a little longer to find a way to forgive you for leaving me behind. Even though I suppose I can understand why you felt you had to."

"*Ja*, this is not bad. You must take time." He released her and spread his arms wide. "There is time for you to take. I will wait."

This time the smile came naturally. He really was awfully charming. Not to mention handsomer than she remembered. Not that his looks mattered one way or another. But this glimpse of the old Fritz made her think that perhaps she could find it in her heart to forgive this new version of him.

Garland packed up the files he'd been poring over in what turned out to be a fruitless search for Fritz. Who would have guessed the guy would just show up one day? Of course, there was still the question of what, exactly, happened to put Marie Spencer in an empty grave that night. The easy answer was that Harold White had killed her for a variety of possible reasons—jealousy, frustration, anger—yet Wayne was never one to be satisfied by easy answers. Garland had hoped once Fritz made his statement, they could consider this case closed. But Wayne said it would remain open until they had some real evidence that Harold had done something more than cover up a tragic accident. *"It's too easy to pin this on a dead man, and we're not taking the easy way out,"* he'd said. Drat his hide.

As he slid the last file into the last box, he heard a hulla-baloo at the front desk. Curious, he eased down the hall to see if he wanted to stick his nose in or not. He peered around the corner, then slammed himself flat against the wall, his breath coming in gasps. He did *not* want to get involved.

He began inching away, trying to think how he could escape. There was a back door, but he'd have to pass the sheriff's office to get to it. Maybe he could just slip into the dark file room and wait it out.

"Deputy Jones."

Garland froze. He didn't need to turn his head to recognize that bass voice. "Yes, sir?"

"I believe there's someone out front looking for you."

Garland peeled away from the wall and turned to face his boss. "Wayne, I promised to visit her once a week with an update. My next visit isn't due until the day after tomorrow. Can't someone tell her I'm out?"

"Why, Deputy Jones, that would be an untruth." There was a gleam in Wayne's eye Garland didn't like. "And you actually have some new information to share this time. I'd say there's no time like the present." He stepped forward and gripped Garland's shoulder. Tight enough to hurt. "As a matter of fact, why don't we set the two of you up in the kitchen. You can make Miss Spencer a cup of tea while you fill her in." He squeezed harder. "It'll be cozy."

"Yes, sir," Garland croaked. "That sounds like a good plan."

"Excellent." Wayne released him, and Garland tried not to rub his bruised shoulder. "You go ahead, and I'll show the lady in."

Garland shuffled down the hall to the kitchen. It occurred to him that he could slip out the back door without Wayne seeing him. Of course, that would be the end of his career, the end of their friendship, and quite possibly his general ruination.

Still. He was tempted.

"What's this I hear about Fritz Meyer showing up at that ridiculous new college in Black Mountain, alive and well?" Lucy's voice was a screech skittering around his skull. She burst into the room, and the phrase *mad as a wet hen* popped into his head. That's exactly what she looked like. A chicken with its feathers in a twist.

"Well?" The one word communicated paragraphs of information.

"Would you care to have a seat? I'll make you a cup of tea while we talk."

She narrowed her eyes but slid into a chair at the scarred table they all shared. "I like plenty of sugar and cream."

"Yes, ma'am." Of course she did. Though sugar was scarce these days, he'd give her what they had. Wayne liked sugar, too. Maybe this would teach him not to foist angry old maids off on him. "Here you go," he said, placing the doctored cup in front of her. She eyed it as if she thought it might be poisoned.

"So . . ." He settled in the chair opposite her, scooting it back from the table a few feet. "I guess you've heard the good news."

"Good news?" She sipped some tea and glared at him.

"That Fritz Meyer is alive and well."

"I'm supposed to be glad he's alive and my sister isn't?"

Garland paused. He'd thought coming at the topic like it was a happy circumstance would keep her off-balance. Now he was the one teetering on uncertainty. "Well, no. Of course not."

"He was around the night someone killed my sister and left her in the grave marked for him." She shook her head as though he were a simpleton. "Have you arrested him?"

"Hold on there. We don't have any evidence that Fritz had anything to do with your sister's death."

Lucy plunked down her cup on the table, splashing liquid over the side. "He was there, wasn't he? I hear you were there that night, too. Would you rather I accuse you? Maybe you shouldn't be the one investigating this business."

"How about Harold White?" Garland blurted. He grimaced. He'd better get ahold of himself before he said something even more foolish. "What I mean to say is, the investigation is ongoing, and thus far nothing suggests that Fritz was involved in foul play as it regards your sister. He did escape from the internment camp, but that's a matter for the army to take up. What little evidence we have points to Harold White."

"Well then, how about Harold? What is this *evidence*," she asked, exaggerating the word, "that he was involved in foul play?"

Garland cleared his throat. "I'm sorry, but I can't discuss that with you. We're still wrapping up the investigation."

"I want justice for my sister."

Was that the glint of tears in her eyes? "That's what we all want," he said.

"I'm not at all certain that's true. No one's cared for the past fifteen years, and now that you have someone who was part of whatever happened to her, you're practically celebrating the fact that he's alive and my sister isn't."

Yes, those were tears. Garland steeled himself, determined to continue disliking Lucy Spencer. She was angry, abrupt, and cold. He swallowed hard. And maybe sad about her sister. Hedda had helped him see that.

"Look, I can't begin to imagine how hard this must be for you. Seems like you thought your sister had just gone gadding off all those years ago, so it's got to be tough learning the truth now. But honestly, there's no reason to think Fritz was directly involved in her death. At worst, I think he took advantage of a terrible circumstance to gain his own freedom."

She knuckled a tear away, looking at him as though daring him to feel sorry for her. "That, at least, sounds like you're paying attention. I'm not at all satisfied, but perhaps I can trust you and the sheriff to get to the bottom of this." She glared at him. "Can I?"

"Yes, ma'am."

"And I'd like to meet this Fritz fellow. Talk to him myself."

"I don't think that would be appropriate." He didn't want her quizzing poor Fritz.

"Frankly, I don't care whether you think it's appropriate or not. Unless he's in custody, I assume he's free to speak to whomever he likes." She sounded triumphant. "There. Now maybe you're wishing you'd arrested him."

"No, ma'am. You're right, he's free to talk to anyone he chooses." Garland smiled weakly and tossed back a slug of his own now-tepid tea. He made a face. He hated tea. And while he didn't wish he'd arrested Fritz, if Lucy Spencer tracked him down, Fritz might wish he were safely behind bars.

26

BLACK MOUNTAIN, NORTH CAROLINA

Fritz sat on the edge of his bed in a small room on the second floor of Lee Hall. It was much nicer than the bunk room he'd shared with a dozen other men while an internee in Hot Springs all those years ago. He hated to admit it, but in some ways those had been good days for him. At first he'd felt an utter loss of control. Then when he was transported from New York to North Carolina, it felt as though he was getting further and further away from any hope of returning to the life he knew.

While stranded in Hot Springs, though, slowly he'd found his footing. He'd made friends. He'd been allowed to build his own cottage in the village they constructed using driftwood and castoff supplies. The satisfaction of making something beautiful had been heightened by the fact that they were limited in their materials. Making art from the leftover detritus of life had been its own reward.

And he could paint. While he didn't have access to high-quality supplies, what he did have was creative freedom. This had delighted him, making him feel freer behind a high fence than he had when on the high seas.

Fritz moved to the window and took in the view of the mountains, where summer's green had given way to the colorful riot of autumn. He particularly loved the maples, which varied so widely from vibrant yellows to brilliant reds and oranges.

That's what he would paint in the studio this afternoon. That's what he would discuss with Josef. The way the colors of the leaves changed against the varying blues of the sky—one color when the sky was a soft gray like now, and another when it was the cerulean blue of a robin's egg as he hoped it would be this afternoon.

Could he capture that? He would try. He knew how that felt. The heightening of the senses with the dawning of the light. Intensity. It's what he'd felt when he got off the train in Bethania and discovered the miracle of people who accepted him as he was.

Of course, he also knew the guilt of having to abandon his mother and Hedda. He hoped *Mutter* understood. She had yet to answer the letter he'd written in which he'd poured out his heart. He'd included a sketch of himself so she could see how he'd changed since she last saw him. He shared his regret over not writing to her sooner and his feeling that, given what was happening in Germany now, it would be unwise for him to come home. He would have liked to write more plainly but feared censors might be reading the mail. He couldn't risk saying too much, such as sharing the details about his new family—he would save that for another letter. Assuming she wrote back and wanted to hear more.

His mother had been so determined that he would become

an important man, perhaps the captain of his own ship one day. His family had been well-to-do before the war to end all wars took his father's life. Afterward, it seemed everyone struggled to regain their footing. *Vater* had never approved of his art, and *Mutter* feared that if Fritz pursued it, he would be poor always. And she was most likely right.

Now that he was in his thirties with a family of his own, Fritz could better understand her fears and concerns. Still, he had made his way in Bethania with a combination of manual labor and art. Most of the families there owned at least one of his paintings, landscapes and portraits mostly. He was good at portraits, although he didn't like painting them as much as the impressionistic work he'd been exploring in his landscapes. Those were less popular with his friends, however. Having Josef and Anni to talk to about art was a dream come true. He hoped *Mutter* would forgive the missing years and be happy to know him as he was now.

Perhaps there would be a letter from her soon. Fritz ran his fingers through his short hair and headed for the classroom, where Josef would be lecturing about color theory. He inhaled the cool, fresh air, letting it expand his chest and enliven his spirit. He thought about Ezekiel prophesying over the dry bones until they had sinews, flesh, skin, and finally breath. The very breath of *Gott. Ja.* That's how he felt today, as though new life had been breathed into him.

"Are you Fritz Meyer?"

He turned to see a small, dark woman speaking. Her black hair was pulled back so tight it seemed to stretch her face. Her frown gave him pause. "I am Fritz."

She moved faster than he expected, darting forward to jab him in the chest with her finger. "Aha! Now I've got you."

He chuckled, a low rumble in his chest. This pixie of a

woman was all flame and no tinder. "Yes, you got me," he agreed.

She flushed, which improved her looks. "Tell me what happened to my sister."

A ribbon of dread bloomed in Fritz's chest. "I do not know your sister."

"Marie Spencer. You were there the night she died. Deputy Jones has failed to give me the answers I need. He claims you didn't have anything to do with Marie's demise, but I'd like to hear it from the horse's mouth."

Fritz frowned. He was both surprised and pleased that the deputy would so plainly state his innocence. "Garland, he tells you true."

"You look like you could kill someone if you wanted to."

Fritz flinched. "I would not want to."

"Who did it, then? What did you see or hear that you have yet to tell anyone?"

Fritz sagged. "Maybe it was Harold White. I don't know. I helped him put Marie in a coffin that he pretended was for me. Then he helped me run away."

She glared at him, and he thought maybe she wasn't as fragile as he'd first thought. "There's something off about this whole business. Seems to me a dead man is an awfully handy scapegoat. Weren't you suspicious?" she asked. "Didn't you care that no one would know what happened to Marie?"

Of course he'd known what he did wasn't right. He'd thought of himself as incredibly lucky all those years ago when the chance to escape presented itself. And then even luckier when his wrong turn landed him in a place where he'd felt more at home than he had anywhere else in his life. But he was beginning to see that he'd left a great deal of sadness and confusion in his wake, intentional or not.

"I am a prisoner," he said, trying to think how best to express himself. "What choice do I have? If I help, maybe I am doing wrong. If I do not help, maybe I am in great trouble." He sighed. "I think it is best not to ask questions."

Lucy stared at him like he'd sprouted a second head. She nodded. "Yes. I know what you mean. Sometimes the world leaves you without any good choices. Tell me, did you know my sister at all?"

"A little. I am driving her places sometimes and she talks to me, but my English is not good then." He smiled at the memory. "She is nice. Even to prisoners. Even though we are meant to be her enemy." He chuckled. "Sweets. I forget that she brings sweets and says"—he raised his voice to a falsetto—"'don't tell on me.'"

A laugh burst from the woman, which seemed to take her by surprise. She slapped a hand over her mouth, her eyes wide. "She used to say that when we were girls, snitching cookies when Mother wasn't looking. It was always her idea, as I was too afraid. But she'd give me a cookie and say, 'Don't tell on me.'" Tears formed in her eyes. "And I never did."

"This is a good thing to remember."

"Yes. Yes, it is." She tilted her head as though reconsidering him. "Thank you for reminding me. I guess maybe I believe that you weren't involved in her death. You're the first person to have anything nice to say about her in a very long time." She paused. "And that includes me."

Fritz looked across the lawn to where he could see Josef bringing his students outside into the fresh air. He was pointing and talking animatedly while Hedda stood beside him, translating for the students. Fritz ached to join them. He would be one of the few to really understand what the teacher was saying.

"Come with me and hear about art," he said to the woman.

"What?"

He pointed at the group. "They are talking about color, how it can change like magic. Come hear this thing."

"But I'm not a student. It wouldn't be appropriate."

"Who is to care?" Fritz asked with a shrug.

The woman laughed. "Alright, but just for a minute." She got a mischievous look in her now-dry eyes. "But don't tell on me."

Fritz laughed, a great, free, uproarious sound that lifted to the sky like a rainbow of colors.

27

BLACK MOUNTAIN, NORTH CAROLINA

There was to be a dance this evening and Hedda would play. The college's first semester had just a few weeks remaining, and everyone wanted to celebrate. Dr. Rice had assured them all that there would be enough money not only for the spring but for a second year after Blue Ridge Assembly hosted its summer retreats for churches.

And Hedda was worried.

She'd been in America for several months past her visa. She'd been meaning to apply for a work visa now that she was employed, but if she was honest, she was afraid they would send her back despite her job. And she was afraid if she left now, she would never be able to return to this place and this life that made her feel alive in a way she hadn't since she'd watched Fritz sail away on a ship, carrying her dreams with him. Relations between America and Germany continued to be strained as Herr Hitler followed Japan in withdrawing from the League of Nations. It did not seem like a good time for a German to hope to find favor in America.

Dr. Rice said she was welcome to return in the spring, but she'd have to find a place to spend the holidays. He added that he was considering making her a member of the faculty, which filled her with hope. Perhaps she should wait until he'd decided for certain. Surely her position would be stronger if she were a college instructor and not just a piano teacher. Initially, she'd hoped that attempting to learn what happened to Fritz would be a good enough reason to extend her stay. But now . . . now! Not only was there no body to return to German soil but Fritz was alive and had presumably stayed in the United States without permission as well. Not something that she thought would be helpful to mention.

What a *Gewirr*—a tangle.

Hedda finished arranging her hair and smoothed her dress, shifting her mind from her worries to the pleasant evening ahead. Eleanor had loaned her a lovely frock. The small amount she earned teaching piano certainly didn't extend to new clothes. While her limited wardrobe was perfectly serviceable and had seen her through, it was nice to wear something different for once. The dress was pink silk, shot through with a deeper rose thread in a diamond pattern. It had a flutter collar high in the front that dipped to a deep vee in the back and short flutter sleeves that allowed her to play unhindered. The skirt had lovely ruffles down the back that she supposed no one would see since she'd be sitting on a piano bench most of the evening. Still, she felt feminine and, dare she say, pretty?

Not that she had anyone to impress, she reminded herself, even as several faces rose to the surface of her mind. Indeed, if someone else took a turn at the piano, she might be persuaded to dance with Garland, should he turn up. And then there was Fritz. A dance for old time's sake?

A tender smile curved her lips. Yes. A dance with Fritz would be nice.

Hedda gave herself one last glance in the mirror and then hurried off to Lee Hall to take her place. She decided to set her worries firmly to the side for now. She'd had little enough frivolity in her life, and the students at Black Mountain College took their fun seriously. As would she.

Inside the hall, a handful of faculty and students had already gathered to chat and put the finishing touches on the food and decorations. The room was filled with excitement and energy, making Hedda eager to play a lively tune. Even though the dance wasn't set to start for another thirty minutes, she decided to warm up a little with some simple, heartwarming music.

As she slid onto the piano bench, she saw Fritz enter from the rear of the space. And if she wasn't mistaken, he did a double take upon seeing her. She tried not to let the smile of satisfaction show. Perhaps he was regretting his decision not to return to her in Germany. She let her fingers dance lightly over the keys. Better late than never? Perhaps this time she would be the one to leave him feeling uncertain.

A sense of power surged through Hedda. It was something she couldn't remember ever feeling before. She'd long seen herself as the poor, pitiful girl whose one true love had disappeared in a time of war. But she wasn't that girl any longer.

She glanced at Fritz out of the corner of her eye and caught him watching her. She turned to smile, and he flushed before looking away and talking animatedly to Josef. Hedda giggled and played a bit more allegro.

Fritz was glad to have Josef to talk to in German. He kept up his English with other students and with Hedda, but it was a relief to simply speak without considering what the right word would be. Sometimes he gave up trying to express more complex thoughts or ideas because he simply couldn't find the words.

Of course, tonight he was feeling tongue-tied because Hedda was distracting him. The years they had been apart had been kind to her. He'd forgotten how lovely she was, especially when absorbed in her music. And that dress. The way it dipped lower in the back, showcasing her slender neck and porcelain skin . . .

Josef elbowed him. "Are you listening?"

"What? Oh, sorry. I was . . . thinking."

"Thinking?" Josef chuckled. "That's one name for it. Anni says you were to marry Hedda once. Perhaps it isn't too late."

Fritz flushed and turned so he couldn't see Hedda anymore. "There is 'too much water under the bridge,' as they say in America. I think it's too late for us."

"Perhaps. Perhaps not. These are strange days, and I say find happiness where you can." Josef frowned. "Is that Eleanor? She's waving at us."

Fritz looked as well and saw Hedda's friend standing at the far door and motioning at them before glancing outside. "Let's go see," he said.

When they reached Eleanor, she grabbed each of them by the arm and tugged them outside. She dropped her voice almost to a whisper. "There's a man in Dr. Rice's office, asking about Germans and if they have the proper papers."

"What is this?" Josef's eyes widened, and he braced himself against the side of the building. "But Anni and I, we have the proper papers."

"Good." She looked at Fritz. "And you?"

The blood had already drained from Fritz's head until he felt a buzzing in his ears. "I-I have not needed papers."

"That's as I feared. And Hedda?"

Fritz shrugged. "I do not know."

Eleanor shook her head. "My guess is she's stayed longer in America than she was meant to. The two of you aren't teachers here, so Dr. Rice wouldn't need to have checked your papers. Maybe it would be smart not to be around if this man comes looking for Germans."

Fritz nodded. "I'll get Hedda, and we will go for a long walk."

"Yes, good. Don't come back until it's dark. If all is well, I'll stand here on the porch, drinking punch. If I'm not here, stay away."

Again, Fritz nodded. Now, how to get Hedda to leave with him without alarming her? "Who else can play the piano?"

"Amanda Stalling plays. I'll ask her to take over." Eleanor darted inside and spoke to one of the students, who smiled and nodded.

Fritz hurried over to the piano and stood there, uncertain whether he should interrupt Hedda. But she saw him and quickly brought the piece she was playing to an end. She smiled as if she knew something he didn't when it was just the opposite.

He cleared his throat. "Hedda, will you come with me? There's something I must tell you."

Her brow furrowed. "But the dance is about to begin."

Amanda approached the piano. "Hedda, do you mind if I start things off? I'm desperately in need of the practice. You can play after me so that no one will realize how much better you play until it's too late." She laughed lightly.

Still looking confused, Hedda stood and let Fritz lead her

to the back of the room. He drew her toward an exit door marked FOR STAFF ONLY.

"Fritz, what are you doing? Why are you being so *seltsam* . . . so strange?"

Once they were in the shadows, Fritz stopped and glanced back across the room. He saw Eleanor, Josef, and now Anni together. A stranger in a dark suit approached them. "Come, walk with me," he said, pulling her outside into the dusk. He led her along a path toward a wooded area. Before they reached it, she stopped.

"*Genug* . . . enough. Tell me what this is about."

"There is a man asking for papers of the Germans. Your papers, are they right?"

Her face slackened, and she swayed. He put an arm around her waist and hurried her away on the curving path until they were out of sight of Lee Hall. He pushed deeper among the trees toward a rustic bench. He eased her onto it and sat beside her. She was shaking.

"Will they arrest me?" she asked in a small voice. "My time here has been up for a month or two now."

Fritz shook his head. "I do not know. I have no papers. What will they do to me?"

She turned wide, frightened eyes on him. Her look of helplessness ignited something inside him so that he pushed aside his fear. "It is not to worry," he assured her. "We are safe here, and Josef, he will not tell."

Hedda buried her face in her hands, muffling her voice. "I don't want to go back." She lifted her face and closed her eyes tight. "I stayed to learn what had happened to you. I should go home now. Comfort your mother. Return to my students." She blinked rapidly. "But I don't want to. I've found such freedom here. It's unlike anything I've known since—" she paused, then glanced at him—"since you left me."

Fritz flinched. "I did not think that I was leaving you. I thought only to save myself from Harold White." Her eyes hardened. "I see now that is what I did. *Mutter* too."

"Has she answered your letter?"

"*Nein*. It is three weeks. I think she must be angry."

Hedda frowned. "I haven't heard from her either. Do you think she's alright?"

"Ach. I had not thought of this. What if . . . ?" He couldn't bring himself to say it.

Hedda laid a soothing hand on his arm. "No, a friend would have written to tell me." Her face pinched. "Unless there's a problem with the post. Times are strange in Germany. It wouldn't surprise me if letters were being held or censored." She sighed and slumped against his shoulder. "Another reason I don't wish to return."

Fritz tried to focus even as her closeness distracted him. "I am thinking I cannot go home even if I want." The reminder settled like a heavy fog, enveloping him. "I have no papers, and this would bring attention to *Mutter* that is not wanted in these days."

Hedda nodded. "That's true. You would need papers to leave America as well as to enter Germany." She straightened and considered him. "But did you want to? And what do you mean about bringing attention to Lotte?"

"I think maybe I should not have written to *Mutter*. It might be better if she thought I was *Verstorben*." He said no more, thinking this wasn't the right time to share his family's secrets with Hedda. There was a man asking questions about Germans and their right to be in America. He couldn't risk being sent away now.

"Maybe we can send a telegram to check on her," Hedda suggested. "It's expensive, but I think worth it."

"I do not want you to have this expense," said Fritz. "I will do it." He reached out and took Hedda's hand. "I am happy you are here, and I am here even if you do not forgive me."

"Oh, Fritz, I think I do forgive you. As much as I suffered in the beginning, coming here now has been *wunderbar*." She laughed lightly and lifted her free hand to indicate the forest around them. "Of course, I may be in difficulty. But I think it's worth the trouble to have found this place where I can play music and learn and be with people who are so very interesting."

Fritz wanted to ask who in particular she found interesting but thought it was not the time. As a matter of fact, the coming of night made him realize it was time to see if it was safe to return to Lee Hall.

"Come, we will go back and see if the man is not here." He stood and tugged her up with their still-clasped hands. Once she stood, she looked at him long enough to stop the breath in his chest. Then she released his hand and started back along the path. He hurried to catch up to her. "We have a *Zeichen*, Eleanor and me."

"A sign?" She laughed nervously. "We'll be taken for spies yet."

They circled around to the front of Lee Hall, sticking to the shadowy edge of the trees. Fritz peered up at the porch and saw Eleanor, punch cup in hand, strolling along in the light spilling from windows and doors open to the boisterous dancers inside. Music rolled across the lawn to reach their ears.

He grinned. "All is well, *Fräulein*." He bowed, suddenly feeling lighthearted. "Will you dance?"

She laughed, and he could hear the relief in it, the fear falling away. "*Danke*," she said, holding out her hand.

He took it and spun her into a dance on the dew-wet lawn, both delighting in the transition from fear to joy. She felt right in his arms, like she'd always fit there, and he wondered how he'd walked away from her so easily.

When a pause in the music came, they stopped. She pulled away only a little and said, "Do you remember the dance before you left on your first voyage?"

"*Ja*, I remember."

"You said you would carry the feel of me in your arms all the way to America."

"*Ja*. And so I did."

She took a step back, breaking contact. "But not all the way to a camp in the mountains of North Carolina, I think."

He was opening his mouth to protest when someone cleared their throat. He whirled toward the sound, raising his fists. "*Wer ist da*," he barked into the night.

28

Hedda released the air trapped in her lungs when Eleanor stepped close enough to be seen. "It's just me. I thought I saw you out here in the dark. You can come back inside now. The fellow from the immigration and naturalization office is gone."

"Thank goodness," Hedda said and began walking toward the hall without sparing Fritz a look. She was flustered to have been found in his arms. What did he want from her? What did she want from him?

Eleanor fell into step beside her. "Someone reported that there are Germans at the college without papers. They sent this man to look into it."

Hedda stopped and stared. "Who would do this?"

"I don't know," Eleanor said, "but the Alberses' papers were in order, which I think satisfied this fellow. I got the feeling he was checking just to humor whoever made the report. He asked if we had any other Germans on staff, and we told him—truthfully—that we don't."

"I'm glad the danger is past now," Hedda said. "Still, I

think I must do something about my papers." She darted a look at Fritz, grateful that she at least had papers to work with. "Maybe I can change them to work or immigration papers."

Eleanor frowned. "I don't think it's that easy."

"Maybe not, but I must do something. I have decided I will stay in America, and I would like to do this in the right way." She nodded to herself. Yes, taking action was the right thing to do.

"Maybe we should look into it before you go and do something you can't take back," Eleanor said as they neared the whirl of the dance. Hedda could hear that whoever was playing was making mistakes, and she itched to resume her seat at the piano.

"Yes, I'm sure you're right," she said, then hurried inside without a glance at either of her escorts. She told herself it was her eagerness to play that made her rush and not the way her body still tingled where Fritz had clasped her waist and where she had rested her hand on his strong shoulder.

The next morning, Hedda took a bus to Marshall. She'd thought to go directly to the federal courthouse in Asheville to learn how to change from being a visitor to an immigrant. But the notion felt so very daunting. Then it occurred to her that having someone in authority might facilitate the process. And who better than a sheriff's deputy? So instead of the courthouse, she set out to find Garland at the sheriff's office in the county seat.

When she was shown into his cramped office, he looked genuinely glad to see her. He hopped up and cleared off a chair, waving her to have a seat. Hedda settled herself, feeling a little flustered now that she was here. She realized her visit had been presumptuous and perhaps a bit forward.

"I hope you don't mind my turning up like this," she said. "I should have sent a note first."

"No, it's fine. I'm glad to see you. I was thinking I'd stop by the college the next time I headed down that way, and here you've saved me the trouble." He flushed and she thought that maybe he was feeling off-kilter as well.

Best to get to the point. "I'm hoping that you can help me," she began.

He resumed his seat behind the desk. "I'd be happy to. What can I do for you?"

"I would like to become an American."

"Well, that's terrific!" His grin suggested he was delighted by the notion. Which gave her courage to continue.

"I'm glad you think so. You see, when I got my travel papers in Germany, they were only for a visit to collect . . . well, to collect a body and bring it home." She raised her hands, palms up. "But now there is no body, and with Herr Hitler making such changes, I don't wish to return. But how to stay? This is what I need your help to learn."

Garland nodded and tapped a finger on his desk blotter. "Do you have your papers with you? I'm not an expert on this sort of thing, but I can find the right person to talk to."

"*Ja.* Here they are." She handed over the carefully folded documents along with her passport. In Germany it was best to always have your papers at the ready. She marveled that Americans hardly gave such documentation a second thought.

Garland unfolded the pages and smoothed them on top of a stack of other papers. As he read over them, his brow furrowed. He flipped back and forth between the sheets, looking more and more concerned. Finally, he raised his eyes to meet Hedda's. "Unless I'm mistaken, and I hope I am, you've overstayed your visa."

"Yes, this is why I would like to change my status. A man came to the college yesterday checking the papers of any Germans working there. Josef and Anni were able to show him their papers, but I did not dare."

Garland stared at her. "What did you do?"

"Fritz and I went into the woods and didn't come back until he had gone away. But I am thinking it would be good to sort this out in case he comes back."

Garland gaped at her, making her feel uneasy. "So Fritz doesn't have any papers at all? What's he plan to do?" He snorted. "Does he think he can just become an American as well?"

"This I don't know, but you're making me think it may be a difficulty."

Garland flopped back in his chair and blinked at the ceiling. He groaned, then took a deep breath and sat forward again. "You're putting me in a tough spot here." He thumped her papers with the back of his hand. "As I understand it, you should be deported since your time here is up. And having overstayed, you probably can't come back for a long time, if ever. Especially these days." He rubbed both hands over his face. "You can't just come as a visitor and then decide you want to stay permanently. That's not how it works."

Hedda felt dizzy. "You're going to send me back?"

"Not me. But as an officer of the law, I sure as shooting ought to turn you in." He groaned again. "I'd really hate to do that. But if I don't, it could cost me."

Hedda couldn't stop the tears that began to track her cheeks. She ducked her head and tried to wipe them away before Garland saw.

"Hey. Don't cry." He came around his desk and squatted beside her, offering a handkerchief. "I'm not going to turn you in. Shoot, that would mean I'd have to turn Fritz in, too, and that's a can of worms I sure as heck don't want to open."

"Worms?"

Garland chuckled. "Sorry. It's an American expression that means something's a big mess."

"*Ja*, this is a mess," she agreed.

Garland stood and leaned against the front of his desk. "So here's what I'm thinking. I'll ask around, do a little research, and see if there's some way you can stay. Some loophole. How's that sound?"

She nodded and mopped her face with the handkerchief. "You're very kind. Will this cause you trouble?"

He grimaced and scratched the back of his head. "Nah. Should be fine. But don't mention this to anyone else. And it'd probably be good if we acted like you didn't mention this to me. It'll be our secret."

"I don't like secrets," said Hedda. "Fritz, he's been a secret for a very long time, and now I think he must remain so. But I understand. It's like in Germany where being a Jew must be a secret. It's why I want to stay in America."

"Yeah, the newspapers say things are real bad for lots of people in Germany right now." He rapped his knuckles on the desktop. "Alright then. We'll figure out how to make sure you stay here in good ol' North Carolina. I'm sure there's a way."

Hedda sniffed and smiled, grateful that she'd come to Garland instead of going to the courthouse in Asheville. From the sound of things, if she had, she would have been sent back to Germany in short order. And much to her surprise, the thought that she might never go back there hardly troubled her at all.

197

Garland put Hedda on a bus back to Black Mountain, then immediately headed for the courthouse in Marshall. He'd talked a good game, but he wasn't at all certain that there was a way for Hedda to legally become an American. No matter how much he wished there were. And if Wayne found out Garland was covering for her, he might not get to choose whether he turned her over to immigration or not. Which would be bad for them both.

At the courthouse, he poked his head into the clerk's office. Penny Crane was a sweetheart, but she was also tough as nails when she needed to be. Working with judges seemed to have rubbed off on her. He figured if anyone knew about immigration laws, it would be Penny.

"Hey, doll," she said as soon as she saw him. "What brings you around this side of the law? Just missing me, I hope."

Garland chuckled. Penny was old enough to be his mother, but that never kept her from flirting with him. Or any of the other deputies. "You know it. Never can get enough of you."

Penny chortled and waved him in. "In my dreams. Now seriously, what can I do for ya?"

"I've got a hypothetical question."

"Ooh, I love those. Sock it to me."

"Let's say someone came to this country from Europe just for a visit but then didn't go home when they were supposed to. Now they'd like to stay, but of course are going to have a hard time becoming a legal immigrant after breaking the rules." He tried to gauge what Penny was thinking, but she had a great poker face. "Any loopholes you can think of to get around that?"

Penny waggled her eyebrows at him. "Interesting. Well,

these days asylum might be one way to go—if this person would be in danger if they went back home. That's a tough one. Or, if they had family members who are United States citizens and it would be an undue hardship for them to leave, like if they had kids or a sick parent who's American, then there's a case to be made."

Garland nodded along. Hedda definitely didn't have family in the U.S., and he doubted she'd be in danger if she went back home. At least not any more danger than anyone was these days. "Got it. Anything else?"

Penny gave him a devilish grin. "You could always marry the girl."

"What?" Garland choked on the word.

"Aw, I'm just giving you a hard time. But seriously, marrying an American is probably the simplest way for a foreigner to stick around. Although it's not altogether simple. There's still paperwork involved and hoops to jump through, but hey, once the knot's tied, even the U.S. government can't do much about it."

Garland felt woozy all of a sudden. "Right," he said. "Guess that answers my question."

Penny laid a hand on his arm. "Say, you aren't thinking about doing something crazy, are you?"

"No. Like I said, it's purely hypothetical."

"Well, don't forget to send me a hypothetical invitation to the wedding." She winked. "You know as well as I do that getting hitched at the courthouse is always an option." She laughed. "Although maybe not for someone who isn't supposed to be in the country to begin with!"

Garland managed a weak chuckle. "Right you are. That *would* be crazy."

29

ASHEVILLE, NORTH CAROLINA

It was good to be in a familiar place for Christmas. Hedda was grateful that Eleanor didn't mind sharing the one room currently available at the Wolfe boardinghouse in Asheville. Mrs. Wolfe told them it was unusual for her to rent a room for such a short stay but agreed since they'd been good tenants previously and the room was, after all, vacant.

"You'd think she was doing us a favor by taking our money," Eleanor laughed as she shoved freshly laundered clothing into the wardrobe. When Hedda didn't respond, she crossed the room and plopped onto the bed, where Hedda sat woolgathering. "Cheer up. We're going to figure out how to keep you here in America, I know we are."

Hedda forced a smile. "I shouldn't fret. There is still much to love about my country, and I do miss the café where I would have *Kaffee* and watch the world go by. I also miss my students—especially Liesl, who has such promise. And it would be good to see Lotte again. I worry for her health. Although her sister is staying with her now, so I'm not sure where they would put me." She didn't mention that Garland would be stopping by to tell her what he'd learned about ways for her to remain in America. She didn't want to get her hopes up.

There was a knock at the door. Mrs. Wolfe pushed it open without waiting for an invitation. "I forgot that I received a letter for you a while back. I suppose the sender didn't know you were at Black Mountain College." She handed the envelope to Hedda. "I apologize that I didn't think of it sooner, but it was buried on my desk." Mrs. Wolfe swept from the room.

"It's from Lotte. Maybe this explains why I haven't heard from her." Hedda clapped a hand over her mouth. "Oh! I was going to send her a telegram. All this business with my papers made me forget."

"Well, read the letter before you worry over that," Eleanor said. "Perhaps you won't need to now."

Hedda opened the envelope and slid out the crinkly paper with Lotte's fine, sloping script. She read it through quickly.

"Well? Did she get Fritz's letter? What does she have to say?"

Hedda shook her head. "I think she must not have received it. She writes of the usual sorts of things with no mention of Fritz."

"What's the date?"

Hedda checked. "Even with the mail slow and jumbled, it would be surprising if she hadn't received his letter before she wrote this." She reread the letter, then lowered the page and stared out the window. "I can't believe she wouldn't mention it to me if she'd received his letter."

"Did *you* write to her about Fritz?"

"No, I thought it best to let him break the news to her."

"Where is Fritz these days?" Eleanor asked. "Did he go back to Bethania for Christmas?"

"He's staying at the college. They needed a handyman to do some extra work, and he was happy to stay on."

Eleanor's eyes twinkled. "Maybe because he didn't want to let the girl he was once engaged to slip through his fingers a second time."

Hedda pinched her lips in a frown. "That is silly talk."

"Maybe." Eleanor stood at the window, watching the street outside. "Well, speak of the devil . . ."

"That's an expression I have never cared for. Why do you say it?" Hedda tried to keep her frustration from making her cross with her young friend.

"Because Fritz just stepped onto the front porch, and I'd be awfully surprised if he's here to see me."

"What?" Hedda hopped up and joined Eleanor at the window.

"Can't see him now. I expect he's in the parlor and asking someone to let you know you have a visitor."

Hedda's hand went to her hair and began twirling a strand round and round. She tried to sound confident. "This is good. I want to ask him about that letter to his *Mutter*."

"Right." Eleanor reached over and stilled Hedda's hand. "You're making a mess of your hair. That won't do. Here, let me pin it up for you."

Hedda grimaced. "Thank you, no. I'll go down before Mrs. Wolfe grows annoyed with delivering messages."

Before she could change her mind, she smoothed her skirt and marched downstairs. She ignored Eleanor, whom she knew was trailing after her. Very well, she had no secrets. She nearly collided with Fritz as she entered the parlor.

"*Wie bitte*," he said. "Oh, Hedda, it is you. I have come to speak to you."

Hedda glanced at Eleanor, who was smirking. "Have you? That's good because I'd like to speak to you." She gestured to a pair of comfortable-looking chairs. "Perhaps we can sit over there, where we will have some *privacy*." She shot a look at Eleanor as she stressed the last word. Her friend grinned before turning and disappearing back down the hall.

"*Danke.*" Fritz followed her to the chairs. He waited for Hedda to sit before settling himself. "You will speak first and then I will, *ja*?"

"That's probably best." Hedda drew Lotte's letter from her pocket. "Your mother wrote to me here. That's why I hadn't heard from her in a while. But even though she would have certainly received your letter before writing this, she doesn't mention you."

Fritz paled. "That is strange. Could it be my letter did not arrive? There is much trouble in Germany now. Or could it have been taken by the government?" He swallowed hard and began tapping his fingers against the arm of his chair.

Hedda nodded. "I suppose either of those are possible. Now I think it's more important than ever to send her a telegram. She deserves to know you're alive as soon as possible."

Fritz bowed his head. "Can I read her writing?"

Hedda handed the sheet of paper over. She noticed that Fritz's hand was shaking as he took it. As he read, tears began to well in his eyes. One spilled over and fell to the page, marring the ink. He jumped to his feet, holding the page up. "Ah, I have spoiled it." He thrust it into Hedda's hands. "*Es tut mir leid.*" Tears continued to fall as he turned his back to her.

Hedda stood and rested a tentative hand on Fritz's shoulder. "You don't need to be sorry. The paper will dry."

He began to cry harder. Hedda didn't know what to do. Seeing this mountain of a man sobbing touched something inside her that she thought she'd long ago put to rest. "Fritz, it's alright," she said.

He took a shuddering breath, pulled out a handkerchief, and mopped his face. After blowing his nose, he turned and sat back down, motioning for her to do the same. They sat in silence for a few moments while he continued to compose himself.

"I have tried hard to not think what I . . . how do you say, *geopfort?*"

"Sacrificed," Hedda supplied.

"*Ja.* Sacrificed. But now there is you, and there is *Mutter.*" He waved at the letter. "And I am knowing I have lost much."

Hedda felt tears prickle her own eyes. She nodded encouragingly.

"This is what I am sorry about."

The words were simple, yet the look in his eyes was everything Hedda had longed for in those years after she lost him. Everything she'd dared to hope might be found again. That hope had died somewhere along the way, and having it rekindled now caused a sweet pain she wasn't sure she could bear.

"Fritz . . ." What did she want to say to him? She wasn't certain.

"*Nein.* It is better that you do not speak now. Now I must send *Mutter* a telegram." He stood, straightened his shoulders, and stuffed his handkerchief back in his pocket. "Do you think—?" He stopped, then started again. "Will you come with me?"

"*Ja, ich werde mit dir kommen.*" She blinked back tears and repeated herself in English, "Yes, I will come with you."

He took her hand, and his smile made her close her eyes against the delicious agony of hope rekindled.

Fritz's heart soared. He'd begun to hope that he might win Hedda's forgiveness. Now he wondered if he dared hope that he might win her heart, too. It had been his once. Perhaps it could be again. He'd been foolish to let her go, although at the time he hadn't known what else to do.

And then there was the matter of his mother. All those years ago he'd told himself it was better to let her think he'd died than to risk being sent to prison as a murderer and an escaped enemy alien. He convinced himself that it would be easier for her.

Reconnecting with Hedda and learning that she'd been there for his mother when he hadn't filled him with regret. He'd thought, ever so briefly, of how he might return to see her, but with Germany as it was, drawing such attention now would be dangerous. He supposed he would never see her again, would never hear her voice or feel the touch of her hand. But he could at least tell her he was well and that he loved her. What seemed inevitable when he was twenty-three, he now keenly realized, had turned out to be a cruel trick of fate.

He glanced at Hedda, waiting patiently for the clerk at the telegraph office to take his message. She would help him know what to say. She would be—had been—a salve to the pain he'd caused. She looked up at him, and he smiled, his heart swelling in his chest. Yes, he'd been a frightened boy once who made foolish choices while in the grip of uncertainty. Now he was a man who knew better.

"What do I say?" he asked her.

Hedda tilted her head and twirled a strand of hair. He remembered her doing that when they first met. It was comforting to know that some things stayed the same. "It will be a shock no matter what you say. Tell her you are alive and you're sorry you did not contact her sooner. Say you will write a letter telling her everything. Say that you love her. It will have to be enough for now."

Fritz nodded. "*Ja*, I will say I am sorry and that I love her." He gazed deeply into Hedda's warm, brown eyes, hoping she understood. "I hope this is enough."

Hedda glanced away and then looked back at him. "I think it will be. Eventually," she said and slipped her hand into his.

30

HOT SPRINGS, NORTH CAROLINA
DECEMBER 1933

Garland struggled to pay attention to the service as the pastor gave his weekly sermon and the choir launched into "Hark! The Herald Angels Sing." Garland normally enjoyed the fellowship of his little country church and got a lot out of it, but today he was too distracted. He'd sent word to Hedda that he would visit her that afternoon to discuss how they might address her "problem." But he still wasn't sure what he was going to tell her.

Or rather what he was going to ask her.

"Please join me in the closing prayer," Pastor Heavner said.

Garland ducked his head and squeezed his eyes shut, barely registering what the pastor prayed. A few moments later, he shuffled outside and stood blinking in the frigid air that felt like snow. Normally, he'd head for his aunt's house for a big Sunday dinner with his cousins and their children, but today he had no appetite. They would barely miss him, the bachelor cousin who tagged along because his parents were gone and his only brother had run off to California.

What advice would his big brother Wendell have for him today? They barely kept in touch, writing a letter once or twice a year. And it had been at least five years since they'd seen each other. Shoot, Wendell would almost certainly tell him he was being a fool. And most likely he was. But he'd been a fool before, and it hadn't killed him. Yet.

It was almost two o'clock by the time Garland arrived at the boardinghouse to see Hedda. He had spotted mistletoe along the road during the drive and stopped to help himself to it. He'd cut holly and some pine boughs as well to make a winter bouquet. The branches filled his automobile with their rich, spicy scent. He felt a little foolish but in a happy sort of way.

As he pulled up, several figures stood on the wide front porch as though they'd just returned from somewhere. He grinned when he saw one of them was Hedda. Was she eager to see him? Her friend Eleanor was also there, and the third figure was a broad-shouldered man. He frowned when he realized it was Fritz. Hadn't that man caused enough trouble?

He hesitated to carry the greenery with him, but then decided it was as good a way as any to stake the territory he hoped he might claim. He scooped everything up, pricking his finger on a holly leaf. Blood welled, ruby red, and he flicked it away.

Hedda spotted him and hurried over to greet him. "Oh, Garland, what is this you've brought?"

He grinned, knowing the greenery had been a good idea. "Saw 'em on the way and thought you might like some."

She drew near and breathed in the aroma of cedar and pine. "*Wunderbar! Danke.*"

He frowned to hear her speak German. He guessed that was Fritz's influence, and he didn't like it.

"Come, sit with us. We can talk about our business after we have visited together."

His frown deepened. He'd rather have Hedda to himself. Eleanor was all right and could be trusted to leave them to discuss Hedda's situation. But he didn't like Fritz being there. The fewer people involved in sorting out Hedda's troubles, the better. Especially since one particular solution was weighing heavily on his mind. "I was thinking we could go for a walk and talk over what I learned."

She gave him a sunny smile. "Yes, soon, but first we are planning to enjoy spiced cider that Eleanor has prepared for us."

He sighed and followed her inside, where Eleanor was setting out cups and cinnamon sticks. Hedda poured steaming liquid and pressed a hot mug into Garland's cold hands while Eleanor scooped up the greenery and disappeared through the kitchen door. Garland nodded at Fritz and settled into a rocking chair.

All was quiet.

About the time the silence was getting uncomfortable, Eleanor burst back into the room with the mistletoe dangling from a length of ribbon. With a giggle, she fastened it in an open doorway. "There, that oughta make things more interesting around here. Garland, you're the cat's pajamas."

Fritz snorted. "This is a silly thing to say."

Eleanor's laugh rose to the rafters. "Can't argue with that."

Fritz sipped his cider, then shook his head. "Speaking English is hard enough without this nonsense."

"But you've been in America for, what, sixteen years now? Surely it's gotten easier." Eleanor picked up her mug and moved to the settee.

"In Bethania there are so many Germans, we do not need to speak English except to outsiders."

"Tell me about the Moravians," Hedda said.

The big man's face lit up. "They are very good people. They come from Moravia and Bohemia long ago and find refuge in Germany before they come to America. They teach me about our Lord and Savior Jesus Christ. I am a new man because of Jesus. He has forgiven me everything." He spread his arms wide.

Hedda stared. "I didn't realize you were so passionate about your faith."

"*Ja*, it is what has saved me from my sin." He looked directly at Garland, then at Hedda. "And I have much sin."

Garland snorted. "That's good. I'm glad for you. I'm a churchgoing man myself. But no amount of forgiveness will keep you from facing the consequences for the bad things you've done."

Fritz's smile dimmed. "You are right. This is why I asked forgiveness from Hedda." He squinted at Garland. "I think that night at the camp was a bad night for us all."

Garland cleared his throat. "Yeah, well, I'm not sure any of us were thinking clearly back then."

Fritz leaned forward and stuck out a big, meaty hand. "Will you forgive me?"

"I, uh . . ." Garland was flummoxed. He didn't know what to make of this. He was a churchgoing, Bible-believing man, but he'd never encountered such a simple and straightforward faith like what Fritz had expressed.

As he was trying to formulate a response, he glanced out

the window and saw a man approaching from the street—a young person, thirteen or fourteen years old. He trotted up onto the porch and knocked on the door.

Fritz answered the door, and his face split with a huge grin. "Denis! You are here!" His smile dimmed. "But I thought you would come to the college. I have not had a time to tell my friends you are coming for Christmas. How have you found me?"

The boy grinned back. "That nice Mrs. Albers sent me over on the bus."

"Ah, this is good. I am so happy that you are here. Now we will have a *frohe Weihnachten*."

Garland gaped, finding this sudden turn of events both mysterious and intriguing. As did Eleanor and Hedda, gauging by their expressions.

Fritz wrapped an arm around the young man. "This is a good time to find me. Now I will show you to my friends." He beamed like a man handing out twenty-dollar bills.

"Introduce me, Dad, not show me."

Garland froze and looked at Hedda, who was ghostly pale and gripping the arms of her chair.

Fritz turned to face the group, nearly lifting the boy from the floor in his excitement. "Remember how I tell you I have a new family? This is my son, Denis. He is a good boy." He chuckled. "Mostly."

Hedda sat in the room she shared with Eleanor, her chin propped in her hand, elbow resting on the windowsill. The cold evening air still carried the scents of the city—food, automobiles, horses. It was like Berlin and yet it wasn't. She couldn't put her finger on why, but pondering that mystery suited her better than thinking about the fact that Fritz had a son.

"You okay?" Eleanor came in from finishing her evening toilette and laid a hand on her shoulder.

"Yes. I think so."

"Quite the shock, huh?"

Hedda turned to consider her friend. She wished she could talk to Anni, but the urge to get out her thoughts was too pressing to wait. "Yes."

"You didn't have any idea, then? Seems odd that he didn't mention he had a kid."

"When I think back on it, he mentioned his new family, but I thought he meant the people of Bethania—the Moravian community. I asked him, and Fritz said he didn't mention Denis in the beginning because he thought he might be in trouble and didn't want to bring his son into it. Then when the sheriff said he wasn't a suspect anymore, he decided it would be a good time for us to meet." She shook her head, feeling dazed. "He has a son, but his . . . wife is dead several years now."

"What's the worst of it?" Eleanor sat and folded her hands in her lap, waiting.

Hedda started to protest that she didn't understand the question, but on second thought supposed she did. "He did not wait for me. Not even one year. Not even six months. When I was still hoping for his return, he was wooing another. Marrying. Having a child."

Eleanor nodded. "Yeah. That's tough to swallow." She tilted her head. "What else did he say after Garland and I took Denis to see the city?"

Hedda stood and paced the room. "He said he realized his having a son might give me a shock." She gave a hollow laugh. "At least he had that much sense." She rolled her eyes heavenward. "He said he hoped I would like Denis, and Denis would like me. He also said that his w-wife"—she choked on the word—"was a good woman. She died when Denis was ten. Not so long ago." She lifted her gaze to Eleanor, eyes wide. "He said I would have liked his wife and that it would be good for his son to have a German mother."

"Well, that's putting it out there," Eleanor said. "I thought he might be courting you. How d'you feel about that?"

Hedda flopped into an armchair. "I confess I thought I might welcome it. But that was before . . ."

"Before you knew he'd married someone else," Eleanor finished for her.

"*Ja*. This is true."

Eleanor chuckled. "And right after he was telling us about being forgiven. Guess he knows what that's all about."

Hedda laughed softly, too. "I'm very confused."

"Yeah, I guess so." Eleanor stretched and stood. "Let's go for a walk. Clear our heads. It's not like you have to figure this all out tonight."

"Yes, I'd like a walk."

"And hey, maybe some handsome stranger will kiss one of us under the mistletoe along the way." Eleanor giggled and held her hand out to Hedda. "Seems like you've got more than one man confusing you these days."

Hedda shook her head and closed her eyes. "You don't need to remind me of this."

31

Asheville, North Carolina

That hadn't gone as planned. Garland loitered in the street near the boardinghouse. He should just pack it up and go home, but he still hoped he might get in a word with Hedda.

Assuming she wanted to speak to him or anyone after the surprise of the afternoon. He paced to the corner and back, trying to talk himself into knocking on the door and asking to see her. If she sent him away, so be it.

He started up the front steps as the door opened and Eleanor appeared with Hedda right behind her, tucking a scarf into her coat. They stopped and stared, as did he.

Eleanor was the first to find her voice. "Thought you'd left ages ago."

Garland felt his neck grow hot. "I was, uh, hoping to, uh, speak with Hedda."

Eleanor braced a hand on her jutted-out hip and opened her mouth, but Hedda put a hand on her shoulder. "It's okay," she said. "We can talk."

"Want me to stick around?" Eleanor asked.

"No, that's alright." She looked at Garland. "I was going for a walk. You will join me?"

"Yeah. Yes, that'd be good."

She came down the steps and began walking toward College Street. Garland trotted to catch up with her, falling into step. She walked with her head down and hands deep in her coat pockets. He shoved his own cold hands in his pockets and tried to think what to say.

"Guess that was a big surprise for you."

"That my fiancé wed and had a child? Yes. It was. But let's not speak about that." They walked on in silence for a few beats. "Thank you again for the branches. They're beautiful."

"You're welcome," he mumbled. "Guess maybe you're wondering why I wanted to see you today."

She glanced at him and laughed lightly. "I might wonder if I were not so . . . I think the word is *flustered*?"

"That's a good word for it," Garland said with a chuckle. "I sure would be if I were you." He pushed his hands deeper in his pockets. "The thing is, I did a little digging into how you might stay in the United States." He peered at her from the corner of his eye. "Assuming you still want to stay."

"I do. That hasn't changed."

He took a deep breath. His original plan didn't seem like such a good idea anymore, yet he still wanted to help her, to give her hope. "I don't guess you have any family here relying on you?"

She laughed. "No. I have no family in America, and almost none anywhere else." Her voice sounded hollow. He wanted to touch her, to comfort her in some way, but didn't know how.

215

"Is there any chance you could ask for asylum for some reason? Would you be in danger if you went back to Germany?"

She looked thoughtful. "No. Perhaps if I were a Jew. Times are very difficult for them right now, but I think I would be safe enough."

She stumbled on an uneven brick paver, and he reached out to steady her. She smiled her thanks. They resumed walking, taking a circuitous route that would lead back to the boardinghouse.

"Is there another way for me to remain here?" she asked.

He rubbed the back of his neck. He'd worked out how to talk about this but needed to rethink it now. "Well, seems like if you were married to an American, that would give you standing."

Her burst of laughter took him by surprise. "Oh, that is most funny. To think that I came looking for the body of the man I was meant to marry. A man who wed an American, I think, since his wife was born here. Does that make him more able to stay than me?"

Garland hadn't thought of that angle. Would Fritz's marriage to an American give him standing? And would the fact that he had a son who had yet to reach the age of majority help as well? "I guess maybe it would. Although he'd still have to sort out the bit about escaping from an enemy alien camp."

She shook her head. "Maybe I should return to Germany. I think I'm causing too much trouble here. I can help take care of Lotte, and now that I know the truth about Fritz . . . well, I think I will live differently."

Garland wet his lips. "I'd be sorry to see you go." He held his breath. Would she understand what he meant by that?

216

"You are kind to say so. I think Anni and Josef would be sorry, too, but . . ." She sighed. "I must not bring trouble to them. They have seen enough of it already."

They had walked a circle that returned them to the Wolfe boardinghouse. Garland scrambled for something to say, something that would keep her here. It's not like he could just grab her hand and ask her to marry him.

Could he?

"Thank you, Garland, for trying to find a way to help me." She shook her head. "I've made a tangle of things." She grasped his arm and squeezed it once before climbing the porch steps. "I'm grateful you're my friend, but I think you have done enough for me. I'll make a plan of my own now."

Garland watched her disappear into the house, lifting a hand to wave as she went. He waved back, then stood there wishing he were a braver man.

Hedda hurried to her room and peeked out the window. Garland was just now walking back to his automobile, head low. She had the sense he wanted something from her, but she had no idea what it might be. She was sorry to disappoint him but was too tired, too overwhelmed to try to understand him.

As she watched Garland drive away, Hedda saw a young man in some sort of uniform hurry down the street and up to the front door. Moments later, Eleanor appeared with an envelope in her hand.

"You have a telegram," she said. "How exciting! Do you think Lotte's answered already?"

"It could be. Fritz gave the address here when he sent his message."

Eleanor handed it over and showed no inclination to leave Hedda to read the missive on her own. But what did it matter? It wasn't as though there would be any private information. Hedda slit the envelope with a nail file and scanned the contents:

Praise God, my son is alive. It is enough. Stay in U.S.

Lotte Meyer

The message tore at Hedda's heart. "She's glad to know Fritz is alive but wants us to stay here."

Eleanor peeked over Hedda's shoulder at the thin telegram paper. "'It is enough.' Sounds kind of ominous."

Hedda sighed. "She's ill—has been for a while now. It's likely she's gotten worse."

"Will you do as she says? Will Fritz?" ·

Hedda moved to the window to stare out at nothing. "I don't know that I'll have a choice. Fritz may have more right to become an American than I do since he was married to a citizen and has a son who depends on him. I doubt he'd want to risk all that by returning to Germany."

Eleanor snorted. "I'm not sure that kid depends on him. Fritz sure didn't mind leaving him to fend for himself while he ran off to Black Mountain."

"He left him in the care of his aunt and uncle."

"I talked to Denis while you and Fritz were sorting things out. He's a hoot! Sounds like he was pretty bored helping his family on the farm back there in Bethania. He's super excited to be in Asheville. Talks like it's a big city to him."

"It must be hard for Fritz to raise a son on his own," Hedda said. Was she defending him?

Eleanor nodded absently. "Do you think you could fall in love with him again?"

Hedda jerked back from the window as if she'd been stung. "I . . . I have not thought of such a thing."

"Haven't you? I thought maybe that had something to do with how shocked you were to find out he'd gotten married so fast. Because you still cared about him."

Hedda glanced at her young friend. Love seemed so simple when you were young. She'd thought so, and it seemed Eleanor did as well. "There's so much more to consider now than when we were engaged in 1914. This situation has become very complex."

Eleanor reached over and took the telegram Hedda still held in her hand. "But not for Lotte. Seems like her situation has gotten very simple. I bet she wishes she could see her son one more time before she dies."

Grief stabbed Hedda. Yes. Things would be simple for Lotte. Her life had narrowed down to the confines of her house, and from the sound of her last letter, perhaps even to her bedroom. Time was short. That was true for them all. And thinking this way made her realize it was high time she decided what she wanted her own future to hold.

32

MARSHALL, NORTH CAROLINA

Y ou have a message from that man over at the library." Margo, the department's secretary, scowled at him over the glasses perpetually perched on the end of her nose. "Mr. Noth," she added as if his name tasted bad.

"Thanks." Garland held out his hand.

Margo held the paper close. "What does he want with you?"

"I don't know. Does the message say?" Garland crossed his arms. Margo always acted like she was doing them a favor by coming to work, but they all knew she loved rooting around in everyone's dirty laundry.

"It does not," she answered with a pucker and a sniff. She slid the piece of paper across the desk. "He wants you to stop by. As if you have time to be at his beck and call. He always was too full of himself."

Garland scooped up the paper. "As it happens, I do have time to run over there. Shall I give you a full report when I return?"

Her eyes lit for a moment, but then she caught on and glared at him. "Hope it's not a wild-goose chase," she said.

"Yeah," Garland said. "There's something we can agree on."

Settling his favorite hat on his head at a jaunty angle, he turned around and headed for the library. He didn't have anything else pressing now, and it satisfied him to let Margo see him behaving as though Martin Noth really was important to his case. And who knew? Maybe he was. He'd sure been helpful in tracking down those photos. Maybe he'd dug up something else.

Once at the library, he headed for Martin's office. As soon as he stuck his head through the door, the librarian lit up. "Good, you received my message."

"I did. Whatcha got for me? More pictures?"

"Better than that." The man was almost quivering with excitement. It was contagious. Garland felt his pulse tick up a notch. Maybe Martin really did have something important to share.

"What could be better than more photographs?" Garland asked.

"How about the photographer?" Martin's face bloomed in a huge smile. "Adolph Thierbach. I've found him."

"You . . . what?"

"The man who took the photographs in the enemy alien encampment." Martin clasped his hands, first one way and then another, as though he couldn't keep still. He spoke in a rush. "I thought to myself that perhaps he would be helpful to your investigation and what harm could it do to see if he's still about. He did leave his album with us, so I had his old contact information. And when I investigated, it was quite simple. His former landlady had his forwarding address, and

221

he is in Blowing Rock—not so very far. He is taking photographs at Grandfather Mountain. Wonderful images, I'm sure. I wouldn't mind seeing them."

"Hold on there." Garland finally got a word in edgewise. "You're telling me the fellow who took those pictures of Fritz is still around?"

Martin nodded. "That is precisely the situation. I thought you would want to speak to him. Am I correct?"

Garland took a moment to process this new information. "You know, I think I would," he said at last. Maybe this photographer would remember something, or better yet, have more images that could help sort everything out. "Can't hurt," he added.

Martin Noth clapped his hands ever so softly.

Fritz swung the axe to split another stick of firewood. Sweat streamed down his face even on this chill December morning, but he didn't mind. It felt good to do physical work, to pour his frustration and uncertainty into a task he could easily see accomplished.

Soon students would return to Black Mountain College, and Hedda would be among them. She'd contacted him the day after Denis arrived to tell him his mother had sent a return telegram. There wasn't much to it, but it was clear she didn't want Fritz to come home. And for good reason, he knew.

He'd gone to speak to Hedda and to see the telegram. He'd thought they might sit in the parlor or go for a walk so they could continue renewing their friendship and hopefully rekindling their love. Instead, they discussed *Mutter* and her failing health. Afterward, he'd written another letter, finding himself eager to share the missing years with his mother. And realizing how much he longed to see her, especially now that she understood why he could not.

Hedda was convinced that Lotte didn't have much longer to live and thought Fritz should go against her wishes and return to Germany. She pointed out that with his marriage to an American, and his son living in North Carolina, he had a good chance of being allowed to become a citizen, free to come and go. Once the sheriff cleared him of any wrongdoing, surely it would be simple, or so she thought.

He wanted to see *Mutter*, he really did. But it would be dangerous for him to return now. Not only for himself, but for *Mutter* as well. If he'd returned home when the war ended, when he might have been absolved from escaping from the camp in Hot Springs, then he could have persuaded *Mutter* to leave Germany when the tide began to turn. Now, though, it was too late. Too dangerous. The window of opportunity had closed.

He brought the axe down so fiercely it split the log and stuck deep into the stump beneath. He took satisfaction in the feel of his muscles flexing and the weak winter sun warming his skin. He wanted to tell Hedda everything: all the reasons why it would be difficult for him to return to Germany, especially now. She would understand and would be sympathetic. This is what he would do, he decided. But it would come as a surprise, and she'd already had several of those. So he would give her a little time to get used to the surprise of his marriage and his son. Then he would tell her the rest.

He looked around, wondering what had become of Denis. He'd sent the boy for water, and he should be back by now. Shading his eyes with his hand, he saw two men walking toward him. As they drew near, he recognized

Sheriff Fitzsimmons and Garland. He stretched his back and watched them approach. What could the sheriff want with him? Would it be something good or something bad?

"My grandaddy always said chopping wood warms a man twice." The sheriff smiled, and Fritz dared hope this was not something bad.

"This is a thing my grandfather said as well. I guess we are not so different then."

"No, in my experience people are people the world over, for better or, all too often, for worse." Sheriff Fitzsimmons shook Fritz's hand and grinned. "But today is one of those better days. I came out here to let you know we found a witness who's let you off the hook. For good."

Fritz stared, wondering if he was failing to understand these words. "I think . . . I want to know more."

The sheriff chuckled while Garland's smile was a little less broad. Still, they both looked pleased. "Do you remember Adolph Thierbach?"

"*Ja*. He takes *das Fotos*."

"Right. Garland here tracked him down, and it turns out he was paying close attention even when he wasn't taking pictures. He saw Harold White strike Marie Spencer."

Fritz stumbled backward as if he'd been shoved. He sat down on a log without planning to and tried to catch his breath. "*Was ist das?*"

Sheriff Fitzsimmons crouched down beside him. "Steady there. Guess that was a big piece of news." He looked up at Garland. "Tell Fritz here what Herr Thierbach shared in a sworn statement."

Garland began speaking. "He was out for a walk that night. The night Marie died and you ran away. He saw a light on in Harold's hut and, as he put it, 'found the contrast between the dark of the night and the light in the window striking.'" Garland frowned. "Not the best choice of words there," he mumbled. "Anyway, he was admiring the 'artistic composition of two figures in the room' when he realized they were arguing. Harold grabbed Marie by the wrist and twisted her arm up behind her. As best he could tell, she stumbled and fell. Adolph went closer to see if he could help and saw that she was lying on the floor, bloodied and unmoving. At that point, as a prisoner, he was too frightened to linger any longer."

Fritz looked from one man to the other, unsure exactly what this meant for him.

The sheriff put a hand on his arm. "It's enough, Fritz. Enough to put you in the clear and close this case. And since the federal boys don't seem to want to go airing dirty laundry from fifteen years ago, I don't see that there's anything left for us to talk about." He straightened and offered a hand to help Fritz to his feet. "Now, if you decide you want to clear up your immigration status, that's a whole other ball of wax I ain't messing with."

Fritz felt joy bubbling up inside him like a rush of warm, yellow light. He wanted to spill it across a canvas, to show the world how good it felt to finally be free of a fear he'd carried so long he hadn't even realized it was still with him. He grabbed the sheriff in a bear hug, released him and then grabbed Garland, too.

"I am free!" he crowed. "The truth has set me free as the Good Book says. This day is *wunderbar!*"

The two men chuckled and slapped him on the back. "Congratulations, Fritz," Sheriff Fitzsimmons said. "Now keep your nose clean."

"*Ja,*" he agreed. "I will do this."

33

Hedda knocked on Dr. Rice's open door. She rubbed damp palms on her skirt and gave him her best smile. "Hello, do you have a moment to speak with me?"

He tossed a pen down and waved her toward a chair he'd dragged in from the dining hall. "You just caught me. I was about to leave to join Nell and the kids in South Carolina for Christmas. They've already left, but I had a few things to finish up. What can I do for you?"

"I would like to be a proper teacher when the next period of study begins." There. No dithering or uncertainty. She'd simply stated her desire. "You said you would consider this, and so I am asking for your decision."

His eyebrows flicked up, then settled into his usual expression. "Indeed. And why should we make this change?"

"I have been effectively filling the role these past months. Several students have studied with me, and I play almost every day for entertainment and edification. The other teachers have said I am a natural when it comes to working with the students." She wanted to go on but stopped there. Better not to say too much and regret it.

"Professors."

"I beg your pardon?" She furrowed her brow.

"We're not teachers, we're professors. And we are professors because we have studied long and worked hard to become so." Hedda cringed inwardly, thinking she'd upset him. "However, I can see that you, too, have worked hard and studied long. And we are nothing if not innovative here at Black Mountain College." He gave her a tight smile. "Very well. I suppose you have earned the right to be more than a volunteer or hanger-on." Hedda tried not to flinch at that. "Bring me your papers in January and we'll make it official." His smile widened, and he raised a pen high in the air. "I dub you *professor* of music at Black Mountain College. I'll expect you to delve into musical theory as well as teach the mechanics. I understand you can do that."

"Yes, sir," Hedda managed. "Thank you." She hurried from the room before he could change his mind or say anything more. At the end of the hall, she paused to catch her breath. She'd done it. Then she closed her eyes and groaned. But what exactly had she done in gaining a position that required papers she did not possess?

As soon as Garland and the sheriff left, Fritz went in search of his son. He finally found him in their shared room and told him the wonderful news. Denis was elated but not to the degree Fritz expected. Was something wrong? He noticed a newspaper spread across his son's bed.

"What do you have there?" he asked in German. Denis preferred speaking English, while Fritz wanted to make sure his son retained his father's language.

"It's today's newspaper. Saw this headline and it made me

think of that girl Hedda said she used to teach to play the piano. The one with only one foot." He answered in English, but when he held out the paper, Fritz forgot to chastise him.

There it was in the middle of page two: *Nazi Germany Will Sterilize 400,000 Defectives*. Fritz scanned the article, glad that his ability to read English was better than his ability to speak it. Chancellor Hitler and his Nazi Party would "improve the Germanic stock" by sterilizing anyone they deemed defective. He shuddered. What might come next?

"What does it mean?" Denis asked. "It sounds really bad."

Fritz considered the question. He'd tried to ignore the news from his home country for a long time, but being reunited with Hedda, spending time with the Alberses, and now wishing he could go home to see his mother had opened his eyes to how much had changed in recent years.

"I am not certain." He answered in English this time, for the German language suddenly felt heavy on his tongue. "But it is something Germany has not seen before, and I think it very bad." He sat, folded the paper, and laid it aside. "It is good that we are not there. I wish your *Großmutter* were not there either." He looked at his son. Would the echoes of the past touch him as well?

"I'd like to go to Germany to take care of her. I never get to go anywhere."

Fritz smiled despite himself. "You are here. This is somewhere, and it is much safer for you."

Denis flopped down next to him and made a face. "You know what I mean. I want to see the world, have some adventure. You were a sailor. You know what it's like to travel to far-off places. Don't you want that for me?"

"*Nein*," Fritz said. "I did not want it for me. I want to

learn art and travel here." He tapped his head. "And here." He tapped his chest. "There is much in here."

Denis rolled his eyes and leaned back against the headboard. "Hedda said my grandmother's sick. She's your mom—don't you think you should go see her?" He looked away. "I'd give just about anything to see Mom again."

Ach. Why hadn't Fritz thought of this? "Yes," he said, taking time to find the right words, "I want to see *Mutter.* But we have been apart a long time. And going back, it is not simple." He nudged the folded newspaper. "Deutschland is much changed. Maybe I could not come back here again. Maybe I would bring trouble to *Mutter.*"

"Guess I'd better go with you, then," Denis said.

"*Nein!*" The word came out louder than Fritz intended. He softened his voice. "No, you and I will stay where it is safe."

"Safe? You know people give me a rough time because I'm half German, right? Seems like some people can't get over the war that was, what, twenty years ago?"

"Not so long as that," Fritz said, rubbing his forehead. "Soon fifteen years will seem like nothing to you."

"Yeah, well, I wasn't even alive then. Seems like I shouldn't have to take guff for something I wasn't around for."

"*Mutter* would like you." Fritz traced the pattern on the coverlet. "After *Vater* died, she wants me to do what makes my heart glad, but she also wants me to be safe."

"Did you do what made you glad?" Denis leaned forward, bracing his elbows on his knees.

Fritz chuckled. "My heart is glad to make sure *Mutter* has food to eat and medicine for making her well. My heart is glad to marry Hedda, who will take care of *Mutter* when I am away." He rolled his shoulders and looked out the window. "If my heart is sad not to make art, what is that when the people I love are well? I think there will be time for art later."

"I get why you didn't go back in the beginning, but why don't you go back now? Especially now that you're in the clear over that woman being killed."

"This is the hard question," Fritz said. He gripped his son's shoulder, squeezing it. "I would be sad to not see you, but I would do it if it were good for you. I think *Mutter* is the same. Decisions like this are never simple. There is good in one hand and bad in the other."

Denis shrugged his hand away. "Sounds to me like you're making excuses. Even if your mom wanted you to have a better life in America, what about Hedda? She seems great, and you just left her to wonder what happened to you. I get that you were scared and thought you might end up in jail, but isn't true love worth the risk?"

Fritz wanted to laugh at his romantic son but knew better. "*Ja.* I am sorry I am not more brave then. But I think maybe I can be different now."

Denis laughed. "And I thought I was clueless about women. Dad, if you think she wants you back, I'm betting you're in for a rude awakening."

Fritz frowned and stood. "You are young. What can you know about it? Now come and help me work. There is much to do."

Denis stood as well. "Alright, I know when you've said all you're going to say."

"This is true. I have said all there is to say."

34

Hedda sat in the tiny room, staring at her hands tightly clasped on the table in front of her. *Deportation.* That's the word the man in the dark suit had dropped like a firecracker in the small room. She'd been so certain that now that she had a real job at a college, getting work papers would be relatively simple. Oh, she'd assumed there would be some paperwork, perhaps a delay, but not this. Not deportation.

She turned toward a scuffling sound at the door and heard a muffled voice say, "I have her things. Just let me see her." Then the door popped open, and Eleanor flew into the room. She dropped Hedda's bag and flung her arms around her. "Garland is coming. He'll fix this," she murmured against Hedda's ear. "Hang tight."

Hedda did just that, clinging to Eleanor as if she were drowning. "Can it be fixed? Have I ruined everything?"

Eleanor extricated herself and dragged the only other chair beside Hedda's closer. She sat and twined her fingers with her friend's. "Of course it can be fixed. Just you wait and see," she said with a too-bright smile. It's good you telephoned me. I called Garland—he'll be here any moment."

Hedda fell silent. Should she explain how she'd come to the federal courthouse to sort out her papers? How quickly she'd been shunted into this small, windowless room, where the man in the suit peppered her with questions and then, with no fanfare or hesitation, sentenced her to go back to Germany with no hope of returning to America for, how long had he said, ten years?

As Hedda stifled a whimper, Eleanor squeezed her hand and smiled that same forced smile that did nothing to loosen the twist in Hedda's belly. She remembered the day she'd arrived in Asheville, hoping to recover the body of her beloved, almost a year ago now. How strange that in that time she'd come to feel more at home among these blue mountains than she ever had in bustling Berlin.

The door opened again, and this time it was a woman in a gray dress with graying hair. She didn't even try to smile but just said, "Come with me," and led them down a long hallway to a cramped office, where the man in the suit—she couldn't remember his name—sat behind a desk with his hands steepled in front of him. Garland stood nearby, his expression much too serious.

"Please have a seat," the man said. "Deputy Jones has made a compelling argument for you, Miss Schlagel, but I'm afraid there's nothing to be done." He didn't make eye contact with any of them but spoke as if addressing the dreary landscape painting on the back wall. "Even if teaching music were a critical job, the fact that you've already overstayed your travel visa means we have no choice but to deport you to your country of origin." He wet his lips. "As a result, you cannot return to America for a minimum of ten years."

Hedda felt the room spin. Only Eleanor's steadying grip kept her from sliding to the floor.

The man cleared his throat. "I understand your friend has brought your luggage." He glanced at the bag someone had deposited inside his door. "Travel arrangements are being made as we speak. You will be escorted by train to the nearest port, where you will be placed on a ship for the return trip to Germany."

"Now hold on just a minute," Garland protested.

The man shot him a dark look. "Your protestation has been noted." He frowned more deeply. "And will be shared with your superiors." He turned back to Hedda. "Say your goodbyes."

Hedda choked on a sob. Eleanor's arms slipped around her shoulders, and she gave up any pretense of stoicism, weeping until her friend's sweater was soaked through. She felt a large but gentle hand against her shoulder. "Come with me, Hedda."

She lifted red-rimmed eyes to see Garland. "Is there nothing to be done?" she asked. "Oh, I have made such a tangle." Her voice sounded ragged.

"I'm going to keep trying, believe me. But for now, I can't stop this." Now Garland looked as though he might cry. "No matter how much I want to."

The woman in gray returned to the room and handed the man behind the desk a folder. He flipped it open and scanned the contents. He stood and cleared his throat again. "Miss Schlagel, Mrs. Everett will accompany you by train to the port of Charleston, South Carolina. From there you will be taken into the custody of the ship's captain and returned to Germany."

"What then?" she whispered.

"That is up to the German authorities." There was a slight softening of his features. "I'm sorry. I know this is difficult, but you should have come here as soon as you knew you wanted to stay longer."

"Would that have made a difference?" Eleanor snapped.

The man's face hardened. "Most likely not. You"—he pointed at Eleanor—"will need to take your leave now."

Eleanor's chin quivered, but she raised it high and turned to Hedda. "Fine. Write to me as soon as you arrive. Let me know you're well. And keep writing until you can come back to America." She gave Hedda a fierce hug that almost hurt in its intensity. Or maybe that was just her heart aching.

"Thank you. For everything," Hedda whispered. "Keep taking pictures. Don't let your dreams die."

"I won't," Eleanor murmured. She attempted a laugh. "I notice you said to keep taking pictures and not to keep playing the piano." Sobering again she added, "I'll miss you. I love you."

Hedda's throat was almost too tight to speak. "I love you, too," she managed.

Garland stood glowering at the suited man. "I'll escort the ladies to the train station," he said in a voice that suggested there was no question he had the right to do so.

"Fine," the man snapped. "I'll include that in my report."

Garland nodded and scooped up Hedda's bag. He held the door open for the two women. Hedda felt as though her feet and her head were no longer connected. She walked out the door and along the corridor without feeling the floor. The train station was just a few blocks away. Mrs. Everett trudged along with them, clearly not much happier about how her day was turning out.

None of them spoke until they arrived at the station. Mrs.

Everett sighed and nodded at the ticket agent. "There should be two tickets waiting for us. I'll get those while you say your goodbyes." She gave Garland a sharp look. "Don't leave my sight."

Drawing himself to his full height, Garland nodded once. He led Hedda to a bench where they sat, her bag at his feet. "I can't believe this is happening," she said.

Garland placed his hand over hers, clasping it as though he could hold her there. "Marry me."

The words hung in the air, and she turned her head slowly to look at him. "What is this?"

"It's your best bet for being able to stay. Or to come back if we can't sort this out today. Your surest way to become an American. If you marry me, you'll have standing."

She gently pulled away and stared at the empty tracks. She could feel tension rolling off him in waves. Was he afraid that she'd turn him down? Or that she'd say yes?

"I can't do this," she said at last, turning back with tears in her eyes. "It's wonderful of you to offer such a sacrifice. If I ever marry, it will be because of love. Not because I want to get around the rules."

"It's not like that," Garland protested. His eyes were wild. It felt like she was seated beside a coiled spring about to go flying into the air.

"Thank you, Garland. I think you're brave to ask such a question. I'm grateful for all you've done and for your friendship." She smiled that sad smile again. "I'll write to you from Germany. It will be good to have friends in America who will write back."

He looked like he wanted to protest, but instead he squeezed his eyes shut and opened them again. "I'll answer every letter," he said, and she knew, without a doubt, he would.

Fritz stood outside Lee Hall staring at Eleanor, unable to take in what she was telling him. He'd been on his way to supper with Denis in tow when she flagged him down. "She is gone? Sent back to Germany? But . . . but this is not right."

"She tried to get the papers to stay here and teach, but they ordered that she be sent back to Germany instead. And I guess there's some business about not being able to return for ten years now that she's broken the rules."

Denis jumped in. "Dad, you should go after her—to Germany. I'll go with you. We'll see your mom. You'd like that, wouldn't you?" He got a sly look. "And I know you like Hedda. This'll let her know you mean business."

Fritz shook his head, his thoughts muddled. "*Nein.* There are many reasons why I cannot go back. I am sorry about Hedda." He glanced at Eleanor. "There is no way to undo this?"

"Garland tried, and if an officer of the law can't get around it, I don't know who could."

"*Danke* for telling me. Will she go to *mein Mutter?*"

"I assume so. We didn't get to talk about her plans."

"I will write to *Mutter* again and hope that Hedda is with her soon. That at least will be a comfort."

Eleanor looked at him like she was disappointed, but what could he do? Nothing. So many times in his life he'd been forced into positions where his choices were limited or nonexistent. He had to put art aside and become a sailor so he could afford to marry. He had to live in an enemy alien encampment. He had to go along with Harold White or face being sent to jail for killing Marie Spencer. He had to make his way in America with little hope of ever seeing his family or Hedda again. He could guess how Hedda felt, buffeted by circumstances beyond her control.

He gazed out at the mountains, which looked bleak in the chill of winter. Tree branches stood in dark contrast to snowy slopes. A flock of blackbirds lifted from a nearby tree, their clamor sharpening the cold air.

"What will you do next?" Eleanor asked.

"I will make art." Fritz nodded. "There is so much I cannot do, so much that is not for me to control. So I will do the things I most love to do. I will make art, I will spend time with Denis, and I will write letters to *Mutter* and to Hedda if she is there with her. And I will see what God has in mind for me."

Eleanor and Denis both stared at him with their mouths open, as if seeking God's mind on the matter were the most preposterous thing they'd ever heard. But Fritz felt as though, at long last, he was making the one decision that was right.

35

MARSHALL, NORTH CAROLINA

What now? Garland stared at his shoes. He'd pol-
ished them to a high shine the night before. He
hadn't had anything else to do and needed to
keep his hands busy.

So much had happened in the last few days. He'd finally
cracked the Marie Spencer case, Fritz's name had been
cleared once and for all, Hedda had been summarily deported, and he'd proposed marriage. None of this was what
he'd had in mind a week ago. Highs and lows. Mountaintops
and valleys. Only this valley seemed deeper than any he'd
walked before.

"What're you doing here?" Wayne did a double take as
he walked by.

"I work here," Garland snapped, immediately regretting
his tone. Wayne always had his back. No need to take his
peevishness out on him.

The sheriff shifted to fill the doorway and gave him a hard
look before seeming to decide to let the moment pass. "What

I mean is, why aren't you in Black Mountain, telling Lucy the news about her sister? I know you've had a lot to sort through the last couple of days, and I'm real sorry about Hedda, but don't you think Lucy should know the truth?"

Garland felt a stab of shame. He'd been so wrapped up in his own frustrations, he'd forgotten about Lucy. "Right, boss. Don't know what I was thinking." He stood and slapped his hat on his head, but Wayne didn't move from the door.

"Garland, word is you offered to marry Hedda to keep her in the country." Garland flinched. How'd Wayne know that? "I guess the woman escorting Hedda wasn't as far out of earshot as you maybe thought. She wasn't much impressed by your attempt to circumvent the law."

"I should have asked sooner."

"What's that?" Wayne narrowed his eyes. "Are you saying you really would have married the gal?"

Garland chewed on that a minute. "I think so."

"Well, 'I think so' isn't good enough." Wayne heaved a sigh and crossed his arms over his chest. "I don't know that there's anything you can do for Hedda now that she's gone." He looked Garland in the eye. "Just wanted to say I realize how hard this is. If you need some time away or, now that the Eighteenth Amendment has been repealed, someone to get drunk with, let me know."

Garland felt a knot in his chest. He swallowed hard. "Thanks, boss. Appreciate the offer, but I'm alright." He attempted a lopsided grin. "Not the first time I've made a fool of myself with a woman. Probably won't be the last either."

Wayne nodded and gripped his shoulder. "Being a fool for the right woman was the best thing that ever happened to me. Hope it happens for you, too, one of these days." He squeezed hard and released Garland. "Now, go see what Lucy

Spencer has to say about her sister's case being solved. I for one am curious to hear how she takes it."

Lucy greeted Garland with her usual frown. She peered around him as though looking for something. "Did you bring Hedda?"

He groaned inwardly. He'd have to tell her that news, too. Best to get it over with. "I have a couple of . . . pieces of news to share with you."

She harrumphed and opened the door wider. "Wipe your shoes on the mat." He did so. "You can sit on that sofa since you fixed the leg." She settled on an armchair near the window. "What do you have to tell me?"

"Well, your sister's case has been resolved," he began. Her eyes went wide, and she inhaled sharply but didn't speak. "We found a witness who saw what happened that night. It seems Marie and Harold were having an argument, and he grabbed her in a way that caused her to fall and hit her head. From what the witness said, she didn't suffer."

Lucy fell back against the cushions. "So it *was* murder," she whispered.

"Manslaughter, technically. Sounds like Harold didn't plan to kill her. But yes, he did it."

She looked him in the eye. "Did you know? Did Fritz?"

He shook his head. "I didn't know. Looking back on it now, I must admit I was a bit naive and maybe too willing to accept what Harold told me, but I had no idea that Marie was even there that night until recently." He took a deep breath. "As for Fritz, he was just in the wrong place at the wrong time. He saw his chance to be free of the camp, and he took it. I don't guess either of us was particularly noble that night, but in the end it was a terrible accident that up-ended all of our lives."

"Including mine." Lucy's words were barely audible. She rubbed her forehead and closed her eyes. "I wanted to think the worst of Marie. I was jealous of the way Momma loved her and the way she got on with people when I didn't. I always imagined that whatever happened to her, it was no more than she deserved." She gave Garland a pleading look. "But she didn't deserve it, did she?"

"No, ma'am. I don't think she did."

Lucy nodded. "What now?"

"Now we close the case. Fritz is no longer a person of interest in this investigation. Your sister's remains will be released to you."

"I can bury her with Momma and Poppa?"

"Absolutely."

"Good." Her eyes flicked to him and away. "Will you help me?"

Garland swallowed past a new lump. "Yeah. I can do that."

"And Hedda, she'll help too, don't you think?"

Garland flinched. "About that. She's been deported."

Lucy gripped the arms of her chair. "What? Why?"

"She tried to sort out her visa to no avail, and the immigration folks sent her home. It was . . . sudden."

"But she has a place here. With us. I don't understand."

"Neither do I," Garland admitted. "I tried to help, but there was nothing I could do."

"You'll go after her, then." Lucy said this as though it were a foregone conclusion. "You'll bring her back to us."

"I-I don't think I can."

Lucy frowned. "You discovered what happened to my sister all those years ago. I'm sure you can handle this, too."

She stood, and Garland did as well. "I'll confess I have not thought well of Germans in the past, but knowing Hedda and, oddly enough, Fritz has made me reconsider. While I still think that awful Hitler is ruining Germany, if not the world, I see now I must not paint all Germans with the same brush." She gave him a steely look. "I trust you'll sort this out for us."

"Yes, ma'am," he said. "I'll do my best." And while he still had no idea how he might bring Hedda back to America, he realized that, more than anything, he wanted to try.

36

BERLIN, GERMANY

Hedda spooned broth into Lotte's mouth. The older woman opened her lips like a baby bird ready to receive her bit of nourishment. And it was little enough nourishment at that. Hedda had been shocked to see how small Lotte had become.

She'd been back in Germany for two weeks now. Her return had been fraught. Officials on both sides of the Atlantic had been wildly displeased with how she'd overstayed her visa. At one point she'd even wondered if she would be allowed to return home, or if she would be tossed into one of the concentration camps that had sprung up like poison mushrooms while she was away. Returning to America was no longer an option for her, at least not for a very long time.

Lotte held up a hand, motioning that she'd had enough.

"Come now, we've only just begun. You have much more soup to eat," Hedda cajoled.

"You finish it. You are too thin," Lotte countered.

Hedda laughed. Her friend was right. She seemed to have

left her appetite in America. She thought of Jack's peach cobbler and the fresh corn on the cob from the garden at Black Mountain College. It had dripped with creamy butter.

She looked down into the bowl of beef broth with a little cabbage. No wonder Lotte saw no reason to try to eat more.

"I wish you had married your deputy." Lotte's words came with a sigh. "Germany is no place for you anymore."

Hedda took her friend's hand and squeezed it. She shouldn't have told her about Garland's last-minute proposal, but she'd needed to talk it through so badly. Now the woman who had once expected to be her mother-in-law wished she'd married another man.

And as for Germany not being a place for her, Lotte was right. Of her six students, only two remained. Three had found others to instruct them, and sweet Liesl had been sent to Switzerland to live with an aunt. Her mother said it was so Liesl could be a help with her younger cousins, but Hedda knew the real reason had to do with the way children like Liesl—handicapped in any way—were being rounded up and sterilized. Or worse. Such stories were told in whispers with darting eyes. No. Germany was no place for her or for Lotte either.

"Perhaps not," she said lightly. "Still, I'm glad to be here with you."

Lotte smiled and closed her eyes, tilting her head back for a nap. But before she could drift off, a fit of coughing racked her body. She pressed a handkerchief to her lips, frowning when it came away tinged with pink. This no longer alarmed Hedda. It was simply the progression of the disease that would soon steal Lotte away from her.

And then what?

She was once again living with Lotte in the woman's small

cottage. It was familiar, and her being there meant Lotte's sister could return to her own home. But what would happen when the inevitable occurred?

She looked to her friend, who had composed herself and was now watching her with bright, birdlike eyes.

Restless, Hedda moved aimlessly about the house, finally ending up in front of the piano, which Lotte had kept in tune. She rested her fingertips on the cool, dark wood of the case. It would take so little effort to sit and play something soft and light to soothe them both. She lifted her fingers, clenching them into fists.

"*Nein*," she whispered. There wasn't any music in her today. It was her desire to pursue music, to teach it at Black Mountain College, that had condemned her to being deported.

Lotte stirred. "Tell me about Fritz." The words drew her back to the moment. "How did he look?" Even as Lotte grew smaller, her eyes grew larger. And the pleading Hedda saw in them was something she could not refuse. She'd already told Lotte everything she could remember and a few things she'd embellished. But the dying woman wanted to hear it all again and again.

"He was handsome when I knew him long ago, but he's even more so now." Hedda was surprised how the words didn't sting anymore. "I think he must have grown taller in America. Perhaps it's the good food and the sunshine. His shoulders are very broad, and he's a hard worker."

"And the people who took him in. Tell me who they are again?"

"I don't know very much about them, but Fritz called them Moravians. I think they were persecuted for their faith."

"They are good people, then?" Lotte's expression was so earnest.

Initially, Hedda had hesitated to say, not having met them. Now she had no such qualms. "They're very good people, yes. They shared their faith with Fritz, and he is a godly man now." These words had also caused her grief in the beginning, but now she was glad to see how they brought Lotte comfort. Fritz's letters to his mother had cheered Lotte, especially the news that he was pursuing his dream of being an artist. And she was content knowing he was safe in America with her grandson.

"This gives me greater joy than you can know," Lotte said.

Hedda moved to the window overlooking the street. She saw two men in Nazi brown shirts strolling along as if they owned the city streets. She supposed, in a way, they did.

"It must be very confusing for you to learn the man you once loved went on to have a life without you. That he has a son and had a wife for a time. This is understandable." Lotte's voice was almost too soft to hear.

Hedda turned to face her friend. "What about you? How does it make you feel to know he carried on without his mother?" She wanted to take the words back immediately. It seemed cruel to say such a thing to a dying woman, yet she needed to know.

Lotte nodded. "Ah, this is your hurt speaking. It is good to let it out, and so I will tell you how I feel." Her eyes grew brighter. "I feel happy knowing that he has been laughing and living and loving in all the years he was taken from me." She patted the chair Hedda had just left. "Sit with me a moment. I will tell you something you don't know."

Hedda didn't want to sit. She wanted to walk, to run, to keep herself too busy to think about all she'd left behind in America. All she'd lost before she'd quite realized it was hers to hold on to. Even so, she obeyed, sitting with muscles tensed as though to spring into action. "What do you want to tell me?"

Lotte lowered her voice even more. "I have not dared to say before, but now, when I have so little time left, I want you to understand why I am glad my son and my grandson are not here with me." She looked around as though someone else might be listening, then leaned closer to Hedda. "I was born a Jew."

37

Black Mountain, North Carolina

Fritz held his brush loosely, feathering color onto the canvas. Josef Albers's classes had opened his mind to using color in new ways, and he couldn't get enough of experimenting with palette knife and brush. He stepped back to take in the effect. So satisfying. So inspiring.

As he reached for more yellow paint, someone tapped on the doorframe. Without looking, he said, "*Ja*, who is it?"

"*Vater*, you've missed the evening meal again."

Fritz now turned and answered, "Ah, Denis, I have nearly finished for today."

"You're always busy. I thought maybe things would be different here, away from Bethania and your work, but it's worse than it ever was."

Fritz sighed and squinted at the dark sky. His light was gone, and he would get no more peace today. He stowed his palette and moved to a sink to clean his brushes. "I do not understand what you say. What is worse?"

"You."

Fritz glanced at his son's sullen face. He was tall and broad-shouldered like Fritz but with his mother's olive skin and dark eyes. Fritz suspected he was being impertinent, yet the joy of this afternoon of painting softened him enough that he didn't scold the boy. "I am the same."

"No, you're not. At least back home you'd take breaks sometimes and we'd do things together. Go fishing or something. Now you're always with those professors—that or painting."

"I am also working to make it possible for you and me to stay here." Fritz slung water from the brushes, then blotted them against a bit of toweling. "I thought you did not want to return to Bethania."

"That's not what I'm talking about at all." Denis kicked the doorjamb. "Sometimes I think you just act like you don't understand because it's easier."

Fritz frowned. Though there might be some truth to that, he wouldn't say so. "What is it that you want?"

"Nothing. Never mind." Denis turned to go.

Fritz darted across the room and caught his son's elbow. "Wait. Come and sit." He waved to a couple of mismatched chairs. "I want to tell you something."

Denis slumped into a chair, all knees and elbows. Fritz tried to remember what he'd been like at fourteen. He'd been a hard worker intent on stealing time to sketch on any surface he could find. He'd left school to work in his uncle's lumberyard, always dreaming of studying art. Of course, that was before he met Hedda. Before he jumped at the opportunity to become a sailor so he could earn enough money to wed. Before he'd learned that dreams were often just that, *dreams*.

"Do you see what I am doing here?" Fritz wanted to resort

to German to express himself, knowing he would do a better job in his native tongue, but for Denis he would speak English. Especially now.

"Painting?" Denis communicated a world of scorn in the single word.

"*Ja*, yes, painting. But it is more than that." He tilted his head to one side. "What is it you want to do with your life?"

Denis frowned and tugged at a thread on his cuff. "I want to see the world. I want to go places and have adventures."

"That is not very, how do you say, precise?"

Denis dropped his chin into his collar. He mumbled, "I could write about the stuff I do. Like Daniel Defoe."

"Ah, this is better. When I am the age you are, I want to paint. Like Kandinsky." He turned to the canvas on its easel and admired how the colors changed in the fading light. "And I cannot. I must work instead. I have waited a long time to do this." He nodded at the painting. "And I find I am almost as happy as I have ever been. Maybe more happy because I must wait so long."

"I don't get what you mean." Denis looked interested in spite of his words.

"I am not saying it right, I think." Fritz wanted to switch to German so badly. Perhaps—

"You said 'almost as happy.' Why almost?"

"Ah, this is the point. I am happiest the day you are born. I did not know it that day, but now, even as I am very happy, I remember that I am happier once."

Denis tilted his head, and Fritz realized it was a mirror of his own listening pose. "I think I will not paint tomorrow. Maybe we will climb to the top of a mountain together while there are no leaves and we can see very far. *Ja?*"

"*Ja*," Denis agreed, giving a half smile. "And then maybe

you can show me this thing with color you're doing. Might as well learn something while I'm here."

Fritz grinned. "Good. Now, I could eat a herd." Denis gave him a confused look. "Is this not the saying? *Ich bin so hungrig, ich konnte ein Pferd essen?*"

Denis began laughing. "*Pferd* is horse, not herd. But maybe if you're very hungry, you could eat a herd of horses."

Fritz guffawed at his mistake, and the joy of laughing with his son truly was the greatest happiness he could imagine.

Garland wound his way up the hillside to the Odd Fellows Cemetery, where nothing remained but disturbed soil and ruts full of water and mud from the melting snow. The Germans buried here had been relocated to Tennessee, and he hoped they were at peace there.

He found the plot where he'd shoveled dirt over the coffin he now knew held the body of Marie Spencer. It was sad to think of Marie meeting with such a terrible end. At least now Lucy knew what had become of her sister.

The memory of Hedda standing here came to him, her expression one of hope and grief mingled together. He missed her. He'd written several letters to her in Germany, laboring to fill each one with happy and cheerful things. What he really wanted to tell her was that he loved her and that his offer to marry her hadn't been some sort of misguided chivalry.

"Garland, is that you?"

He whipped around, astonished to see two men approaching. How had he failed to hear them before they drew so close?

He stiffened when he recognized the broad shoulders and

shock of light hair on one of the men. "Fritz? What in the world are you doing here?"

"I have brought Denis to see the place where I am staying while in America before."

Denis stepped forward. "I asked Dad to bring me here so I could see where he was held prisoner."

Garland bristled at this. "He was an enemy alien during the war. It's not like he was in jail."

Fritz grunted. "It feels like jail. It feels like I am trapped in a cage."

Garland didn't want to get into a debate. This was ancient history. "The camp was on the other side of town," he pointed out. "Why'd you come here?"

"This is true. But Denis is asking to see where I was not buried. Next we will see the camp."

Garland snorted. What a way to put it. "Not much of the camp left. If anything."

"This is what I have been told." Fritz looked sad. "I am sorry to remember the *Karussell* and the *Kirche* that are gone now. I think it is sad not to keep them."

"I rode on that carousel once." Garland smiled at the memory. "It sure was something. How'd you fellas figure out how to make it go around?"

Fritz shrugged. "We have not much else to do." He grinned. "Making the *Karussell* go makes the time go, too."

Garland chuckled. "Say, wasn't there a picture of a ship painted on there?"

"*Ja*. I paint it. I am very proud, and now"—Fritz shrugged—"so much is gone."

Garland kicked at a clump of mud. Fritz was right. So much was gone. And he feared there was more to be lost. He'd never been a fan of politics, but with Hedda in Germany he'd become more aware. Lately, Winston Churchill, a member of Parliament in England, had been warning that Germany was gearing up for war. Garland didn't know if this Churchill fellow could be trusted, but the things he said struck a chord of fear.

"You hear from Hedda lately?"

Fritz looked surprised. "*Nein*. I write to *Mutter* often, and she tells me that Hedda is well and taking very good care of her. I am glad for this even though I am sorry she has been sent back there."

Garland was sorry, too, but he didn't feel like talking about it with Fritz. "I'm heading back to town. Can I give you two a ride?"

"*Nein*," Fritz said. "We are here to walk and to see the land." He grinned at Denis. "We are here to be together."

Denis's face lit up as the two headed down a trail that led to Hot Springs and then on to the old camp. Garland watched them go, feeling annoyance, relief, and maybe just a touch of envy.

38

BERLIN, GERMANY

Hedda clutched her shopping basket like a shield. She kept her head down, not making eye contact with anyone. It was good that she'd kept to herself in those days before she left for America. While she knew shopkeepers' names and recognized neighbors, they didn't expect her to be chatty.

Her hand shook as she reached to accept a packet of beef bones she would use to make soup for Lotte. Meat was difficult to come by, and she didn't dare push Herr Stefan, the butcher, to set aside a special order for her ill friend. That would be drawing attention to herself—and to Lotte. And attention was the last thing either of them wanted.

Lotte had kept her secret for a very long time. But what if someone knew? What if someone remembered that her parents were Jewish? Lotte's husband had been Lutheran, and she'd converted before marrying him. Much to her parents' horror and shame. But for the Nazis, being a Jew wasn't a matter of faith, it was a matter of blood, of a lineage that couldn't be changed by conversion.

Hedda shuffled out of the butcher shop and headed for the grocer's at the end of the block. She hoped for some fruit— maybe apples that were only a little soft—but knew it was unlikely this time of year. She'd settle for her usual cabbage and perhaps rutabagas as a change from potatoes. As she flitted from shadow to shadow in the gray, overcast day, she felt as though eyes were following her, searching her heart and mind for the frightening secret Lotte had entrusted to her.

It was a relief to finally return to Lotte's cottage, where she only had a few minutes to spare before fourteen-year-old Herrman was due for his lesson. Although he was one of her less promising students, she was nonetheless grateful to still have the little bit of income his parents paid her, along with the distraction of teaching. Her desire to play for her own enjoyment had withered, and it was only for the sake of her students that she played at all.

"Lotte? Do you need anything? Herrman will be here any moment." She pasted on a cheerful face as she put away their few groceries and tidied her hair.

"Hedda, come sit with me."

"I can't, Lotte. I must prepare for the lesson." She scooped up her sheet music and turned to check on her friend. Tears tracked the older woman's face. "What is it? Are you in pain?"

Lotte patted the cushion beside her. "Herrman's mother came while you were out. Sit."

Confused, Hedda sank onto the worn cushion. "What is it? Is Herrman well?"

"He's well, but he's not coming for his lesson. He has joined the Hitler Youth movement, and his mother came to say he no longer has time for such frivolous pursuits as music."

"Oh. I-I don't know what to say." Hedda felt as though Herrman somehow knew Lotte's secret and had turned against them. But that was just her own paranoia, surely. "I thought his mother wanted him to be a concert pianist?" Her voice sounded so small.

"I think now she hopes he will find a greater future in following the Führer. She spoke of Herrman's activities with great pride." Lotte choked on a sob. "She said he reported their neighbors—a Jewish family—to the authorities, and they . . . they have been forced to leave the building where they have lived all their lives." She buried her face in her hands.

Hedda stared, unseeing. She went to Lotte and wrapped an arm around her shoulders, patting softly and murmuring what she hoped were comforting words, although she hardly knew what she said. All she could think was that if the truth were known about Lotte, the two of them would be forced to leave as well.

Her crying finished for now, Lotte fell back against the sofa cushions, clearly exhausted.

"Come, you should lie down." Hedda held out a hand to help Lotte to her feet. Although she was only sixty-three, Lotte shuffled along like a woman of ninety. Surely she wouldn't live much longer.

The thought pierced Hedda. Was she wishing death for Lotte? As she guided her friend's thin frame toward the ailing woman's bed, she decided *no*. She didn't wish Lotte dead, but she feared others did.

39

MARSHALL, NORTH CAROLINA

The envelope sitting on his desk seemed out of place to Garland. For a moment he thought perhaps Hedda had written to him here instead of at home. Their correspondence, which he'd thought was off to a good start, had nearly stopped. His last three letters remained unanswered. He told himself it was the postal service, but he feared it was likelier that Hedda had simply stopped writing back. Her last letter had been short, and she no longer shared anything personal. It was little more than a recitation of the weather.

He checked the return address. No international postmarks, rather one from Black Mountain. He slit the envelope open with a penknife, taking in the sloping, feminine handwriting.

Garland,
  I want to thank you again for helping to resolve the mystery of Marie's death. I knew it had weighed on me

all these years, but I didn't realize how much until that weight was finally lifted.

As a gesture of goodwill, I'm writing to invite you to a play being performed at Black Mountain College. Thornton Wilder, the playwright, visited the college last year, and they've been determined to put on one of his plays ever since. They selected The Long Christmas Dinner, *not, I think, because it's a favorite, but because it has the most roles of his one-act plays. At any rate, I hope you will come and be my guest.*

Jack and Rubye are preparing refreshments to enjoy after the play. I'll expect you at six unless you send word otherwise.

> *Your friend, Lucy*

Garland chuckled. His friend indeed. How had that happened? He remembered the first time he laid eyes on Lucy Spencer. It was the day he'd turned up on her doorstep to tell her they'd discovered her sister's remains. She'd been so very angry. And with good reason, he supposed.

Well, all right then. He'd go to this silly play. If nothing else, it would give him an excuse to write to Hedda one more time. And if she didn't answer this time, well, he'd let it go. He'd let *her* go.

He knew just what Lucy meant about not realizing how heavy a weight had become over time. He'd carried the weight of the night Fritz and Marie disappeared without even realizing it. Now that that weight had been lifted, he knew better than to pick up a new one.

Fritz added the final touches to the backdrop for the play being performed that evening. While most of the students had been angling to play specific roles, all he'd wanted was a chance to help create the set. While the makeshift stage was simply set with a dining table and chairs, it was the entrance representing birth, and the exit representing death, that Fritz wanted to get his hands on. And so he had, with the help of other students passionate about color and design. And now, shortly before the performance, he added his surprise: a false window showing a bare branch encased in ice. He'd painted it in a way that made it appear as though the light had been captured in the ice, causing it to gleam.

He hung the window behind the table, which was set as if for a feast. Standing back to take it all in, the light seemed to flicker in the ice just as he intended. Even if no one else noticed this special touch, he was well pleased.

He'd read the play, and while he knew his English was far from perfect, he thought he understood what Mr. Wilder was trying to say about time, how the past and the future were contained in the present moment—like the branch encased in ice.

"Well. That is very nearly perfect."

He turned toward the voice to find Anni Albers standing with hands clasped, taking in the set.

"You have a gift for bringing out the light. I'm glad you've stayed on here. Josef enjoys all his students, but I think he especially enjoys you." She laughed lightly. "And not only because you do not expect him to speak English."

Fritz flushed and ducked his head. "*Danke*. I have waited a very long time to do this work. And now I am only glad the waiting is over."

"Do you miss Germany?" Anni asked the question with her head tilted and her dark eyes scanning him intently.

Fritz shrugged. "I do not think about this. It is many years since I am there."

"I miss it, but what I miss is how it used to be. I think maybe the Germany I knew is gone now." She sighed. "Which makes me miss it all the more." She stepped closer, resting a hand on his sleeve. "My parents knew yours."

Fritz froze under her touch. "I did not know this."

"I don't think they knew each other well, but our grand-mothers, they went to temple together." She squeezed his arm. "I understand why you do not go home, why you cannot draw attention to your *Mutter*. I know that even here, in America, being known as a Jew can cause difficulty. I am sorry."

Fritz felt emotion swell in his chest. He'd kept this secret for so long. At first he'd kept it not as a secret, but simply because it didn't seem important. Then, as Germany became less and less friendly to Jews, he kept it for his own sake and for Denis's. It was difficult enough for his son to be seen as half German—adding Jewish heritage to that wouldn't help. And now he kept the secret because he feared for his mother half a world way. The last thing she needed as she grew sicker was to have someone stumble upon her parentage.

He hung his head. "I should go back to her when the Great War stops, maybe in 1920. But I am afraid for Harold White to say bad things about me. And I have *Frau und Kind* by then. Denis, he is young, and . . . we are happy. I tell my wife my family is dead so she will not ask questions. I think if you tell a lie for a long time, you believe it is true."

Anni nodded sadly. "Yes, I understand. But you are writing letters now? And your mother, she understands?"

"*Ja*." Fritz raised his chin. "We must not write the words so plain, but she is forgiving me and is glad to know her *Sohn* has a *Sohn*."

Anni smiled. "*Das ist gut.* Now we will find a place to sit. The play will be starting soon, and I am excited to see it."

"*Danke*," Fritz said, grateful to at last have someone who understood the sorrow he carried.

Garland put on a suit and tie for the play performance. While the students and instructors at the college often wore relaxed clothing for classes, he knew they still dressed nicely for their evening gatherings.

Lucy greeted him on the wide porch of Lee Hall, wearing a long peach-colored dress with draping at the neck that actually made her look . . . nice. She motioned for him to hurry. "They're starting soon. I thought it was up to the lady to keep the gentleman waiting, but here you are squeaking in at the last moment."

"Sorry," he mumbled, checking his watch. Looked to him like he was right on time.

Lucy led him to a seat near the front of the room. Fritz was there, as were the Alberses. They all smiled in greeting—even Fritz, although he looked worn down.

"Fritz designed the set," Lucy announced with pride.

"*Nein*, not design. I build and paint these," Fritz corrected. But his expression warmed. "It is my entertainment to make the place for entertainment."

Lucy chuckled and swatted the big man's arm. "Your English is getting better every day. Even making plays on words. How clever you are!"

Fritz flushed. Garland just stared, wondering what had happened to the dried-up husk of a woman Lucy Spencer had been when they first met.

Lost in thought, Garland had trouble following the play.

Though the entire thing was performed around the same table set for Christmas dinner, it apparently covered decades of time—one Christmas after another—as the characters aged, died, and had children. He did notice, as the play came to an end, how it had come full circle, ending in much the way it began. He found that idea troubling. He liked to think his story would end differently from the way it had started. As a matter of fact, he was determined that it would.

The applause made Garland jump. He quickly joined in, refraining from the whistling and foot stomping some of the students indulged in.

The audience began to break up, moving toward tables set with punch and cookies. As he fell into the flow, Garland noticed that Denis wasn't part of their group. "Fritz, I'm surprised Denis isn't here."

Fritz looked around with a puzzled expression. "You are right. This is a surprise."

"Oh, he's probably off with his own friends," Lucy said. She took Fritz's arm. "Let's have some punch and find a place to sit."

Fritz moved toward the table, then stopped. "*Nein*. He is to be here. I will look for him."

The rest of the group chatted and nibbled Jack's shortbread while sipping punch that tasted suspiciously like someone had added an extra "kick." Garland was beginning to wonder why he'd bothered to come. All the evening had done was remind him that Hedda wasn't there.

He was edging toward the door when a disheveled Fritz returned, his face a mask of worry. "Denis is gone. I cannot find him."

"What do you mean?" Garland asked. "Where's he supposed to be?"

"Here. He is supposed to be here. I seek everywhere but do not find him."

"Maybe he just went for a walk and is back in your room by now," Lucy suggested. "Let's go look."

"I have already done this."

"Won't hurt to check again," Garland said. "Maybe we'll find a note or something."

Fritz frowned deeply but led the way to the room he shared with his son. They crowded in—Anni, Josef, Lucy, Garland, and Fritz—even though it was immediately obvious that Denis wasn't there.

"Where are his things?" Garland asked.

Fritz pointed at a narrow chest of drawers with a shaving mirror on top. Garland slid open the top drawer. Empty. Fritz rushed to his side and opened the next two drawers. The first was also empty, while the second contained a folded slip of paper. He fumbled trying to open it. They all stared at him as he read the note aloud, slowly.

> "*Vater,*
>
> *I have gone to Germany to see my grandmother. I think it's not right that you won't go to see her even though you say she's dying. I figure if I want to know anything about my family, I'd better go now. I took some of the money from your wallet. I promise I'll pay you back. I'll write to you as soon as I get to my grandmother's house. Don't worry about me.*
>
> *Denis*"

Fritz staggered and sat heavily on the edge of the bed. "There is nothing for me to do now but worry."

"For heaven's sake, why don't you go after him?" Garland was dumbfounded by the German's reluctance to go to his family. "Your mother's dying, your son's run off, and Hedda's there. You're no longer under suspicion in America. What's more important than the people you love the most?"

The big man closed his eyes and let his head fall back. "Nothing is more important."

"Well then? Pack a bag. I'll take you to the station myself."

Garland felt a hand on his arm. He turned to see Anni Albers gazing at him with sad eyes. "He must not go. He has no papers."

Garland saw the sense of that but continued to press. "We'll get him some papers. Sheriff Fitzsimmons can help. We'll all attest to who he is. It might take a little time to sort out, but if we play it right, he just might return to Germany a hero. A former prisoner in America returned to his homeland at last. They'll probably throw him a parade." Garland guessed half of what he was saying was impractical nonsense. Probably his own desire to go after Hedda was coloring his opinion.

"This is the fear," Anni said. She looked at Fritz. "I think you must tell Garland why you cannot go home. Why even now it is not good that Denis is trying to go there."

Fritz inhaled deeply and let the air out slowly. "*Mein Mutter ist Juden.*"

"What?" Garland took a step back.

Lucy's hand went to her mouth. "Then you're Jewish, too."

"I am Moravian," Fritz said. "But in Germany I think this does not matter. *Mutter* gives up being Jewish when she weds *Vater*, but I think this does not matter to the Nazis."

"Do her friends know she's Jewish?" Lucy asked.

264

"They do not know when I am growing up. I hope they do not know still."

"But if you went home and drew attention to your family . . ." Lucy left her sentence hanging.

Garland rolled this new information around in his head. Would he have the guts to go to Germany if he were half Jewish? He wasn't at all certain he would.

"I'm not Jewish," he said. Heads turned to stare at him. "What I mean is, I could go after Denis without causing a ruckus. All the way to Germany if need be."

Fritz stepped closer and grabbed his arm. "You would do this?"

"I . . . well . . ." Garland hadn't thought it through. Would he really do such a thing? Why not? He'd made a mess of things with Fritz's escape, helping to hide Marie's death, not telling Wayne the whole truth, and letting Hedda go. "Yeah. Yeah, I'll go. Our best bet is to catch him before he leaves the country. He'll have a tough time doing that without a passport. That means I should leave immediately."

Fritz flung his arms around Garland's neck, nearly tackling him to the ground. "*Wunderbar!*"

Garland staggered and recovered, patting the big man on the back.

"You must find Denis before he leaves for Germany. This would be best," said Anni. "Go now. He will take the train to New York, I think. With luck you will catch him before he does something foolish like stow away on a ship."

"I will go with you as far as I can," Fritz said. "Papers are not needed if I do not leave the country. And Anni is right—maybe we will catch him before he goes too far. Two can look more than one can."

"Right," Garland agreed. "We'll head out on the first train."

40

PORT OF NEW YORK

The people.

Garland had forgotten how many people crammed into big cities like this. It had been years since he left western North Carolina, and he was none too happy to be away from there now, especially with a big German in tow, making people nervous with his questions about a teenage boy. He scanned the crowd at the port once more. How were they going to find Denis amid this crush?

Mike Morris at the train station had been downright delighted to fill Garland in about the golden-haired boy with the wide shoulders who had bought a ticket and then clung to the shadows. "Figured he was runnin' away from something." Mike's eyes lit up with the hope of hearing a good story. Garland didn't offer details, which wouldn't win him any points the next time he needed information from the ticket agent.

Thankfully, Denis's train had left just four hours ahead of theirs, and Mike assured him there was a layover in Washington, D.C., that would give them time to catch up. Garland had hoped to run the boy down there, assuming the late hour meant fewer people, but he'd been wrong. Now, here he was, hungry, rumpled, and tired after grabbing just a few hours of sleep on the train. He was pretty sure Fritz hadn't slept at all, and he looked like it.

Garland sighed and finger-combed his hair, hoping he looked more like a man with authority than he felt. He guessed Denis would try to book passage to Germany, so they would start there.

He flashed his badge at a worker and got directions to the nearest place to purchase transatlantic passage. He wasn't too worried about Denis boarding a ship since he was pretty sure he didn't have either identification papers or enough money to buy a ticket. Still, all sorts of things could happen to a naive boy in a place like this. If Denis became desperate, someone could easily take advantage of him. Or he might try to stow away.

"Fritz, you head down to the farthest pier, and I'll start with this one here. We can meet in the middle. Hopefully one of us will have corralled your boy."

Fritz nodded and set off at a trot. Garland worried he might cause trouble but figured splitting up was the best way to cover as much ground as possible. He tossed a prayer heavenward. Something he was out of the habit of doing but now seemed like the time to start again.

Garland patted the passport in his pocket. He trusted he wouldn't need it. Still, better to have it than not. The smells of the port made his head spin and his stomach churn. He'd had a terrible cup of coffee on the train, and now it felt as though it were eating through the lining of his stomach. What he wouldn't give for a biscuit with butter and strawberry jelly about now.

He trudged toward the closest international pier, forcing himself to take in his surroundings and be on the lookout for a boy in way over his head. Which made him almost miss the clump of men cheering and jostling in the shadow of a towering ship. He drew closer and saw that they were betting on two men in a wrestling match. He was about to move on when he glimpsed a shock of blond hair and realized the man who appeared to be winning wasn't a man at all but rather a half-German boy.

Garland elbowed his way through the seething mass just as Denis pinned his opponent to the ground and the crowd erupted in cheers. Denis released the man he'd been wrestling and sprang to his feet, raising his arms in victory. Other men clapped him on the back, and one approached him making a show of counting out bills as he spewed a stream of oily words. "Good show. Figured you could do it. But that was just a taste of what's to come. You stick with me, boy, and you'll be rich soon enough."

Denis grinned. "That's alright. Just needed enough to book passage to Germany. Now where's my hat?"

As Denis looked around, Garland saw the other man's eyes narrow and sharpen. He had a scar across his forehead that interrupted one eyebrow. Garland guessed he was thinking he'd found a cash cow, and he wasn't going to let Denis go so easily.

"Denis." Garland touched the brim of his hat for luck and drew up to his full height. He spoke in a booming voice. "I'm here to take you into custody."

Just as he'd hoped, the word *custody* drew the attention of every man there. Most of them found some other place to be. The one with the cash shoved the money in his pocket and left his hand there, hidden from view. Garland kept an eye on that hand.

"And who might you be?" the man asked, his face inscrutable.

"Deputy Garland Jones. This kid is a runaway, and I'm here to take him home."

"Kid. He's big enough to be a man. And holds his own like one, too. Guess he can decide for himself where he goes."

Denis found his hat where it had been stepped on and dusted it off. "That's right, Garland. I can decide for myself."

Garland wanted to snag the boy by the ear, but he controlled the urge. "Sure. You're going to see your grandmother in Germany. Has this fella given you the money you need to do that?" He jerked a thumb toward the man with his hand still in his pocket.

"He was about to when you busted in," Denis said, his elation at winning the match beginning to fade.

"That right?" Garland asked the guy with the scar.

The man smoothly extricated his hand and offered Denis some crumpled bills. "That's right," he said with a smirk.

Denis nodded and counted the money. "Wait, I thought there'd be more. Didn't you say there'd be more?"

"And there will be. Lots more. Soon as you tussle with a few more like that last one. Word will get around and then we can win the big money. This fella here's just trying to hold you back. Probably jealous since he's not half the man you are, even if he is three times as old."

Garland stiffened but didn't take the bait. He was pretty sure Denis would see what was happening, and he was hoping to get out of here without any real trouble.

Denis darted a look at Garland, then back at the other man. "I just wanted to make some quick money so I could pay for passage on a ship. I'm not looking for a job. Especially not one fighting all day long."

"You a coward like this one?" He jerked his chin toward Garland, who noticed the man's hand was back in his lumpy pocket.

Denis shifted from foot to foot as though he couldn't decide what to do or how to answer. "Look," he said at last, "I want to go to Germany. I'm not looking to stick around." He sidled closer to Garland as he spoke.

"Your funeral," the man said, jerking his hand out of his pocket and pointing his index finger at Denis. He dropped his thumb as if lowering the hammer on a pistol. Denis flinched and stood frozen as the man cackled. "You ever change your mind, you come ask for ol' Spinner. I ain't hard to find." He shot Garland a look. "So long as you ain't a copper." He turned and melted into the crowd.

As soon as the man was out of sight, Denis grimaced. "Guess that wasn't the smartest idea I've ever had." He slid his gaze to Garland. "You gonna help me find a ship? Help me go see my grandmother?" He sounded so hopeful, Garland almost hated to let him down.

"Like I said, I'm here to take you home. Your dad shared an interesting piece of information with us that makes your going to Germany—a bad idea to begin with—even worse." He slung an arm around the kid's shoulders. "C'mon. Those few bucks aren't gonna get you to Germany, but they will buy train fare back to North Carolina. Maybe some breakfast, too. Your dad is searching the other piers for you. Let's find him, buy return tickets, grab a bite, and have a talk. In that order. Trust me, your dad only wants what's best for you."

Denis took in the wharf, the piers, and the ships waiting to take people to far-off lands. "Dad came after me?"

"He did. He's really worried about you."

Denis rubbed his shoulder where he'd likely twisted it

in the wrestling match. "Yeah. Okay. I don't have a better choice right now, and I guess I should hear Dad out. I can't believe he came all this way. I thought he wouldn't leave North Carolina."

Garland smiled. "What, you don't want to be a fighter in ol' Spinner's club?"

Denis grunted. "Pretty stupid, huh?"

"Yeah, but I was the same kind of stupid once. Still can be if I'm not careful."

"You gonna tell me those stories?" Denis asked a little too eagerly.

"Not today," Garland said with a chuckle. "Maybe one day, though."

41

MADISON COUNTY, NORTH CAROLINA

Garland stood in front of the sheriff's desk, hat in hand. Literally and figuratively.

"It didn't occur to you to clear this with me?" Wayne growled.

"I thought if I left immediately, I could catch him. And I did."

"What crime did he commit?" Wayne spoke in a low, even voice that Garland thought was worse than yelling.

"No crime."

"Right. So why is it you were the man to chase him down?"

Garland gripped his hat hard to still his hands. "It's not safe for Fritz to go, and there wasn't anyone else."

"I doubt that. Seems like I heard Fritz went with you, and don't tell me again that you were the only one with papers. Fritz didn't need papers to catch a train to New York. I also doubt that the need to run this kid to ground was as urgent as you seemed to think." Now Wayne's voice rose. "And now you want to take time off so you can travel to Germany to check on Hedda and to see if you can do anything to help Fritz's mother." He glared at Garland. "Do I have that right?"

Garland had to admit it sounded a bit thin coming from the sheriff's lips. "Yes, sir. It's just that we're all so worried about Hedda, and with the way things are in Germany these days . . ." He trailed off.

"We're all worried, are we? Seems to me this may have something to do with a certain *Fräulein* you developed a soft spot for before she got herself deported back to Germany." His eyes bore into Garland's. "Am I right?"

Garland figured it was no good pretending otherwise. That was the root of the matter. "You're right."

The air went out of Wayne, and he sagged back in his chair. "For Pete's sake, Garland. I know I said I felt bad for how things ended up, but why this girl? Why now? It'd be much more convenient if you fell in love with someone else."

Garland felt the blood drain into his feet. In love? Was he in love? "I . . . I never said I loved her."

Wayne began to laugh. It started small, just a chuckle, then built into a knee-slapping guffaw. Garland stared. Finally, the sheriff got a hold of himself. He wiped his eyes and shook his head. "If you're not, then why in blue blazes would you ask her to marry you, waste who knows how much money, and travel halfway around the world to . . . what, tell Hedda you miss her and check on some kid's grandmother?"

Garland felt all that blood rush back into his face, reddening his cheeks.

"What's her name?"

Garland frowned in confusion. "Whose name?"

"This grandmother of Denis's you're so all-fired determined to look in on."

Garland opened his mouth to reply, his brain a scramble.

Hedda had told him the name. So had Fritz. Why couldn't he think of it now? "I, uh, her name escapes me at the moment, sir."

"Right. Good to see how much you care." He slapped the desk and stood. "The answer is no. As you well know, the county doesn't allow for extended leave. It's a miracle we get Christmas Day off. I couldn't say yes even if I wanted to."

Was that a glint in Wayne's eye? He seemed to be saying something without saying it. Garland took a step forward, holding out his hand. "But I—"

"One more word and you won't need leave." Wayne's voice was steady, pleasant. It didn't sound like a threat.

"But I just want to—"

"Right. You are now officially on indefinite leave without pay. That, the county allows." Wayne marched to the door and opened it, clearly inviting Garland to leave. "I believe the appropriate phrase here is '*Auf wiedersehen.*'"

Garland scuttled through the opening, head down. The door came nigh to catching his heel as Wayne clicked it shut.

He stood in the hall a moment, blinking and trying to think what had just happened. Had he been fired? He looked back at the closed door. Or maybe his boss—his friend—was giving him a gift. He jogged down the hall, already thinking about how to pack light for his journey overseas.

After a long transatlantic voyage, Garland was now standing in Berlin on a foreign train platform. He decided that *foreign* was the right word for everything he was feeling. The countryside he'd passed through by train looked similar enough to North Carolina's hills, fields, and trees.

But the high jagged mountains capped with snow and ice he'd seen in the distance were something else altogether. They looked threatening to him, especially when he imagined them beside the undulating folds of his beloved Blue Ridge Mountains.

The mountains here loomed and gave him a bad feeling. Or maybe that was just the fact that he was spending money he wasn't sure he would be able to replace anytime soon.

He looked around, trying to think what to do or where to go next.

"American?"

The one-word question came from a tall man with a decidedly American accent. He had a broad, white forehead and somewhat disheveled dark hair sticking up in the back. His expression was solemn but friendly. Garland resisted the urge to grab his arm and never let go.

"I am. From North Carolina."

"Are you? I hail from there as well. Asheville. Not that they want me back there ever again. Coming from London at the moment."

"I've come from Hot Springs, just up the mountain." The mixture of relief and joy Garland felt at encountering this bit of home almost swamped him. He pulled out a slip of paper. "I'm looking for this address. Any idea where I should start?"

The man took the paper. "Oh, sure. I can direct you."

Garland grinned foolishly. "Much obliged." He stuck his hand out. "I'm Garland Jones."

The man took his hand with cool, sturdy fingers. "Thomas Wolfe. If you've heard of me, no need to say so. And if you haven't, I'd just as soon you didn't mention that either."

Garland was soon headed in the right direction, thanks to Mr. Wolfe. He did tell his new acquaintance that he'd not only heard of him but knew his mother.

"Doesn't everyone?" was Mr. Wolfe's response. Garland wished he had someone to tell about his encounter and then realized he soon would. Hedda would be interested surely, for she'd stayed with Mrs. Wolfe. And it would be a good topic of conversation as they became reacquainted.

Before too long, he arrived at the small cottage on a street that looked like it had once been prosperous but was now a bit down-at-the-heel. The houses were close together, although they were set back from the street with tidy fences and flowers blooming in window boxes. He felt his heart begin to pound as he neared the address Fritz had given him.

He strode up to the house and knocked on the front door.

42

BERLIN, GERMANY

Hedda sat at the piano. Today she would play. No more swimming in sorrow. No more wishing things were different. Music had always been her balm, and it was high time she used it to soothe the wounded places in her heart. This piano, this house, even her life might be demanded of her any day now. She must seize every moment and not give in to grief.

As she lifted her hands to begin, she heard a knock at the door. She clenched her fingers, stood, and went to see who had come and what they might require of her.

Hedda stared in stunned silence when she opened the door to find Garland standing there, a goofy smile on his face.

"Bet you're surprised to see me," he said.

"I . . . *ja*. Very surprised." The words in English felt dusty on her tongue. She'd been speaking only German for so long now. Not only because she was once again in Berlin but because there was a patriotic fervor that looked with suspicion upon anyone not speaking German. "Come in," she added.

Garland removed his hat—that same hat she'd noticed the first time they met—as he entered the cottage. Hedda tried seeing the room through his eyes. She supposed it must seem stiff and formal with Lotte's antiques and collection of art objects.

"Why have you come? How have you come?" She flinched. Did that sound unfriendly? He couldn't know about Lotte, could he? She'd written to Fritz only two days ago.

Garland didn't appear to be offended. "It's quite a story. I don't suppose you could offer me a cup of coffee while I tell you about it?"

"I'm sorry. Of course. Come with me to the kitchen while I prepare it." She noticed that Garland was looking all around as they moved through the rooms. Right. He didn't know about Lotte.

"I sent Fritz a letter day before last. You must have been already traveling by then." She wasn't telling this right, but she was so flustered. "Lotte died."

"Oh." Garland froze. "Oh. I'm sorry." He took a deep breath. "Real sorry. I got the idea to come here because Fritz and Denis couldn't." He frowned and looked around as though someone might be listening. "You know why they can't, right?"

"If you mean Lotte's family history, then yes, I do."

He twisted his hat in his hands. "Did it cause you any trouble? Do people know?"

"I don't know. No one has said anything, but still, I must be very careful."

Hedda busied herself adding precious coffee to a percolator and getting out cups and saucers. She uncovered a plate of Springerle she'd made the day before. She'd gone without sugar for weeks to save enough to make the anise-flavored cookies, hoping they would tempt Lotte. Too late. Now she was glad she'd baked them in her friend's memory.

Garland propped one hip against the counter and watched her. "I'm sorry about Lotte, but it sure is good to see a familiar face and to hear someone speaking English. Although I did run into Julia Wolfe's son at the train station. He helped me figure out how to get here."

"Thomas Wolfe, the writer? His book is quite popular here. How extraordinary."

"Isn't it? To come all this way and run into somebody from back home. Although I guess he hasn't been in Asheville for a long time. Nice fella."

Hedda poured the coffee, which she'd stretched with some dried chicory. She sat at the small table where she and Lotte had eaten so many meals. Now that she thought about it, it had been weeks since they'd sat here. "Tell me about your journey. This is quite unexpected." She drew in a deep draft of air and let it out slowly. "Unexpected but so very welcome."

Garland basked in the pleasure of being in Hedda's company. He was bumfuzzled by it all. The journey, the luck of running into an American from Asheville, finding Hedda. And now here they sat drinking coffee and chatting like months and miles hadn't separated them. Good gracious but he cared about this woman. If he'd had doubts before, they were gone now.

After a full hour of catching up on the news from home, Hedda pushed her chair back. "I must go and see if I can find something for our supper. There is not much in the pantry, and these sweets, they're not enough."

"I'll go with you," Garland offered.

"*Nein*. It will bring too much attention. It's better if you stay here."

She led Garland to the parlor and offered him her copy of *Look Homeward, Angel*. He wanted to protest, but it felt good to let himself sink into a plush chair. After Hedda left, he began to read this novel by the man who'd given him directions. The next thing he knew, he was jolted awake at the touch of Hedda's hand. She was standing very close. He smelled something nice . . . was it spices from the cookies?

"I'm sorry to wake you," she whispered. "It's getting late, and I've prepared some food."

Before Garland could even think of a response, his stomach let out a gurgle as though speaking for him. He clapped a hand across his middle and looked at her, wide-eyed. "Pardon me."

She bit her lip, although merriment danced in her eyes. "It's a universal language," she said. "Come and I'll give my answer."

Garland stood and stretched, noticing that the hour was growing late. He was weighing whether he should go and find lodging for the night when the aroma of something beefy made up his mind for him. A few moments later, he sat opposite Hedda, breathing in the steam from a bowl of beef-and-barley soup. He ate more quickly than he intended, mopping up every drop with a crust of brown bread.

Hedda watched with a pleased look on her face. "Lotte ate so little. It's good to see you have an appetite."

Garland flushed. "Guess I was pretty hungry after all the traveling."

Smiling, Hedda took his empty bowl and slid the plate of Springerle toward him. He considered politely declining but couldn't resist. He was biting into his second cookie when someone knocked at the door.

Stiffening, Hedda tiptoed over and peered out through the sidelight. She eased the door open and spoke German in soft tones. Finally, she closed the door and returned to the table.

Garland dusted cookie crumbs from his fingers onto the plate. "What is it?"

"I saw a friend of Lotte's at the market. It seems Lotte's death has revealed her secret. It is now known that she was born a Jew."

Garland nodded. "It doesn't matter, does it, with her gone now?"

"This is her house. She said the house would come to me when she died, with some of the contents going to her sister. But sometimes the rules are different for Jews. I don't know what will happen to this place . . . to her things. I don't think I'll be allowed to live here."

Garland couldn't think what to say to that. They both knew it wasn't fair, but they also knew saying so wouldn't change anything. He took her hand and held it a moment. It seemed better than words. She smiled at him and blinked back tears. Finally, he stood and looked out the window at the dusky sky. "Guess I'd better find a place to spend the night. But I'll be back first thing in the morning."

Hedda laid her napkin on the table and ran her fingers over it as though it were important to smooth out any wrinkles. Without looking at him, she said, "There is an extra bedroom here where you can sleep. I would feel better if you stayed."

A lump formed in Garland's throat. He tried to speak, then cleared his throat, drawing her attention. He nodded. "Okay" was all he could manage.

43

Garland woke to the sound of music. He blinked, trying to make sense of where he was. Right. Germany. He sat up, swinging his legs to the floor. A window was open just a crack, letting in fresh air that suited the sweet notes rising from somewhere below. From Hedda's piano if he wasn't mistaken. He found the washroom he'd used the night before, quickly completed his morning ablutions, and tiptoed down the stairs.

Hedda sat at the piano, her back to him. Her silvery hair fell loose almost to her waist. It was longer than when he'd last seen her in America. He had no idea what she was playing, but the way her arms swept across the keyboard, her fingers performing a complex dance, was mesmerizing. He stood there transfixed until she finished, the final notes fading away like the scent of lilacs carried on a breeze.

"Bravo." He didn't realize he'd spoken until she turned and smiled.

"Garland. Did you sleep well?"

"I did," he said with surprise.

"There's coffee in the kitchen and some apples. And I would be happy to prepare eggs for you. Our neighbors have chickens. Are you hungry?"

Garland wished he wasn't hungry but feared his stomach would give him away again. "I could eat," he said. He trailed after Hedda into the kitchen, where she busied herself at the stove.

She flashed him a smile. "I still can't believe you are here. I think, in all the telling yesterday, you did not really say why it is you have come so far."

Garland felt his heart rate tick up. "Like I said, because Fritz and Denis couldn't. We were worried about you. And about Lotte." Was it warm in here? "Josef and Anni, they wanted to know you were okay, too." This sounded even thinner than when he'd told it to Wayne. "Plus I had some time off and . . . and I wanted to see you were alright with my own eyes."

Based on her rosy cheeks, Hedda thought it was warm in here, too. "Yes, I see," she said, sounding like she didn't see at all. She shook her head and changed the subject. "I wish Fritz had told me about Lotte's history. It would have been good to know. I wonder why he didn't."

"Pride." The word slipped out of Garland's mouth before he could think about it.

Hedda flashed him a look. "What do you mean?"

Garland ducked his head, sorry he'd spoken. "A man doesn't like to let a woman he cares about know he's afraid of anything."

"And you believe Fritz cares about me?"

Aw, for Pete's sake. This was the last thing Garland had

meant to talk about. "I wouldn't want to speak for another man," he mumbled.

"Hmmm." Hedda added diced onions and potatoes to a skillet. She began cracking eggs into a stoneware bowl. "I thought maybe he did." Garland's heart plummeted. "But then what does it matter"—she caught Garland's eye— "since I no longer care for him?"

He leaned toward her, trying to think of the right words. This was his chance. He'd tell her how much she meant to him, and then they'd figure out what to do next. But before he could speak, there was a knock at the door. "I'll get it," he blurted and turned away.

As he hurried to the door, he considered that this was all wrong for several reasons. First, he was missing his chance to tell Hedda how crazy he was about her. Second, this was not his house, and answering the door was presuming a great deal. Yet he supposed it was too late to do anything else. He opened the door to find a man there, standing stiffly in a brown uniform. He extended his arm in the salute Garland found so odd and said something in German.

There. A third reason he shouldn't be answering the door.

Hedda nudged him from behind. He stepped aside as she responded in German. The official didn't seem happy with whatever Hedda was saying. She spoke rapidly and pressed a packet of Springerle into his hand. At first he seemed reluctant to accept the gift. Then she folded the cloth back, and the sweet, spicy scent seemed to sway him. Or maybe it was the Reichsmark notes Garland spied tucked beneath the cookies.

The uniformed man nodded, held up his finger, and said, "*Eines Tages*." With that, he spun on his heel and marched off toward the street. Hedda was quick to shut the door, locking it. She turned and leaned against the door with her eyes closed.

Garland wanted to take control of the situation, to come to her rescue, but he had no idea how to go about it. "What was that all about?"

"The government is claiming Lotte's house and everything in it." She covered her mouth with her hand, as though by stopping the words she could stop the inevitable. "I know that man. We went to school together. I convinced him to give me one more day before they come. He granted me this but said if anything of value is gone, they will know and will come to find me." She choked on a sob and fell against Garland's chest. "I have nothing," she choked out. "Everything is gone."

He held her as she wept, trying desperately to think of what to do.

They ate breakfast in silence, each of them knowing the food was too precious to waste.

"We have to figure out how to get you to America," Garland said at last. He looked at her cautiously. "I mean, if you want to come back. I guess I'm assuming a lot. Maybe there's nothing there for you anymore and you want to stay here, even though—"

She held her hand up. "Yes. I want to return to America. And yes, there is much there for me now." She hoped he understood her meaning but couldn't bear to speak any more plainly. "We will hope, yes?"

"Okay. Okay, I hear you."

"Do you?" she asked. Then she leaned over and kissed him, soft and fast, on the mouth. His eyes widened.

"Yeah," he whispered. "Yeah, I do."

"We have today," she whispered. "I will play for you. And then I will pack my own things. Surely they cannot deprive me of the few items I brought to this house." A tear slid down her cheek. "My piano I cannot take. I only hope someone else will love it as I have."

Garland nodded mutely. She swallowed the last few bites of egg, pushing them past the lump in her throat. Afterward she piled the dishes in the sink, not bothering to wash them. She was determined to enjoy this day with Garland. It wasn't enough, but it was something.

Garland repacked his few belongings in the satchel he'd borrowed from a friend. Here he was, a world traveler, and he didn't even have his own suitcase. Not that it mattered. He didn't expect to travel anywhere else after this. He'd just be grateful to get back home safely. Hopefully with Hedda in tow. He just had to come up with a way to make that happen. He'd tried to give his full attention to her playing this morning. It had been breathtaking, but every time he found himself caught up in the glory of the music, reality pushed back in.

They could find a place to stay. There were plenty of hotels and tourist lodgings. Surely he could afford something respectable. And she clearly had some funds set aside. He considered that they could pose as husband and wife to save on a second room, but then he quickly dismissed the idea. He wouldn't do that to Hedda. This was difficult enough for her already. He was beginning to believe she returned his feelings, and he didn't want to spoil what he hoped would be more than a fleeting romance. Although *how* it could be was a question he had no answer to.

Hedda appeared in the doorway. "You have packed your things?"

"I have. And you?"

"There isn't much to pack. I think I will dare to take a few mementos that are not worth anything to the Third Reich, as they are calling themselves."

"That's a good idea. It's not as though they have a list of everything here, right?"

She gave him a worried look. "I don't think so, no. But we must be careful all the same."

Garland nodded and watched as Hedda moved through the house, touching a vase here, a framed photo there, running a hand along the spines of the books on the shelves. He guessed all of it was as familiar as her own face and yet none of these things was hers.

Hedda sank into a chair at a mahogany desk that Garland had admired earlier. She began methodically going through the contents, sorting papers, making a stack of letters, and dropping things that weren't important into a wastebasket.

"Have you thought about what you'll do?" Garland asked. "I have some ideas for now, but I'll have to go back to America eventually."

Hedda put on a brave face. "I have friends who I think will let me stay with them until I can find a job. I have a little money. It will be enough." Garland suspected it wouldn't, but he let it go for the moment, thinking hard as he watched Hedda sort through Lotte's papers.

Then he saw it. Their salvation. He pounced on the stack at Hedda's right elbow. He snatched up the papers and knelt at Hedda's feet, taking her hands in his. "Never mind sorting through all of this," he said. "Pack just two bags. Take what matters most to you."

She looked up. "What matters most?"

"Of Lotte's things, of your things. But pack light. We don't want to draw attention. Two bags only."

"What are you talking about?"

"You're coming with me. To America."

Hedda gave a strangled laugh. "I can't. I have no papers. And even if I did, they would say *verboten*."

Garland pulled something out of the stack of papers and handed it to her. Hedda took it and frowned at him. "This is Lotte's passport. It does me no good."

He flipped it open to the page with Lotte's photograph and squinted at it. "This isn't a good picture, which is good." He chuckled nervously, then hurried on. "If your hair were darker, no one could tell it wasn't you. And here . . ." He scanned the words in German, trying to decipher them. "Aha. The date is still valid. The passport is good. Who's to know?"

Hedda shook her head slowly. "But using false papers that belonged to a Jew, this is very risky."

"Riskier than staying here until the Nazis come to take everything away? Riskier than trying to start over with nothing and with no help?"

"Coffee."

Garland drew back. "You want coffee? Now?"

Hedda lurched to her feet. "At school, the girls would darken their hair using strong coffee. We can take the train to Denmark. Once we're out of Germany, we can book passage to America. It will be safer this way."

"Now you're talking," Garland said with a grin.

44

Two hours later, they boarded a train heading for the German/Denmark border. Garland led the way while Hedda, her still-damp hair darkened and mostly tucked beneath a kerchief, followed close behind. She carried two satchels of clothing, what was left of Lotte's jewelry, a couple of her favorite books, and a photograph of Lotte holding a young Fritz on her lap. She had always kept it close in her last days, and Hedda wanted to give it to Fritz. Or at least keep it out of the hands of the Nazis.

They'd left the house tidy and locked up tight. She supposed someone would be there soon enough, breaking the door down and ransacking Lotte's lovely home. But she wouldn't think of that now. Now she needed to think only of escaping her homeland.

"But how will we get passage on a ship?" she asked for the third time. Garland had return passage on a ship leaving Hamburg, but that would do him no good in the Danish port of Esbjerg. He had yet to give her a satisfactory answer, simply saying he'd work it out.

His plan began to take shape for her when he asked about

the topaz ring she no longer wore. "Do you still have that?" he asked.

"I . . . it is the ring Fritz gave to me, so I no longer wear it." She felt her cheeks flushing.

He looked oddly pleased. "Yeah, well, I'm not going to argue with that, but do you still have it on you?"

"In my bag." She dug out the ring and handed it to him. "It has some value, so I did not get rid of it."

He smiled as he took her left hand and slipped the ring onto her finger. "I'll say it has value. We'll tell them we're getting married and beg to be allowed to purchase tickets on short notice."

Hedda's throat felt tight. She struggled to breathe evenly. So much was happening at once. So many pieces of her past mixing and mingling in a confusing whirl. This ring had been her dearest possession for years and then, when she had learned the truth about Fritz, it became a haunting reminder of what might have been. Now it stirred more feelings than she could process. The ring reminded her of Fritz and the dreams they'd once shared. Yet Garland sliding it on her finger gave her hope that marriage might one day be more than a ruse for fleeing the country. And it reminded her of Lotte, who had owned the ring before giving it to Fritz to seal his love for Hedda.

Hedda closed her hand in a fist and looked closely at the topaz stone, the golden fire in its depths. "I think this is a huge risk," she said, "but it might work." She looked up at Garland, whose infinitely tender expression made her pulse quicken. "*Danke*. Thank you for coming here. For finding me."

He nodded, then took her hand, lacing his fingers through hers. "Yeah, it is a risk. Which is why we need to take it now, today, before we lose our nerve. And before anyone thinks to come looking for us."

"Alright," Hedda agreed, pressing her palm to his and daring to hope for the first time in a long time.

Garland had no idea what he was doing. He'd never considered himself a brave man. As a matter of fact, he'd felt cowardly looking back on his failure to ask questions the night Marie Spencer died. But now this was his chance to do what was right—to make a difference, to help someone else.

He looked down at his hand, still linked with Hedda's. Not just someone. *The* one. He was sure of it now. Hedda was the one for him. All he had to do was sneak her out of a country hostile to the woman she was pretending to be lest they both end up in a concentration camp.

No problem.

He told himself the hard part was done. They'd left the city where Lotte and Hedda were known. No one would be any the wiser at the border or in Denmark, and surely they could find a tenderhearted ticket agent who would help them. Even so, each time he saw someone in a uniform with a swastika, he felt like throwing up.

"Garland." Hedda drew his attention. "When we reach the border, the train will stop so that everyone's papers can be checked. I think it would be good if we were not together then. If I am caught, you can continue on."

Garland gripped her hand more tightly, finding this came more naturally than he expected. "Are you kidding? And leave the future Mrs. Garland Jones to fend for herself? Not on your life."

Hope battled with fear in Hedda's eyes. She spoke so

softly he could barely hear her. "It could be your life you risk. I've heard of terrible things happening to people they call 'political enemies.'"

The train began to slow, and passengers shifted in their seats. Garland felt Hedda's hand tighten around his. He looked down at her and smiled. "Ready to do this? Together?"

Hedda's smile wobbled, then steadied. "I cannot think this is a good idea and yet I don't have any other. And so I'm ready."

"Good," Garland said, his heart singing despite the peril they were in. "Now let's look like we're in love."

She nodded, her eyes brimming with tears, as the man in the brown shirt moved down the center aisle, holding his hand out for each passenger's papers.

Garland was pretty sure he'd sweated through his overcoat by the time the German official made it to their seats. He handed over their passports as if he did this sort of thing every day. The man flipped through the pages of the booklets, frowned, and looked sharply at each of them.

"*Sie sind Amerikaner?*"

Garland glanced at Hedda. "He is asking if you are an American."

"Oh. Right. Yes, I'm an American."

"*Sprechen sie Deutsch?*"

He knew that one. "No, afraid not. But my fiancée here is happy to translate for me." He tried to sound jolly about it. "Don't speak Danish either, but I guess we'll manage." He chuckled, but the laughter died on his lips as the man glared at him. The German official spewed a stream of words at Hedda, pointing at Garland and shaking his head.

Hedda ducked her head. "*Ja,*" she said. "*Das verstehe ich.*"

Garland began to feel as though he might either pass out or lose his breakfast. Was this man about to haul them off to some gulag? No, that was Russia. In Germany it would be a concentration camp. He felt light-headed and wished he could take his coat off but didn't dare do anything other than pray silently.

Finally, the man made a derisive gesture and tossed their passports into Hedda's lap. "*Der Amerikaner,*" he snarled before moving on down the aisle.

Garland didn't move until the uniformed official exited their train car. Then he sagged, his breath ragged. "What did he tell you?" he asked.

Hedda gave him the tiniest smile. "He lectured me—a good, upstanding German—for being with a disgusting American. He encouraged me to reconsider my choice."

Garland loosened his shirt collar and fanned the lapels of his coat. "Are you reconsidering?"

"*Nein,*" she said and reached for his hand once again.

Once in Esbjerg, they found a ticket agent with no one else in line. Garland envisioned himself swooping in and negotiating a ticket for Hedda. But he forgot he'd have to negotiate in Danish, which of course wasn't possible. Instead, he stood by helplessly as Hedda spoke rapidly, tossing her head and showing off her ring. She pointed at Garland and made a pleading gesture.

The ticket agent with his perfectly knotted tie and slicked-back hair listened with narrowed eyes. He asked a few questions as sweat began to form on Garland's brow.

He wasn't sure how much more stress he could handle. He tried to look confident and self-assured, yet he felt heat climbing up his neck. Hopefully he just looked like a nervous bridegroom.

Hedda seemed to be answering the man's questions to his satisfaction. She leaned close and whispered something, then pushed her passport—Lotte's passport—closer to him.

The man took it and smiled. "You're in luck," he said with a wink in heavily accented English. "I am happy to help the lovers." He slipped Hedda's last Reichsmarks from between the pages before stamping both passports and handing her two tickets with a flourish. "Hurry. There is not much time before the ship departs."

Hedda grabbed the tickets, and she and Garland started rushing toward their ship. He glanced back as he allowed her to pull him along. There was something about the way the man told them to hurry. Garland saw the agent speaking to a man in the dreaded brown uniform. He stumbled and nearly went to his knees.

Hedda hissed, "Don't look back. Denmark cooperates with the German government, but I don't think a Nazi official would have authority here."

Fear rose up in Garland. He'd been afraid the night Harold White had rushed him into burying the coffin he'd thought held Fritz. He'd been afraid when Hedda had been deported. He'd been afraid on the train. But this. This raw fear, so close to freedom, seemed to be an accumulation of all the rest. It made him want to just give up and get whatever terrible thing was about to happen over with. He didn't think he had much fight left in him.

"*Fräulein!*" a voice called out. Garland flinched. He looked over his shoulder to see the soldier hurrying after them, his hand in the air. "*Warten Sie,*" he called. Garland didn't know what that meant, but he could guess.

Hedda tugged at his hand. "Keep moving."

Garland stopped. No. He wouldn't run this time. He'd lived with fear for far too long. He would not live with it any longer.

"Can I help you?" he said to the man, who had caught up to them, panting a little. "I'm an American police officer." He hoped this guy understood English. "Do you have official business?"

"*Was ist das?*"

Garland pulled out his badge. He didn't suppose it meant anything here in Esbjerg, but what did he have to lose? "Policeman. Official business."

The German's eyes went wide. "*Ja, ja,* you are rich American, right? And maybe you are cowboy?" He mimed pulling a pistol and firing it. "Like Tom Mix. I like this hat." He pointed at Garland's favorite pinch-front hat. He'd had it for years, and it fit him perfectly.

Garland laughed, a nervous burst of astonishment and relief. "Sure. I'm a cowboy. Left my horse back home."

"*Das ist gut.* You have something for me?"

Garland looked at Hedda, hoping for help. What did this man want?

Hedda whispered, "I think he wants a 'gift' like I gave the ticket agent."

"We need whatever cash I have left," he murmured. She let her eyes drift up to his head. "No. My hat?" She nodded.

Garland turned back to the man and took off his hat. "You like it?" he asked. The man's eyes lit up. "It's yours." Garland handed over the hat. The man grinned and twirled it on one finger.

He looked at Hedda, who stood clutching Garland's arm. "*Fräulein, Wir wünschen Ihnen alles Gute.*" He gave the Nazi salute. "*Sieg Heil!*" Then he smirked at the pair of them and left.

"What did he say?" Garland asked.

Hedda, visibly shaken, answered, "He said, 'We wish you well.'"

Garland drew in a deep breath and let it out slowly. "Great. Now, let's not give him time to change his mind about that. C'mon, we're headed for America."

45

BLACK MOUNTAIN, NORTH CAROLINA

Fritz finished knocking together another simple book-case. He was making several to go into the students' rooms, and while they weren't elaborately made, it was satisfying to start with a few pieces of lumber and end with a useful item. He stood back and checked to make sure the finished piece was square. Maybe he'd paint the book-cases using Josef's color theories. The students could help. It would be an excellent teaching project.

Moving on to cut and measure the next board, he was grateful for the work that kept his hands and his mind busy. He'd received Hedda's letter letting him know *Mutter* had died. He was surprised at how, in the few months they'd been back in touch, hearing from her had become an important part of his life. And now that was gone forever.

In her last letter to him, she'd mentioned her confidence in heaven and how glad she was that Fritz would join her there one day. While the sorrow of her passing was sharp and deep, he found that he could rejoice in their reconnection and the joy and forgiveness that came with it. He was grateful that she wouldn't have to bear witness to the hard things happening in Germany these days. He feared the situation would get worse yet. Now his greatest worry was for Hedda. What would she do? Was she still living in his mother's house? Was she safe?

It had been nearly two weeks since Garland went to Germany. He hadn't heard anything more from Hedda or Garland. Not that he expected to, although he'd thought Josef and Anni might hear something. He told himself it was the deterioration of the German postal service. Nothing more.

He tidied his tools and made his way to Jack's kitchen, where the scent of bacon lingered. He'd worked up an appetite and, though it wasn't lunchtime, hoped he might find a slice of bread and some butter or one of Rubye's ginger cookies. The memory of his mother's homemade Springerle cookies came to him. What he wouldn't give for one of those.

He grabbed a leftover biscuit and was headed back to work when Jack called to him. "Hold on there, Fritz. There's somebody in the hall to see you." Jack had a twinkle in his eye, but that was often the case. Fritz liked how cheerful the man was.

"Who is it?"

"Do I look like your social secretary?" Jack laughed. "Go and see."

Fritz stuffed the bread into his mouth and washed it down with a swig of water before entering the hall, where he saw three people outlined against the brightly lit windows. He first registered Denis, then realized that was Garland with him, and finally . . . Hedda?

Although he had many questions, Fritz suddenly couldn't

remember his English. He just stared at the woman he thought he would never see again.

Denis broke the silence. "Hey, Dad, guess who's back?"

"When are you returned?" Fritz managed, finding his tongue at last.

"Late last night," Garland said. "We stayed with Josef and Anni in Black Mountain."

Hedda spoke next. "Fritz, did you get my letter?" She spoke in a rush, tears blooming in her eyes. Fritz immediately wanted to stop them.

"Yes," he hurried to reassure her. "I write back, but maybe you do not get my letter before you are gone from there."

Hedda shook her head, the tears falling freely now. "No, I didn't. We had to leave." She glanced at Garland, who handed her a handkerchief. "All of your mother's things, her property, we had to leave it behind. The authorities, they learned she was born a Jew, and they took it all."

Fritz bowed his head. He felt Denis move closer and reached for his son, wrapping an arm around his shoulders. "This does not matter. These things were never mine, and Denis and me, we have no need of them." He squeezed his son. "I am only sorry Denis did not meet his *Großmutter* in this life, but he will meet her in the next one."

Hedda nodded, sniffling and smiling. "That is a good way to look at it." She pulled something from her bag. "I brought you this. I hope it will be a comfort."

Fritz took the photograph and felt joy rise within him. "I remember this day," he said. "I did not want my photo taken alone, so *Mutter* sat with me. She kept it close always." He swiped away tears. "*Danke.* I do not expect anything, but this is what I want. And now I am only glad you are away from

Germany." He frowned. "But how is it that you are here? I am thinking the Germans will not let you leave."

Hedda moved to a chair as though she didn't have the strength to stand any longer. "It's been a difficult journey. I darkened my hair and used your mother's passport to get to Denmark. Garland said we were traveling to America to be wed, and a sympathetic ticket agent let us purchase passage."

Fritz stared at his former fiancée. "This sounds like a foolish thing to do. But here you are, so I cannot think it was wrong."

"Here I am," echoed Hedda.

"And here she's going to stay," Garland chimed in.

Fritz narrowed his eyes. "Because this is true about getting married?"

"No, no," Hedda answered quickly. "That was only to help us get away. I'm not sure what to do now. I'm here without permission, and I can't keep pretending to be Lotte."

Garland, who Fritz thought looked a bit disappointed, squeezed Hedda's arm. "We're going to get you asylum. I'm not exactly sure how that works, but we can sure demonstrate that it's not safe for you to live in Germany. Don't worry, we'll figure it out."

Fritz nodded and touched the tip of one finger to his mother's image. He thought he knew exactly how Garland would like to figure this business with Hedda out. And he supposed, if he were being sensible, he'd wish the couple well. What did he have to offer Hedda after all? Certainly not American citizenship, as Garland perhaps could.

He glanced up at Hedda, who was watching him with such compassion in her eyes. Then again he'd be a fool to make the same mistake twice.

Garland stared at the courthouse door. He'd sent Sheriff Fitzsimmons a letter from New York when they arrived at the port. He guessed Wayne would've received it by now. He'd offered a short summary of his time in Germany and the fact that he was returning with Hedda safe and sound. He mentioned Lotte's passing but skipped the bit about using her passport to bring Hedda back to the U.S. He figured Wayne was probably better off being able to claim he didn't know anything about that. He'd also mentioned seeking asylum with great confidence, though he didn't have the first idea of how to go about getting it.

He took a deep breath and pushed the door open. He was pretty sure Wayne was here. What he wasn't sure of was what he'd say when he saw him. He was still confident that the "leave without pay" business had simply been a means to an end, but he was nervous nonetheless. Margo, in her usual spot at the phone desk, spotted him.

"Where you been?" she asked. "And where's your hat?"

Garland was surprised. He'd assumed everyone would know his business by now. The fact that Margo, who knew everything and then some, seemed unaware gave him hope. "Been on leave. Traveling." Short and sweet, that was best. Margo narrowed her eyes. His already jangled nerves began dancing. "Sheriff in?" he asked.

She pinched her lips and looked him up and down. "He is. But I don't think he's expecting you."

"That's okay. I'll just stick my head in."

Margo stared him down. He began to sweat but gritted his teeth. *Don't elaborate*, he told himself. If he could hold his own against Nazis in Germany and Denmark, surely he could hold up against a nosy secretary.

"Fine," she snapped. "Guess you can keep your business

to yourself if you want." She sniffed and turned back to her typewriter, rolling in a report form with two carbon copies. He opened the door to Wayne's office with the odd sensation that he could feel her eyes on him even though her back was turned.

"The prodigal returns." Wayne leaned back in his chair, making the mechanism squeal. "What can I do for you?"

And just like that, Garland knew what to say. "Do I still have a job?"

"Do you still *want* a job?"

"I do."

"Good. Can I trust that you won't be keeping secrets from me in the future?"

Garland froze. He sure as heck was keeping a secret right here and now. He gnawed at his lip and tried to think. Then he noticed that Wayne saw his hesitation. He straightened his shoulders, held up his chin, and confessed. "Right. Guess I'd better tell you I got Hedda back using false papers. She's in Black Mountain, staying with the Alberses. I'm hoping I can help her stay in the country for good."

Wayne closed his eyes and shook his head. "You sure do have a knack for landing smack-dab in the middle of the most original messes."

"Yes, sir. Reckon I do."

Wayne sighed heavily. "What do you propose to do now?"

"Propose," Garland said.

Wayne frowned. "Right, that's what I want to know."

"I mean, sir, I'm going to propose to Hedda. I want to marry her."

A slow grin spread across the sheriff's face. "Guess you're not finished rounding up trouble for yourself yet. Think she'll go for it?"

Garland fought a wave of nausea. Was he afraid she wouldn't accept? Or that she would? "I've asked her once already, and she acted like I was doing it just to get her out of a tight spot . . . so I don't know."

"Are you?" Wayne asked. "Are you just trying to help her out? Seems to me I've seen you do some foolish things in the name of being 'helpful.'"

Garland gave the question some thought. "Maybe that was true the first time I asked. I felt bad about Marie Spencer and Fritz. And I didn't want her to go back to Germany." He took a deep breath and let it out slowly. "But I don't guess a man chases a woman halfway around the world just for fun. Not to mention that bit where we were on the run from a Nazi officer." He grinned. "I'm pretty sure I'm not just being helpful."

"Alright then." Wayne slapped his hands against the desktop and stood. "So long as you keep your nose clean and invite me to the wedding, I guess you've got your job back." He chuckled. "And I'll expect to hear the *whole* story about outrunning that Nazi officer."

Hedda closed her eyes as Anni finished braiding her hair and draped it over her shoulder. She caught the faint scent of the lavender Anni tucked in among her underthings. It reminded her of her mother, gone many years now.

"You must never go back," Anni said, smoothing a wayward hair into place.

"Never? That's a very long time."

"*Ja.* I know. It's how long I plan to stay away."

Hedda reached up and found her friend's hand. "What if I have no choice in the matter?"

"We will not let that happen."

"But what if I'm discovered? Garland talks of asylum, but I don't know how such things work."

Anni took a seat next to Hedda on the dressing table bench. "I think you have an important choice to make."

"Oh? What's that?"

"Will you marry Fritz and make your home among the Moravians, where perhaps both of you will go unnoticed? Or will you marry Garland and allow him to make you an American?"

Hedda stared at her friend. "These are the choices you see for me?"

Anni shrugged. "They are both good men. There are much worse choices."

"You talk as though I could simply make this choice. It seems Fritz and Garland would have something to say about it."

Anni laughed. "Has not each one asked you already?"

Hedda considered for a moment. "But Fritz asked me many years ago. And Garland only asked me to try and help."

"Ah. You think they do not love you." She sighed deeply. "What is love? For one, it has been dormant for many years but I think could still bloom. For the other, it is a desire to rescue you, to sacrifice for you. Is this not love?" She sighed. "Good marriages have been built on less."

Hedda reached up to twist her hair, only to remember that Anni had braided it. "None of this is as I dreamed when I was a girl."

"Look at me. I did not want to be a weaver, but this is what the *Bauhaus* needed. And now I cannot think what my life would be without it. Perhaps it will be the same for you." She patted Hedda's arm and stood. "No matter. You will always have your music, and that is what you are made for."

Hedda watched her friend exit the room, once more considering her words. She'd lost so much, starting with Fritz all those years ago. Then her parents. Now Lotte and the sense of belonging in her own country. Was it time to gain something? Like a husband?

She wasn't certain. Then again neither of them had asked her, at least not lately. As Anni said, the only thing she knew she had for certain was her music. And so, not knowing what else to do, she would go to the college and play the grand piano Johann had recently donated. That, at least, was something she could do without help or permission or censure.

46

BLACK MOUNTAIN, NORTH CAROLINA

On Monday morning, Hedda settled onto the piano
bench and flexed her fingers. She'd gotten into the
habit of playing hymns to begin the day as the students and professors ate their breakfast in Lee Hall. Dr. Rice,
who had given her the job he'd promised without asking too
many questions or quibbling over her lack of papers, said she
was playing their "matins," and she liked the sound of that.

Each day she half expected to see a policeman or government official march onto campus and demand to see her
papers. While she still had Lotte's passport, her hair had
quickly returned to its natural pale color. She could no longer
pass for her friend. She supposed she should dispose of this
evidence of her dishonesty, but other than the photo she'd
given to Fritz, it was the only image she had of Lotte and
she didn't want to let it go.

She was so absorbed in playing that she failed to notice
when the room emptied out, growing silent around her. As
she struck the final chord, she sat there a moment letting the

sound fade into the corners of the room, as if the walls were soaking up the music to release it again later.

"That was very good."

Hedda turned to see only a few students lingering at a far table, and Denis, who was sitting near her, a folded newspaper in his hand. "*Danke*," she said.

Denis shifted forward, tapping the paper against his knee. "You know I tried to go to Germany. I really wanted to meet my grandmother."

"She would have liked you." Hedda smiled. "No, she would have *loved* you and spoiled you. And you would have loved her back. I'm sorry you were not able to meet her."

"Yeah, I was mad about how no one wanted me to go—especially Dad. But hearing how the Nazis reacted to Grandma Lotte being Jewish, well, now I get it. Have you heard the latest out of Germany?" Denis opened the paper and handed it to her.

There on the front page, sandwiched between an article about tobacco sales and a photograph of two women with the caption "Visitors from Georgia," was the headline NAZI BANKER URGES OUSTING MORE JEWS. The first sentence read, "*Head of Cologne Chamber of Commerce says Jews must be eliminated from all industries and businesses.*"

Hedda scanned the article, her stomach clenching. She was glad she'd yet to eat breakfast. "But this . . . this isn't right. How can they do this?"

Denis shook his head. "I guess they can do whatever they want. And if I were still there, this would apply to me. Dad said I'd be *Mischlinge* rather than Jewish, but I'm betting that wouldn't make things much easier for me." His mouth twisted. "Maybe it's a good thing Grandma Lotte is dead. I think that's what the Nazi Party wants."

Hedda could see that Denis was sullen with anger. She laid a hand on his arm. "Thank you, Denis."

He blinked. "For what? For telling you terrible news?"

"No, for reminding me that I did the right thing in leaving Germany. Even if I'm in America without permission, at least I'm here. I'm glad, too, your father never came home. If he had, you would not have been born. And I would be a German married to a Jew in a country where that is now illegal." She shook her head in dazed wonder. "Perhaps everything has turned out for the best? I don't know." She flashed a smile. "But I'm grateful to be here—playing this beautiful piano, talking to my American friend."

Denis returned the smile. "Yeah. I'm glad too. Guess we'll just have to wait and see how our stories turn out, huh?"

"I think so. And you, you still have so much story ahead of you." She shook off the lingering sorrow she felt for her country. "What's next for you? Will you stay here with your father or go back to Bethania?"

"I'm ready to go back," Denis said. "I thought I wanted a more exciting life, but the past few weeks have been too exciting." He chuckled. "Helping with the spring planting sounds like just the thing about now. And Dad said he'd be coming back at Easter, so maybe I'll go ahead of him and make sure the house and everything's in good shape. We have our own school there, and although I've been keeping up on my own, it'll be nice to spend time with the other kids."

Hedda felt a stab of something unexpected. "Oh? Fritz is leaving the college?"

"Maybe not for good. I'm not sure what his plans are. He loves it here, but he said he needs to make a living. He's going back to woodworking, I think." Denis stood. "I'm glad you're here. Dad likes you, and so do I. I'd hate for you to be stuck in Germany."

Hedda nodded. "*Ja*," she said. "Me too."

Fritz splashed color across his canvas in the makeshift studio. He'd been working to get this piece right for a week now and finally knew how to finish it. His movements might have looked frenzied to someone watching, but even in the rush of creativity he knew what he intended. At last he knew.

He stopped and stood back. There. He'd done it. Thanks to Josef's teaching about color, Fritz had found the right combination to make the blues of this piece jump off the canvas with a pulsing light. He grinned, well pleased with what he'd accomplished. Even if no one else appreciated it, he knew he'd satisfied a longing to create something that expressed what he felt when a blaze of amber leaves against an October sky took him by surprise.

"'The heavens declare the glory of God; and the firmament sheweth his handywork,'" he whispered. Yes. If he never painted again, this would be enough.

Fritz turned at the sound of someone approaching. Josef Albers peered at his canvas, still glistening with wet paint. His teacher spoke in German, "Of course, it must dry before we know for certain, but this looks like excellent work." He thumped Fritz on the shoulder. "You have learned well."

"*Danke*" was all Fritz could manage to say.

After Josef left, Fritz stood near a window, cleaning his brushes. His gaze caught on a stranger who was walking across campus. A very official-looking stranger. He froze.

He knew Hedda was worried about her status in America. Was she a refugee? An illegal alien? If she were discovered, would she be sent back to Germany? Fritz had brushed such concerns aside. He'd lived in the United States for a long time now without anyone asking for his papers. But he paid enough attention to world news to know that the number of people immigrating from Europe to America had been drastically cut in recent years. And there had been that time last year when an official came to check the papers of any Germans working at the college. And now Hedda worked at the college.

Fritz quickly put his supplies away and hurried outside. He'd helped Hedda avoid official notice before. He'd be only too glad to do it again. He found her in the kitchen, helping Jack and Rubye prepare vegetables for lunch. He stopped in the doorway, watching her for a moment. She stood between the Negro husband and wife, her slim paleness more pronounced. He supposed she was just what the Nazi Party looked for when they lifted up the Aryan race. As was he.

She glanced up at him and smiled, reminding him that her eyes were brown. So not the perfect blond-haired, blue-eyed Aryan after all. He smiled back. No, not the perfect German like he would have been had he returned home. Except for being half Jewish. Thank goodness he'd never gone back. He knew himself well enough to recognize that he would have been tempted to support German nationalism and the idea that genetic weakness should be rooted out. It sounded like a fine idea . . . until it applied to you and the people you loved.

That idea of genetic weakness would include people like Anni, Jack, and Rubye. It would include him, too, thanks to his Jewish mother and Jewish grandparents. Would he have hidden his family history? Yes, he thought. He would have tried at any rate.

"Hedda, will you come with me for a walk?" he asked.

Surprise flitted across her face. "Let me finish this first."

He came closer and spoke more softly. "There is a man who looks like the one who comes to see the papers of Germans. I think we should go for a walk."

"Oh." Hedda paled. "Yes. Of course." She glanced at Rubye, who made a shooing motion. "Let's go," she said as she tossed her apron onto a chair.

Moments later they were outside and walking into the shaded woods. Signs of spring were all around, with birds singing and buds just beginning to swell on the branches. Green shoots were popping up here and there, and snowdrops bloomed under the trees. They soon came to the bench they'd shared all those months ago.

Hedda sank down, gripping the rough edge of the seat. "How is it possible that so many months have come and gone since I saw the photo of your grave and began this journey?"

"Much is changed," Fritz said, settling beside her. "And much is the same."

She slanted a look at him. "What do you mean?"

"You are a pianist. I am an artist. This is the same. We are these things when we meet and fall in love. We are these things now."

"But Denis said you were thinking of giving up your pursuit of art to go back to Bethania."

"I think maybe I will go back and earn some money to live. But maybe I will come back again. And I am still an artist. I am this when we are engaged and when I am on a ship and when I am in a camp in Hot Springs. I am this in Germany and in America. This I am always." He leaned back, getting more comfortable on the hard bench. "The Moravians teach me that God creates, God redeems, God blesses. And so we have faith, love, and hope." He sighed heavily. "I am not good at showing you these things, and I am sorry."

"I forgive you," Hedda said and leaned back beside him. "I think I forgave you when I had no choice but to go back to Germany to care for Lotte. I think she was as much my mother as yours by then. And I'm grateful to have been loved by her."

Fritz took her hand. "I have much to thank you for. This will take a long time."

She laughed lightly. "You don't have much time if you're going home at Easter. Paint me a picture and I'll consider myself thanked."

Fritz turned toward her on the bench, now cradling her hand with both of his. "What if there is more time? What if you come with me to Bethania when I go?"

"But what would I do in Bethania? I have a place here at the college—playing, teaching, performing. Dr. Rice has finally given me a proper position. It's true I might be safer in Bethania, but I would have to earn my keep."

"I would keep you," Fritz said. "I think it is time we married." He forced a nervous laugh. "Our engagement is long enough."

Hedda withdrew her hand from his grasp. "This is a big decision to make. I'm not sure what to think."

Fritz scrambled for the right words in English to persuade her. "I am looking for a wife. I am wanting to care for you always. To love you as I did before."

Hedda shifted back on the bench. "So you're saying you love me? That you want to spend the rest of your life with me?"

"*Ja*. You are beautiful and strong and smart." He smiled, remembering their early days of courting. "When we met before, I think you were . . . what is the word? Timid. Nervous. I am in love with you then, but now I see you are stronger, more courageous. We will make a good team. You will help me in my work and play hymns for the people." He warmed to what he was proposing. "This will be very good for us all."

"I-I don't know what to say." Her eyes darted to the path leading back to Lee Hall and Black Mountain College. "You've given me a great deal to think about."

The confidence Fritz had felt that she was about to accept faltered. "You will come with me, then?"

She turned pleading eyes on him. "I need time to think about what you've said. It's a tempting offer." She gripped his arm and squeezed. "You're a good man, and I care for you. But I'm not certain." She sighed and looked away. "As you say, I am still a musician, yes? But so much else has changed." She looked back at him, and he felt his hopes sink. "I'm not the same girl you proposed to before the war."

"*Nein*. You are not. And I think I am foolish not to return to you then."

She shrugged. "Maybe. Maybe not. But here we are now, and I'm honored that you would ask me to be your wife once again."

Before Fritz could say anything more to persuade her, they heard someone coming along the path, whistling. They both froze before Fritz realized he knew that whistle.

"It is Denis," he said.

They sagged back against the bench when they spotted the young man through the trees. As he came around the final bend, he grinned. "Heard you two were out here hiding in the woods. Thought I'd come to tell you there's nothing to fear. The man in the suit is a reporter come to write a story about the crazy college for artists and dreamers. You can come on back now." He laughed. "Although I think you'd better not volunteer to be interviewed."

Fritz gave a chuckle of his own. "*Ja. Danke* for coming to tell us. Now we won't have to miss lunch." He stood and held out a hand to Hedda. She took it long enough for him to help her to her feet, then dropped it as she hurried back toward campus.

Denis looked sideways at his father as they watched her go. "What were you two talking about?" he asked.

"Nothing. We are just passing the time," Fritz said, and he feared he was telling the truth.

47

Garland had every intention of asking Hedda to be his wife. He just hadn't found the right time to do it. Now that he was in Sheriff Fitzsimmons's good graces once more, he'd committed himself to doing his job well, working longer hours and taking less-desired assignments. All of which left little time to travel to Black Mountain College.

But in April there was to be a concert and art show, and he would absolutely make time to attend. Lucy sent him the invitation, which had been a veiled request for him to drive her to and from the campus. An excuse he was only too happy to use to his advantage.

"Aren't you the picture of loveliness?" he said as he held the car door open for her outside her cottage.

"And aren't you the smooth talker? I'm not so very many years older than you," she said with a twinkle in her eye. "You'd best not flirt with me if you don't mean it."

Garland chuckled. "Yes, ma'am. But you really do look nice."

"Thank you," she said, pursing her lips. "I might say the same about you. Is that a new hat?"

He felt heat radiate up his neck. He had taken particular care with his appearance, but he'd prefer it wasn't too obvious. "Haven't had a reason to dress up lately," he mumbled. "Seemed like a good time to break out my suit."

"No need to be embarrassed," said Lucy as she plucked a loose thread from his lapel. "Seems to me you could do worse than to find a smart college girl to woo."

Garland flushed more deeply. "Oh, now, those girls are too young. I'm just along to give you a ride and to see the show."

Lucy looked up at him from the front seat where she'd settled herself. "Too old, too young, you're like Goldilocks. Wonder when you'll find the one that's just right?"

Garland forced a chuckle as he closed the car door. He walked around the back of the automobile slowly, composing himself. Was it obvious that he was interested in Hedda? Probably. Lucy might be nicer than she was when they first met, but she was still a pistol and certainly not above giving him a hard time. For half a minute he considered confiding in her about his plans but then decided against it as he slid behind the wheel.

"You'll do fine," Hedda assured Amanda, one of her students who was nervous about the piece she planned to play for the evening's concert. "You could play this while sleeping, you know it so well."

Amanda giggled. "I think the saying is that I could 'play it in my sleep,' but I appreciate the sentiment." She smiled and added, "Thank you for everything you've taught me."

Hedda shrugged one shoulder. "It's not so much. You

have a talent for it. Now, what is it they say in the theater? 'Go break your leg'?"

"Something like that," Amanda laughed. "Are you playing tonight?"

"Not tonight. This is a time for the students to shine. I'll be watching, though." She gave Amanda a quick hug and went to find a seat in the hall.

They'd set up a makeshift stage with curtains to hide the performers. There was to be music, a short skit, and a dramatic reading. Paintings were hung along one wall for attendees to admire. One of Fritz's paintings stood out from the rest with its vivid, glowing colors. He really was an artist. Hedda realized she was glad for him. Glad he'd finally been able to express himself so beautifully.

Hedda looked around the room, taking it all in, marveling at how far she'd come since leaving Germany. Her life had been so regimented and structured, just as she liked it. Now she had a routine but also plenty of room for surprises. Each day was different, and she sometimes allowed inspiration to spur her to something completely unplanned. Of course, there was also much more uncertainty in her life. She still half expected a government official to come take her away at any moment. But in a way, that added to the delight she felt each day. She understood how fleeting everything was. And she was determined to enjoy every moment she could.

"Halloo, Hedda! Come sit with us." The feminine voice came from the side of the room nearest the fireplace. Hedda spotted Lucy and moved to her side with a smile.

"I'm so glad you've come."

"And look who I brought with me." Lucy waved Garland over from where he was talking to Johann. Hedda felt a flutter in her chest. It had been too long since she'd seen the deputy. He would forever be an important part of her life. Her rescuer in a way. When he saw her, his face bloomed with a smile that caught her breath. The way he looked at her, it gave her an idea. A bold, brazen idea.

"It's good to see you, Hedda," he said. She had the sense he wanted to take her hand or perhaps even hug her, but the air between them was suddenly awkward. She didn't know what to do or say.

"I'm glad to see you as well" was the best she could offer. They looked at each other, neither one speaking, until Lucy clapped her hands.

"Let's sit," she chirped. "I'm here. Hedda, you sit beside me. Garland, you take the chair at the end of the row. You can stretch out those long legs if you need to." Garland colored at that but quickly plunked down in his assigned seat, and Hedda settled next to him. She thought she could feel warmth radiating from his arm so close to hers, but surely that was her imagination. The room was simply overly warm with all the people gathered together.

"I thought you might be playing," Garland said.

"No, tonight is for the students. I'm happy just to listen." As she struggled to think of what else to say, thankfully she was saved by Dr. Rice, who appeared onstage to start the performance.

Over the next hour, she tried to keep her focus on the students but failed miserably. The idea that was taking shape left her palms sweaty, her heart racing, and her nerves a jumbled mess. Finally, the performance ended, and everyone began milling around, drinking punch and eating the oatmeal cookies Jack had baked earlier. Hedda helped with the food, her hands shaking and her eye on Garland. When he neared the door, she grabbed two cookies and intercepted him.

"Will you join me on the porch for a sweet?"

There was that smile again. "Sure thing. I seem to have lost track of Lucy, so I guess she's not in a hurry to head home."

Outside, they each munched a cookie as they strolled toward the far end of the porch, where the light was dim and the crowd was thin. She marveled that Garland seemed to have had the same idea as she had. Or almost the same, she thought, wishing she had a cup of punch to wash down the pastry that had turned to dust in her mouth.

She knew now that Anni had been right. While the two paths before her weren't the only ones, Fritz and Garland could each offer her a way through her troubles. And she was suddenly quite certain she didn't want to go to Bethania with Fritz.

"I've missed seeing you," Garland said as they stepped off the porch and strolled across the lawn. "I've been pretty busy since we got back from Germany."

Hedda dropped the last of her cookie in the bushes, certain she couldn't swallow another bite. "Yes, I've missed seeing you, too." She realized her fingers had found their way to the nape of her neck, where they twirled a strand of hair. She thought she'd broken that habit. She quickly lowered her hand, hoping Garland hadn't noticed.

"You have?" He sounded surprised.

"Yes, you've been such a wonderful friend to me. I can never repay you for all you've done."

Garland's voice dipped low. "There's nothing to repay. It's been my honor."

"I'm glad to hear you say so." Hedda's heart beat so fast she thought Garland could surely hear it. "Because I have a favor to ask of you."

Even in the gathering darkness, she could see him smile. "Ask away. I'd be happy to help any way I can."

"Marry me." She hadn't meant to blurt it out quite so plainly, but how else could she have put it?

Garland froze, staring at her. "What did you say?"

Hedda cleared her throat. "It's very bold of me, I know. But you once offered to marry me so I could become an American. And then we pretended to be engaged to escape Germany. Will you still do this?"

"I . . . I . . ." Garland stuttered, his eyes wide with, what, panic?

"I'm so sorry," Hedda said. "I shouldn't have asked you. Please, will you pretend I didn't?"

"I'll marry you."

"Oh." Hedda felt relief wash through her. "*Danke*. I think there may still be some difficulty since I came here improperly, but once we are wed, what can be done?" She hesitated. "But if you think it would make things difficult for you, we won't do it."

"No, no, I don't think it'll cause any trouble. As a matter of fact, I was going to ask you the same thing." He gave her a lopsided smile.

Hedda laughed, grateful that she had worried for nothing. "I'm so glad. It's too much to ask, but when I thought a government man had come to take me back . . ." She shuddered. "I realized I must do whatever it takes to avoid returning to Germany. Fritz suggested I marry him, but he is also here without permission so perhaps that wouldn't help." She took a calming breath. "You are a good man, Garland. I'm fortunate to know you." She flushed. "The marriage will be, how to say it, in name only? I don't expect . . . that is to say, I don't—"

"Right." Garland cut her off. "We can talk about all that another time."

As he spoke, Lucy came trotting toward them. "There you two are. I hate to interrupt whatever you're doing out here in the dark, but it's high time I went home. Garland, if it's not too much trouble?"

"Sure thing," he said. He looked to Hedda. "I . . . I'll be in touch."

They all three said their goodbyes, and Hedda watched them go with mixed feelings. On one hand, she felt incredible relief that she had a solution to the problem of staying in the United States permanently. On the other hand, she felt oddly confused by Garland's reaction. While he'd agreed to marry her and had even mentioned having the same idea himself, she had the strangest feeling the arrangement wasn't what he wanted after all. Was she foolish to hope a marriage of convenience might become something more?

She headed to her room, trying not to think about it too hard. Most likely something had simply been lost in translation.

48

Could he have bungled that any more thoroughly? Garland kicked himself all the way back to Madison County, barely slept a wink, and dragged himself into the office the following day looking like he'd been on a weeklong bender.

"Good gravy, man, what freight train ran you down last night?" Wayne intercepted him as he staggered down the hall. "Get in here before anyone else sees you."

Garland followed the sheriff into his office and slouched into a chair.

"Are you sick?" Wayne demanded.

"I'm getting married," Garland blurted.

"Oh. Well, that explains a lot." Wayne settled in his own chair and laced his hands across his belly. "Who's the lucky girl? I might've had a guess if you didn't look half dead."

"Hedda." Garland was pretty sure confiding in Wayne Fitzsimmons wasn't his best idea, but then he was flat out of ideas—good or bad.

"I could've sworn you told me she's just the one you wanted to marry. So why the long face?"

"She is the one," Garland said, cradling his head in his hands.

"Son, I've questioned hardened criminals with more success than I'm having right now. How about I quit guessing, and you just go ahead and tell me whatever it is you need to get off your chest."

Garland released a great sigh. "She thinks I'm agreeing to a platonic arrangement so she can become an American."

"Well, are you?"

"No!" Garland jerked his head up, nearly shouting the word. He lowered his voice. "I mean, yes, I guess I am. But that's *not* what I want."

"What do you want, then?"

"I want to marry her proper. I want her to be my wife. I want to have kids with her, if God blesses us with 'em. I want to listen to her play the piano, and I want to teach her how to fish because that's about my favorite thing to do other than be around her. I want her to be my wife, and me to be her husband. I want to give her all the love she's been missing out on since Fritz left her to pine away like the fool he is." Garland took a deep breath. The first one he'd had since Hedda asked him to marry her. It felt good.

Wayne chuckled. "That clears things up for me. Too bad it doesn't do diddly-squat to clear things up for Hedda."

Garland blinked. "You think I should tell her?"

"You know, I thought I was going to have to fire you for not being as forthcoming as you should have been about the night Marie Spencer died, but now I'm thinking I'll have to fire you for being an idiot."

"But what if she doesn't want the same thing?"

"That'd be good to know." Wayne propped his feet up on the corner of his desk. "Of course, it'd be even better to find out she does want the same thing and you've just been too dunderheaded to see it."

Garland surged to his feet. "Don't guess I have any sick leave coming to me."

"The way you look? I would say you'd best hightail it on out of here in case whatever you've got is contagious."

"So I can . . ."

"Git," Wayne said. "And don't come back till you've taken whatever medicine that German gal decides to dish out."

Hedda enjoyed a rare moment to herself in the kitchen at Black Mountain College. Jack and Rubye had the afternoon off, and none of the faculty or students had come to forage among the cold sandwich supplies they'd have for their supper. She decided to make a pot of tea to take back to her room. She knew she should find Fritz and give him a definitive answer to his proposal, but there was something about Garland's agreement to marry her that made her think he might yet change his mind. If he did, would she accept Fritz after all? The thought left her cold.

As the kettle heated up, she rummaged through the cupboards looking for something nicer than the thick pottery mugs they used for coffee. On a shelf in a far corner, she discovered a few mismatched tea things, including a cup with, of all things, violets on it.

She remembered her favorite cup in Lotte's kitchen back in Germany. She'd missed so many things since leaving almost everything behind when Garland helped her escape. She'd missed clothing, mementos, and books, but she'd forgotten about her teacup with its spray of flowers. How long had it been since she'd sipped a *Köppke Tee* in that cozy kitchen?

She placed the cup on a tray with the pot of steeping tea and a few precious cubes of sugar Jack had saved for her. She started to head for her room but then changed her mind and took the tray into the main room of Lee Hall, which was almost always empty at this hour. She settled the tray on a table and poured the amber liquid over a lump of sugar in the pretty cup, watching the crystals dissolve as steam perfumed the air with Darjeeling.

She sat in a chair in a pool of sunlight, lifted the cup, and sipped with a sigh. She let her gaze roam the towering space, so very different from Lotte's kitchen in Germany. She remembered how its coziness had made her feel safe and tucked away. Now she knew she was much safer here in this soaring room with its oversized fireplace and doors that opened out to the beauty of the North Carolina mountains. More importantly, she was freer here. Free from pining away for lost love. Free from worry over Lotte. Free from the fear that had been holding her prisoner for so long she hadn't even noticed.

"You look beautiful."

She turned toward the gentle voice. She had been so absorbed in her thoughts that she hadn't seen Garland enter. She smiled. "Come, sit with me," she said.

He dragged a chair closer and sat across from her. "Would you like some tea?" she asked. "I'll have to find another cup." She laughed. "Although I feel so lazy. We could share this one, so there's no need to go back to the kitchen."

"That's all right," he said with a smile. "I didn't come for tea."

"What then did you come for?" she asked with a coy lilt to her voice. It was to be a marriage of convenience, but who was to say it couldn't become more? She prayed it would become more.

"I've come to turn down your offer of marriage."

She froze with the cup halfway to her lips. She slowly lowered it back to the tray. "Why are you saying this?" The ease she'd been feeling evaporated, replaced by a knot of dread.

Garland slid forward and dropped to one knee in front of her. "Because I want to be the one who asks you to marry me."

She was grateful she'd set the cup down lest she spill tea all over them both. "I don't understand."

He took one of her shaking hands in his. "Hedda Schlagel, I don't want to be your husband 'in name only' so you can be an American. I want to be your husband in every way that matters because I love you and I can't imagine living without you. Will you marry me and really, truly be my wife?"

She felt her free hand cover her mouth. She pulled it away to speak. "But I thought you only wanted to help. I didn't think that you had these feelings for me."

Garland shifted, his smile faltering. "I was afraid that's all you wanted from me. Do you—" he swallowed and started over—"do you have feelings for me?"

Without giving it another thought, Hedda flung herself at him, wrapping her arms around him and nearly toppling him to the floor. As he righted them both, they bumped the table, and the teacup with the violets tumbled to the floor, where it broke into several pieces.

"Oh, we have broken this cup," she said, not releasing him.

Garland stood, pulling her up with him. "Maybe Josef or Anni can put it back together." He tightened his arms around her. "Or maybe they can turn it into art, something completely new."

"*Ja*," she agreed. "*Neu*," she added, whispering the word in German. "That would be even better." And she lifted her mouth to his, certain at last that he'd meet her more than halfway.

Epilogue

Hedda woke with a start. Had she overslept? She'd certainly slept more deeply than she had in months. She swung her legs over the side of the bed, goose bumps erupting as her skin met the cool November air. She glanced at the far side of the bed, not surprised that Garland was already up. She was only surprised that the house was so quiet.

There was to be a party this day.

After making herself presentable, she went to the kitchen in the house in Hot Springs that had once belonged to Garland's grandparents. She remembered how surprised she'd been to learn that the American man who really did love her lived in a fancy house with gingerbread trim and stained-glass windows.

"*Guten Morgen, mein Liebling*," Garland said in his mountain accent. She blinked, then laughed at the scene before her. Her lanky husband sat at the table, spooning applesauce into tiny Zelma's birdlike mouth. When the child, who was turning one that day, saw her mother, she grabbed the spoon and clapped her hands, splattering applesauce across Garland's shirt.

Hedda rushed to the sink to retrieve a damp cloth and began dabbing at the mess. He laughed and stilled her hand, tugging her onto his lap. She squirmed. "Not in front of Zelma," she said as he kissed her neck.

"Who better?" he asked. "She'll know her parents didn't get married for convenience's sake."

Hedda giggled and relaxed against him. Even though she would be forty soon, her husband could make her feel like a girl of seventeen. No, she thought, the girl she'd been at seventeen was silly. She placed a hand on either side of his face and kissed him deeply with a passion and love no young girl could possibly muster.

"Well," Garland said when she released him, "that makes me want to quit my job and wait on you hand and foot all day every day."

"*Gut*," she laughed, moving to a chair so she could resume feeding Zelma. Her bright-eyed daughter watched them intently from her high chair. "Now change your shirt. Our guests will be arriving for Zelma's birthday lunch before we know it."

A few hours later, Josef, Anni, and Lucy were the first to arrive. The Alberses had driven from Black Mountain with Lucy along for the ride. They spilled into the house, bringing with them a gust of cold mountain air. "*Wo ist mein Paten-kind?*" called Josef. Zelma squealed in response and began babbling, holding her arms out. Josef scooped her up and began to speak to her earnestly in German.

Anni, laughing, came to hug Hedda. "He is determined that she will be fluent in German. It is good, I think, for her to know two languages."

"Yes," said Hedda, "although speaking German in public is not so popular these days."

"*Ach*, no." Anni sobered. "Have you heard the news from Germany? I hate to bring it up on such a festive day—"

The sound of someone at the door drew their attention, and Hedda hurried to welcome Fritz and Denis inside. "Come in! We're so glad you could come from Bethania."

"The women of the church sent cookies," Denis said, holding out a large box. "They saved up enough sugar to make dozens and dozens of them."

Garland suddenly materialized at her elbow. "Are you talking about those thin sugar cookies that're so crisp and delicious? Hand 'em over!"

Hedda slapped his hand playfully. "We'll share them with our guests after lunch," she chided.

He dropped a kiss on her head. "Fine. I guess you're sweet enough for now."

Hedda flushed, hoping Fritz wouldn't mind seeing the affection between her and Garland. It had been several years now since they'd parted as friends, but she still worried a little.

"Dad has some news," Denis said with a grin, elbowing his father.

Fritz nodded enthusiastically. "*Ja*. I am to be wed next month," he told the group. "Her name is Martha, and she is *wunderbar*."

"That's great news," Garland said, slapping him on the back. "I for one highly recommend the matrimonial state."

They all moved into the dining room, where Hedda had laid out a feast with Garland's help: roasted chicken sliced on a platter, potato salad with bacon, creamed spinach, crusty bread, and an assortment of pickles. For dessert,

Apfelkuchen, which was like the cakes her mother had made when Hedda was a girl. *And Denis's cookies*, she thought with a smile.

They crowded around the table, with Zelma in her high chair between Hedda and Garland. Everyone held hands while Garland gave thanks for the food, their friends, and their daughter. And then Hedda, stumbling over the foreign words, gave the Jewish blessing she'd looked up for Anni's sake. "*Barukh ata Adonai Eloheinu melekh ha'olam sheha-kol niyah bidvaro.*"

With tears in her eyes, Anni translated, "'Blessed are you, Lord our God, Ruler of the universe, at whose word all came to be.'" She smiled. "*Danke*, Hedda. Today this is even more sweet to hear."

"Oh, that's right. You said there was some hard news out of Germany. Is that what you mean?"

"Let's not discuss it now," Anni said. "Now let us celebrate."

Hedda felt that old knot in her stomach tighten. "No, tell me and let's be done with it."

Josef reached inside his jacket and pulled out a folded copy of the previous day's *Asheville Times* and slid it toward her. Hedda held the newspaper so that she and Garland could read it together. The front-page headline shouted, ANTI-JEWISH VIOLENCE HITS GERMANY, and its heavy black letters weighed her down. She went on to read, "'Nazi Germany today indulged in its greatest wave of anti-Jewish violence since Adolf Hitler came to power in 1933.'"

Though she knew her guests were waiting, she read each word of the article carefully, turning to page three to continue: "'In the east end, gangs wrecked numerous Jewish furniture stores. Mobs pushed pianos into the streets.'" She gasped and said, "I know this music store. Herr Bloch was always so kind to me. He let me play any instrument I liked, even though he knew I couldn't afford to buy any of them." She laid the paper down, unable to read more.

It was Anni who reached over to cover Hedda's hand with her own. "We are both orphaned by the *Vaterland*. The Germany we knew has left us. But we are here now, celebrating a child who is part German and part American." She paused, composing herself. "And you have given her a Jew for a godmother." She reached across Hedda to rest her other hand on Zelma's downy head. "This is the world I will choose to live in."

Tears falling, Hedda leaned over to hug her friend, even as Garland placed a comforting hand on her shoulder.

Fritz stood and lifted his glass. "'When a man's ways please the LORD, he maketh even his enemies to be at peace with him.'" They turned toward the strapping German and one by one raised their own glasses. "It is good we are here together like this," Fritz said. "God is good even when the world is not."

Zelma clapped her hands and laughed her baby laugh of pure joy. Hedda found she couldn't help but laugh with her. Yes, here was something good. Here was hope for tomorrow.

Author's Note

As I write this in early October 2024, western North Carolina is struggling to recover from the devastation of Hurricane Helene. My prayer is that by the time *These Blue Mountains* makes its way to bookstore shelves, our region will have recovered and will be welcoming visitors to one of the most beautiful places in the world once again. Please come see us. We're going to need you.

These Blue Mountains had its genesis in a German enemy alien internment camp in Hot Springs, North Carolina, during WWI. So many people aren't even aware that German citizens, not soldiers, were held captive during the war years. The Germans in Hot Springs, many of them sailors, happened to be in U.S. waters when war broke out in Europe. Their ship, the *Vaterland*, was commandeered, and they were made "comfortable" at the Mountain Park Hotel.

There were more internees than there were citizens of the town, which made residents nervous at first. But once locals grew accustomed to what was referred to as the "German invasion," they took it in stride, even befriending some of the internees. Prisoners included a full orchestra that had performed for passengers on the ship. On Sunday afternoons the townspeople would come and sit outside the fence to enjoy concerts.

But what captured my imagination most was the Bavarian village internees built from driftwood, scrap lumber, and anything else they could get their hands on. Much of it was detritus from the flood of 1916. The village was a feat of engineering with two-story chalets, beautiful gardens, fences, and yes—as mentioned in the story—a small church and a working carousel with hanging chairs and elaborate paintings on the center column. Google it—my description doesn't do it justice.

But as fascinating as the village and the history are, I needed a story. And when I received my copy of *The German Invasion of Western North Carolina*, a pictorial history compiled by Jacqueline Burgin Painter, there it was. Gerda Kostynski's brother, Richard Schlause, went to sea in 1917 and disappeared. Then in 1933, Gerda picked up a copy of *Berlin Radio Magazine* and saw a photo of the German ambassador placing a wreath on a monument to German sailors who'd died in a typhoid outbreak. On a small cross in the foreground of the photo was the name *Richard Schlause*. She had found her missing brother.

So I borrowed Gerda and Richard's story and gave it to Hedda and her fiancé, Fritz. I imagined what might have happened if she'd come to America to recover the remains of a German prisoner of war during those terrifying years of Hitler's rise in Germany.

As always, I enjoyed weaving real history into my imaginary world. Hedda stays at the Wolfe boardinghouse, which is now the Thomas Wolfe Memorial in Asheville, North Carolina—another spot I'd recommend you visit when you come to our mountains. Yes, Wolfe really was in Germany around the time I had him run into Garland. That was too good to pass up.

Black Mountain College, which closed in 1956, offered an intriguing place for Hedda to land. It was on the cutting edge of artistic expression and creativity when it was founded in the 1930s. The school went on to produce influential artists, including Josef and Maria Albers, who did indeed flee Germany, although I played with their timeline a bit. To learn more about it, check out the Black Mountain College Museum + Arts Center. It remains a vibrant community of artists here in western North Carolina.

I hope you enjoyed spending time with Hedda, Garland, Fritz, the Alberses, Lucy, Denis, and all the other characters populating my story. I hope even more that they'll inspire you to explore the real history behind *These Blue Mountains* and to find ways to support western North Carolina by visiting, shopping online, or supporting charities in our region. Two good ones are Black Mountain Home for Children, Youth & Families and Samaritan's Purse. I worked at the children's home for sixteen years, and they were hit particularly hard by Helene. Samaritan's Purse is headquartered in Boone, North Carolina, and has been front and center when it comes to being boots on the ground for the hardest-hit areas.

Thank you for joining me in learning about and caring for the people of these blue mountains.

For more by Sarah Loudin Thomas,
read on for an excerpt from

The Right Kind of Fool

Available wherever books are sold.

1

The day's heat lay close to Loyal like a quilt he couldn't push back. He imagined the cool, dark current of the Tygart River. But Mother would never let him go swimming by himself. He loved diving deep, feeling the pressure of the water press against his face and ears so that he heard a whooshing thrum. At least that was what he thought he heard. He could almost remember . . .

But Mother never let him go anywhere alone. He'd been home from school for weeks and weeks, and she rarely let him leave the house without her. He wasn't a baby. He'd turned thirteen back in May, was well on his way to fourteen. He'd be a man before long. Like Father. He bet Father would let him go swimming. If he were here.

If he were ever here.

Mother was at one of her church meetings. He glanced at the tall clock wagging its tail behind glass. She'd be gone another hour at least. And while she told him not to go any farther than the back garden with its rows of corn, beans, and tomatoes, the thought of disobeying seemed less and less terrible as the airless day hemmed him in. He grunted. He would do it. It was time he acted his age.

Delphy pushed a strand of damp hair back from her face and sighed. Did they really need to discuss plans for decorating the church for Christmas in such detail this far in advance? The discussion as to whether or not to have a "greening of the church" service or to simply put the decorations up on the Saturday after Thanksgiving was grating on her nerves. Didn't they have more important things to discuss?

"Delphy, will you supply the cedar branches?" Genevieve Slater laid a cool hand on her arm. How was her hand cool in this heat?

Delphy pushed a smile up from the place where she stored manufactured emotion. She'd been forcing smiles since the town realized her husband spent more time on his beloved Rich Mountain than he did with his family. He still came down to see them but only on his own indecipherable schedule. Maddening. "Of course," she said. As if she had the only cedar trees in Beverly. Yet it wasn't worth pointing out. She'd learned to save her energy for battles that mattered. And goodness knew the battle she was fighting to convince the town that her family was intact required the bulk of her energy.

Genevieve smiled and turned to a discussion of the Christmas pageant and the timing of the Christmas Eve service. Delphy spotted one of the funeral home fans tucked behind a hymnal and began stirring the thick air. At least no one had made a pointed remark about whether or not Creed would help cut the cedar and bring it to church. She supposed she should be grateful for small blessings.

The cool water was every bit as delicious as Loyal had imagined. His clothes lay piled on the bank next to a piece of toweling he'd found in the ragbag. If he didn't stay too long, Mother would never know he'd been gone. The sheer joy of being alone—of being free—washed over him. It was even more refreshing than the water. He dove again, then surfaced drawing air deep into his lungs. He could smell damp soil and moss. He floated on his back and let the sun bake his face as he watched a few puffy clouds drift through the washed-out sky.

A movement on the far bank drew his attention from the blissful river. He treaded water, watching. It wouldn't do to be caught by someone who would tell Mother. There. A flash in the trees. He moved closer so he could crouch in the edge of the river among water-worn stones where the water lapped at his legs. The figure looked familiar . . . Michael Westfall.

Loyal ducked lower, grateful that Michael was rushing along a path and paying no attention to the river. The older boy had teased Loyal more than once, made fun of how he talked with his hands. Loyal wondered why he was in such a hurry on this hot day.

Michael paused, looked over his shoulder, and beckoned someone on with a *hurry-up* gesture. He glanced around wildly and then stuck something in a rotted-out stump. As he straightened, a girl with russet hair sped into view. It was Michael's sister, who was the same age as Loyal. They would be in the same class too, if Mother would ever let him go to the school in town. He had always found Rebecca to be her brother's opposite. Kind, still, peaceful—always ready with a smile and a wave for him. Plus, she was pretty.

Now, though, the girl was gasping for breath. Her hand pinched her waist as she ran after her brother. She glanced over her shoulder, fear in her eyes. Loyal glimpsed another movement—higher up the mountain—but before he could focus on it, he saw the older boy's hand motions get bigger and his lips move. Loyal saw the word *hurry* take shape over and over. What was wrong? Michael grabbed his sister's hand and tugged her forward, then released her and rushed ahead. Rebecca looked back again and paused, panting. She closed her eyes and bowed her head. When she lifted her face, she turned toward the river, and Loyal had the notion she saw him. Her eyes were full of something . . . a secret maybe? He rose up just a little, and her eyes widened. He lifted a hand the way he would when signing *your*. She lifted her hand in the same way, and he understood that something terrible had happened. Then she turned and sprinted after her brother.

Creed headed out to the only spot near the cabin that got good sun. He planned to pick a mess of beans where they climbed the stalks of corn he'd planted in his garden patch. He wished for Delphy's good pork roast with sweet potatoes, but he'd eat his beans and be glad for them. As a boy there'd been more than one lean year and he knew even now folks in cities were going hungry. The country was in a pickle, and he wasn't so sure President Roosevelt was going to get them out of it.

There'd been rumors in town about some homestead project Eleanor Roosevelt was championing. They were talking about setting one up on mostly empty land out near the Westfall place. Word was, they'd pay good money, but there were plenty of folks who valued their land more than empty government promises. And Hadden Westfall was one of them.

Creed felt an ear of corn to see if the darkening silks were telling the truth about it being ripe. He grunted and added the ear to his galvanized bucket. He might even dig a few early potatoes. He ought to leave them to grow until the tops frosted and the tubers hardened off, but they'd sure be tasty cooked with the beans and a piece of salt pork.

Pausing, he peered down the mountain through the trees to where he could glimpse the Tygart twisting along the wide valley below. He stretched his back and took in the view. It was a good place—the valley shaped like his grandmother's long wooden dough bowl. The bottomland was gentle and rich, softly curving up to the steeper hillsides, offering plenty of room for a man to make a life if he were so inclined.

Creed turned back to his garden. Some days it was lonesome up on Rich Mountain no matter how much he appreciated the peace and quiet. No matter how many times he told himself his family was better off with him up here.

The mountain was where he could keep an eye out for ginseng to dig each fall so he could sell enough to pay Loyal's tuition. No one could accuse him of depending on his wife's inheritance. Then, in the spring, he'd gather the morels folks were happy to trade for, and he could always sell a mess of fish if he needed to buy the boy some new shoes or books for that special school he went to.

Not such a boy anymore. The thought flicked through his mind as he went back to gathering his supper. Loyal had turned thirteen a few months back. Some places he'd be considered a man already, but Loyal was different. He was special.

Creed didn't know what was going to happen to him, what he was going to be. Maybe, if he learned enough, he could be a teacher at that school he went to. He was plenty smart—at least Delphy said he was. Creed hadn't much learned how to shape the boy's language.

He broke off another ear of corn and dug out those potatoes, then strode to the cabin to set everything to cooking. Who'd have thought he'd be the chief cook and bottle washer in his own house? When he married Delphy, he'd supposed she would do that from then on. And then Loyal came along and Creed took his own father's advice too much to heart. Pushed the boy too far. Demanded too much. And now . . . well, it wasn't worth dwelling on. Dad wasn't here to see how far he'd fallen, and that was a relief.

Creed started nipping his beans and breaking them into a pan. They'd need to cook the longest. He lost himself in the rhythm of the simple task, thinking about how many times his grandmother had done the same. She'd stepped in when his mother died bringing him into the world, and she was the only person Creed had ever seen stand up to Dad. He smiled at the memory of the petite woman in her perfectly starched apron, dressing his father down. She'd laugh to see Creed doing women's work now.

No, he thought, she'd fuss. She would not approve of a married man baching it up on a mountain while his wife and son lived just a few miles away. He made a point of going into town to attend church with them most weeks and he even spent the night now and again, but mostly he felt more at ease here on his mountain and suspected Delphy and Loyal were more at ease once he was gone. Still, it might be nice if . . .

Movement along the path leading to the cabin caught

Creed's eye. He noticed a puff of smoke rising from the path and jerked to his feet. Had some fool started a fire?

Setting his pan aside, he laid a hand on the rifle leaning against the doorjamb. He cradled the long gun in the crook of his elbow and watched to see what—beyond the smoke— had drawn his attention. Not many ventured this high up the mountain without having a purpose in mind.

When he saw it was a boy, he relaxed. Then he recognized Loyal and every sense went on alert. Delphy never let the boy wander on his own, and she rarely set foot on the mountain. What in the world?

Loyal got close enough to make Creed out, and his eyes lit with fire. He hurried on, sticking his hand straight out in front of him and flapping it—the funniest-looking wave Creed had ever seen. He formed a fist with his right hand, the thumb sticking up in the air, and smacked it into his left palm. He did this several times, moving both hands toward his chest, eyes pleading with Creed.

"What's the matter, Loyal? What's wrong?" Creed spoke slowly, locking eyes with his son.

Loyal made a sound of frustration. He fanned the fingers of his right hand, touched the thumb to his forehead, and lowered it to his chest. Then he held both hands flat in front of him, one palm up, the other palm down, and flipped them both over to his left as though turning pages.

Creed felt his own frustration rise. He'd never taken the time to understand what Loyal was saying. He knew the boy could understand him by watching his lips, but how to make sense of what Loyal wanted to tell him? He was clearly upset, and Creed realized the boy's hands were shaking as he made those motions over and over, as if Creed would suddenly grasp what they meant.

"Where's your mother? What are you doing here alone?"

Loyal screeched and stomped his foot.

Creed held up both hands toward his son. "Wait," he said. "I know what." He patted the rough boards of the porch. "Sit. I'll be right back."

Loyal groaned and slumped onto the porch as if carrying the weight of the world on his shoulders and expecting his father to relieve him of his burden. Creed might not know sign language, but he knew body language and it tore at his heart to see his son unable to communicate with him.

He darted inside and grabbed several sticks of kindling. Back outside, he crouched down and smoothed a patch of mountain dirt. Loyal brightened and grabbed a stick. He knelt down beside his father and began to mark in the earth.

M-A-N

He made the motion with fanned fingers and thumb touching his forehead, then chest again.

"Right, you want to tell me about a man."

Loyal nodded and looked serious. He made the flipping motion with one hand and then scratched some more.

D-E-A-D

Creed felt his eyebrows shoot up into his hairline. "There's a dead man?"

Loyal nodded like his life depended on it.

"Are you sure he's dead?"

The boy dropped the stick and made the flipping motion some more, frowning and shaking his head. Creed tried the motion himself, and Loyal nodded solemnly.

"You'd best show me where," Creed said.

Sarah Loudin Thomas is the director of Jan Karon's Mitford Museum in Hudson, North Carolina. She holds a bachelor's degree in English from Coastal Carolina University and is the author of the acclaimed novels *The Right Kind of Fool*, winner of the 2021 Selah Book of the Year Award, and *Miracle in a Dry Season*, winner of the 2015 INSPY Award. Sarah has also been a finalist for the Christy Award, the ACFW Carol Award, and the Christian Book of the Year Award. She and her husband live in western North Carolina. Learn more at SarahLoudinThomas.com.

Sign Up for Sarah's Newsletter

Keep up to date with Sarah's latest news on book releases and events by signing up for her email list at the link below.

SarahLoudinThomas.com

FOLLOW SARAH ON SOCIAL MEDIA

Sarah Loudin Thomas

@SarahLoudinThomas